THE
GOODBYE

ALSO BY JOANNE DEMAIO

The Seaside Saga

Blue Jeans and Coffee Beans
The Denim Blue Sea
Beach Blues
Beach Breeze
The Beach Inn
Beach Bliss
Castaway Cottage
Night Beach
Little Beach Bungalow
Every Summer
Salt Air Secrets
Stony Point Summer
The Beachgoers
Shore Road
The Wait
The Goodbye
The Barlows
—And More Seaside Saga Books—

ALSO BY JOANNE DEMAIO

Beach Cottage Series

The Beach Cottage
Back to the Beach Cottage

Standalone Novels

True Blend
Whole Latte Life

The Winter Series

Snowflakes and Coffee Cakes
Snow Deer and Cocoa Cheer
Cardinal Cabin
First Flurries
Eighteen Winters
Winter House
—And More Winter Books—

Copyright © 2022 Joanne DeMaio
All rights reserved.

ISBN: 9798808581210

Joannedemaio.com

the goodbye

BOOK 16

JOANNE DEMAIO

one

THERE'S NO SIGN OF CELIA.

She's not crossing the yard. Not calling out Shane's name. Not rounding the corner of the shingled seaside cottage. Nothing.

So all Shane can do is stand on the evening lawn with Maris and Jason and take in the sight before them.

The shabby round table is set.

Lantern light flickers.

Alongside wild beach grasses, old boat oars are randomly propped in the ground.

Faded paper lanterns strung between those wooden oars softly glow.

And the lavender of twilight makes it almost unreal.

Beyond, the dark water of Long Island Sound spreads to the horizon.

Shane can also make out the splash of distant waves. The whisper of those beach grasses.

But all else is still.

In that uncomfortably quiet pause, he motions for his friends to sit at the table. Jason and Maris do—taking their seats as Shane steals another look over his shoulder for Celia. The yard beyond is eerily empty. *Come on*, Shane thinks. *Don't do it. Don't bail on me.* Grabbing his cell phone from his back pocket, he checks for any messages from her.

There are none.

Just show up, he silently pleads while checking his watch, too. Celia's late. She should be here by now.

But she's not.

Another quick look. And still nothing.

So Shane wipes his palms on his jeans, pulls out a slatted folding chair at the table, and sits. Shifts that chair a little sideways—affording him a view past Jason and Maris to the yard. To the walkway beside the cottage where Celia might approach.

"You nervous?" Jason asks as he slowly turns a crystal glass on the table.

"Yep. I am." Shane takes a linen napkin and dabs at his forehead. "Nervous mostly about what you'll think of her."

"Shane!" Maris pulls her chair in closer. "I'm sure she's wonderful."

"How'd you two meet?" Jason asks now, watching Shane across the table.

"Accidentally."

While they wait there, Maris toys with her long necklace of beads and stones. "Have you been seeing her long?" she presses.

"No. Just started up this summer." Then? Nothing. Because Lord knows he's running out of bluffs. Running out of answers that won't clue these two in to the truth: that they already know—very well—his girl. So Shane checks his watch again. Stands, too, and veers over toward the cottage side yard. Still not a single sign of Celia. He turns back to Jason and Maris. Oh, and there's no missing the way they're looking at *him*. He sees the smiles that come from witnessing the tough lobsterman sweat. Hell, they're actually enjoying his case of nerves.

"Well," Jason says when Shane sits again. "Seems like she's the one, from what I'm seeing here."

Shane doesn't answer. Instead, he blows out a breath, tips his chair back and glances past them once more.

"I'll take that as a yes," Jason tells him. He reaches across the table and gives Shane's arm a slap, too.

"A yes to what?" Shane asks, distracted by Celia's absence.

"She's the *one*, man. It's written all over you. And hey, relax. Maris and I are happy for you."

"It's such a perfect night, too," Maris wistfully goes on. "Look at the weather. And the lanterns. Oh, she's going to *love* what you did here," she adds, motioning to the romantic, lantern-lit table.

Shane nods—but he also hears something. A noise, yes, from behind Jason and Maris. A footstep maybe, on the planked walkway alongside the cottage.

So he looks in that direction. And just like that? The wait is over.

Celia is stepping off the walkway and onto the lawn—where she stops. She wears a fitted white tee with a long faded denim skirt and very low tan ankle boots. Casual and elegant as ever. Several silver chains hang from her neck.

Her beautiful auburn hair is down.

But in the twilight, what Shane sees *most* is her struggle not to cry. Standing there, she blinks a few times. Presses her lips together. Looks quickly away, then back at Shane.

At only Shane.

"There she is," he says to Jason and Maris. They turn quickly in their mismatched chairs and look across the lawn.

But Shane doesn't wait for their reaction. He hurries to Celia and takes her face in both his hands. Stands close and swipes a tear from her cheek, too, before leaning in and kissing her.

"It's okay," he says right into that kiss. "*It's okay.*"

Turning then, he escorts Celia Gray to the glimmering table set beside the sweeping dune grasses. The paper lanterns hang like stars above. Beyond, an endless twilight sky stretches over the Sound. Gently, Shane pulls out her chair and takes Celia's hand as she sits.

⌒⌣

"*No way*," Jason says under his breath. Laughs easy, too.

"Oh my God! *Celia!*" Maris slowly stands. "It's you?"

Celia nods. "It's me."

Maris rushes around the table, bends to Celia in her chair and hugs her.

Jason watches all this—Shane quiet and riveted to Celia; Maris embracing Celia; Celia looking hesitantly to them all, but smiling now, too, as Maris sits again.

"This is actually really hard for me," Celia begins. She looks to Shane seated next to her, reaches out and lightly tugs his vest lapel. "I don't know what to say. Except I'm so nervous."

"Don't be," Jason tells her.

Maris motions to everyone at the table. "It's just us, Cee."

"Exactly," Celia goes on. She gives a little shrug to Shane, who folds a hand over hers. "Shane and I … We didn't have to explain things to anyone before. And as much as I was on the fence about coming here tonight—"

"I was about ready to put up a billboard announcing it," Shane finishes, getting them all to laugh.

Which is when some floodgate opens. The talk starts up in earnest. There are questions. Disbelief, too. Happiness. A toast is made. Wineglasses are raised high, the wine sparkling beneath glowing paper lanterns. A salty breeze lifts off the distant water. The lavender sky deepens in color.

Amidst all that commotion at the table, the food is served, too. Boiled lobster. Fingerling potatoes in olive oil. Steamed corn on the cob. Tomato-and-cucumber salad.

"Elsa's tomatoes," Shane says, holding up a fork speared with a ripe tomato wedge.

Everyone nods knowingly and digs in. Lobster claws are cracked open. Tails are split. Tiny forks dip the tender lobster meat into drawn butter. Lanterns glimmer around it all.

"Once Jason figured there was a girl in my life, I had no choice but to spill it, really," Shane explains. "I felt trapped. Like I do on the boat sometimes—when the rope wraps around my foot and I have do to some fancy footwork to escape it."

"So all this here tonight is your fancy footwork?" Jason asks while lifting a forkful of dripping lobster.

Shane drags a hunk of crusty bread through the butter and olive oil drippings on his plate. "You got it," he says. He bites into that bread and keeps going, too. "Celia and I just got back from spending a few days together in Maine," he manages around chewing.

"You *did*? What about the baby?" Maris asks.

"Aria was with us," Celia tells her, then sips her wine.

"She was?" Maris nibbles a cucumber slice. "How did she like it?"

"My goodness, she *loved* it," Celia says while cracking open a lobster claw. "Oh, she slept so deep. I swear, there's something in the air there. It's really clear ... and powerful, somehow."

Shane's dipping his own lobster meat into the butter. "So we were in Maine, and Celia never even had an authentic lobster dinner there. Thus, tonight."

"If you were up north together," Jason says, "then this really *is* serious?" As he asks, he motions his fork between Shane and Celia.

Celia nods. "It is."

"Believe me," Shane goes on, "it took us as much by surprise as it did you two, tonight."

Jason breaks a hunk of that crusty bread in half. "Yeah, I'll bet," he's saying as he does.

"Right off the bat, there was something there." Shane leans over, then, and presses a kiss to Celia's head.

Maris reaches forward and clasps Celia's arm. "*But what about Elsa?*" she asks in a hushed voice. "What's *she* say about it?"

"Elsa thinks I was at my father's this week," Celia admits.

"Wait." Maris squints through the low misty light. "Are you telling me—"

"Maris." Shane sits back in his chair and looks directly at her. "Elsa's not aware of any of this."

"What?" Maris asks, looking from Shane to Celia.

"*Nobody* knows," Celia adds. "No one."

A quiet settles on them now. The talk doesn't flow as easily with the realization there might be some friction, and resistance, to this relationship.

"And I'm well aware," Shane says, "that there are no secrets at Stony Point. But this one?" He loops an arm around Celia. "This one's a must. For now."

"Why, though?" Jason asks. "You're two adults. You make your own decisions."

"Oh, Jason." Celia butters an ear of corn. "It's *really* complicated. With the baby. And everything with Sal. The last thing I want is to be judged right now. *Or* to hurt Elsa."

"All right. I get that." Jason sits back and looks at the two of them. "Nothing's easy, is it?"

"True words, my friend." Shane lifts his wineglass and toasts him. "And we just don't want to even *go* there yet, telling people. Dealing with the criticism. Or any pushback."

"Pushback?" Maris asks, slipping off her short beige-and-white blazer and draping it over her chair.

"Can't deny it, Maris." Shane reaches for the plate of potatoes.

"I hear you," Jason says, pointing a fork at them. "The new mother and the badass lobsterman? Who lives *hundreds* of miles away?"

7

Shane just turns up his hands.

"Helluva pair," Jason adds.

"Jason!" Maris swats him with a cloth napkin. "No judging!"

"That's okay. But please try to understand," Celia persists. She sets down her corn, wipes her hands on her napkin and leans close over the table. "Right now, we're just *quietly* enjoying what we've found … Seeing where things might take us, you know? And even though we're okay letting you in on this, we're begging that it goes no further. Not yet."

"You don't have to beg," Jason says. "You have our word."

"Definitely," Maris agrees.

After Celia gets up to hug Jason and Maris, Jason stands, too. He turns, then, and manages to slap Shane's shoulder in a way that gets Shane to reach around from where he sits.

"Thanks, man," Shane tells him while shaking his hand. "If someone had to know, glad it was you."

～

Just like that, some ice is broken. All inhibitions are gone as the evening goes on. Wine pours freely. Talk and laughter come easily. Stars emerge in the darkening September sky. Those dune grasses whisper beside them. The air is redolent with salt from the sea. Dishes are somewhat cleared before they're all sidetracked again with some lobstering story Shane tells, or with Maris relaying passages from the novel she's writing. Eventually, Shane and Celia bring out the dessert platter.

"The lemon bars are from the farm stand," Shane says. "And I picked up *those* bad boys at Scoop Shop earlier," he adds, nodding to the other dessert on the platter—cut squares of ice-cream sandwiches. "Some are plain. Some edged in chocolate chips."

Celia bites into one. "*Mmm*, so good," she says around the cold food.

"Pass one my way?" Shane asks. "A chocolate chip."

Maris and Jason reach for the ice-cream sandwiches, too.

"To sweet summer nights," Maris toasts, raising hers before digging in.

And before the grilling resumes.

Just like Shane knew it would. The hows and what-ifs and wheres get tossed around in the glimmering lantern light. In her black halter top and black bell-bottoms, Maris leans back, crosses her arms and shoots questions at them. It seems she and Jason are still floored, the way their questions bubble up; the way they then lean close, squinting at Shane and Celia across the table.

"Have to admit I had *some* suspicions about you two," Jason lets on, drawing a hand along his scarred jawline. "Saw things the night of Kyle's vow renewal."

"Things?" Shane asks.

Jason shrugs. "A few looks."

"A certain slow dance," Maris adds, sipping her wine.

"Yeah," Jason agrees. "One that maybe crossed the friendship line."

"And now that we *know*," Maris says, motioning between Shane and Celia, "if there's anything we can do to help—"

"There *is* something, actually. So hold that thought." Shane stands. He hurries across the lawn, climbs the seven painted porch steps and goes in the cottage. Just for a moment, though. Only long enough to grab a tall and narrow gift box. "You asked if there's anything you can do to help," Shane calls out as the cottage screen door slams shut behind him. "Well, it'd help *everyone*," he says, sitting again and not missing a beat, "if *you* two would just get back to being married. The whole damn beach is worried about you, you know." He sets the gift on the table.

"What's this?" Jason asks, reaching for it.

"Wild blueberry wine," Shane says. "Made in Maine."

"You'll love it," Celia tells them, briefly squeezing Shane's hand as she does. "It has a citrusy taste, with a delicate tartness."

Jason and Maris quiet, then. Noticeably. Maris gives a slight nod across the table.

And Shane feels it—some tension the gift insinuated into the evening. "The wine's carbonated, like a prosecco. And here's what we want," he goes on, his voice low. And serious now. "For you two to privately crack open that Maine bubbly one night. Remember the *good* times, for God's sake—and kill that bottle together." Shane clasps his hands behind his head and leans back in his chair. "Skipper's orders."

Maris, if Shane's not mistaken, fights some sudden tears as Jason opens the gift box and pulls out the bottle. It's rope-wrapped, and the wine inside? A midnight-purple color.

Jason looks up from the wine. "Thanks, guy. We'll put it to good use."

"Excellent," Shane says, still watching them across the table. "That's all I want to hear."

Lantern light flickers around them. Shadows have grown long. That sea breeze barely moves. Jason glances at Maris—who gives only a fleeting, small smile.

Funny thing, Shane notices. Though the salt air is sweet and the night, young? All is not right between those two.

two

LATER, THE CRESCENT MOON HANGS low in the sky. That slice of moon drops a swath of gold on the dark waters of Long Island Sound. Maris thinks the moonlight looks like it's been dabbed with a paintbrush on the sea's water. That wavering gold stretches from the distant, black horizon, across the Sound and straight to the beach— where lapping waves reach onshore.

After their lobster dinner, she and Jason left Shane's and walk along the sand now. They don't say too much. It's been a shake-your-head kind of evening, what with the surprise of Celia and Shane's affair.

"I really have to process all this," Maris tells Jason beside her. "Don't you?"

"In more ways than one," he says, loosening the skinny tie over his utility shirt.

"Can you still believe it?" Maris' sandals are looped through her fingers. Small waves splash at her feet. "I

12

almost died when it was *Celia* walking into that backyard."

"I know." Jason scoops up a beach stone and tosses it out over the water. "But after having dinner with them? I can't picture them apart. Or, Jesus—with anyone else, either."

"True. So true."

They talk little as they walk then. Out on the water, the empty swim raft floats in that swath of moonlight. And on the sand ahead, the last-standing cottage on the beach is mostly dark. Few windows are illuminated there. It's a peaceful night. Still, something about that beautiful lobster dinner, and watching Shane *so* taken with Celia, oddly leaves Maris feeling lonely. She senses that loneliness—brushed across her heart the way that moonlight is brushed on the water. Wavering with the ripple of the waves.

"Unlikely couple, huh?" Jason's voice comes to her in the darkness. He skims another stone far out over the water. "Shane and Celia."

"Think they can make it work? I mean, Shane lives so far away."

"Don't know. It'll be tough." Jason stops near the rocky outcropping past the Fenwick cottage. He turns to the water and pauses, looking out into the darkness. "With the miles about to come between them?" He looks at Maris as she pulls up the short blazer draped over her shoulders. They start walking together back down the beach. "Odds are stacked against them."

～～

Shane and Celia sit alone now at the rickety table.

Beyond the nearby sweeping beach grasses, Long Island

Sound stretches out into the night. Around them, the paper lanterns strung from wooden oar to wooden oar still glow. The salt air is misty. Shane's aware of it all as he sits beside Celia there. He drags his fork across his plate, and presses up crumbs and pieces of lemon bar. Raises his fork to his mouth. Sips his wine.

"Wish you could stay," he says to Celia.

She swirls the wine in her glass. "Me, too. But it's late. And I'm sure Elsa's keeping an eye out for my car."

Shane sits back in his old wooden chair and pushes up his cuffed shirtsleeves. "I know she's got Aria tonight. So where'd you tell her you were going?"

"Out."

"What?"

"I told her I was going out."

"That's it?" Shane leans forward, elbows on his knees now. "Just that you were ... going out?"

Celia nods. "I said she could call or text me, if necessary."

"You didn't lie?" Still leaning on his knees, Shane goes on. "You know, make something up and tell her you were ... I don't know. Visiting Lauren, maybe?"

"No. Elsa doesn't need to know *where* I am. Only that she can reach me."

"Now Celia, that's a change." Shane sits straight and pulls his chair beside hers.

"Well," Celia says, then tips up her wineglass for a sip. "There have *been* some changes lately."

"Like what?"

"Like a little bit of Elsa doing her own thing, and me doing mine, too. At least I was honest with her."

"Can't fault you that."

"No. I told her I was going out tonight—which I was. And she knows how to get in touch," Celia says, matter-of-fact.

Shane watches her in the night's shadows. Lantern light shines on the table, on the lawn. Pale light falls from the crescent moon, too. Celia's face is calm now. She sits close, her legs casually crossed. That long, faded denim skirt she wears is slit in the front and falls open below the knee. In the flickering candlelight, her silver chain necklaces glimmer against her white tee. She's comfortable here. With him. With herself.

But Shane knows. Elsa hurt Celia with her solo decision to keep the inn closed, so now Celia's drawn a line of privacy between them. He says no more about it. "It's freeing, no?" he quietly asks instead, stroking her arm as he does.

"What is?"

"Putting it out there."

"Putting *us* out there?"

"Yeah. To Jason and Maris."

"Little bit." Celia picks up a lemon bar from the dessert platter. "At first I thought it would be a mistake."

"But it wasn't," Shane tells her.

"No." Celia takes a bite of that lemon bar. "It's a relief, actually," she says around the food. "But they're the easy two."

Shane just nods. And moves a strand of hair behind her ear. Touches her face. *"God, am I in love with you."*

Celia takes his hand and kisses it. "Let me help you clean up here before I leave."

"No. I'll get it afterward." Now he leans close, brushes a crumb from her lips and kisses her. Cradling her face, he says then, "I'd rather just sit at this table with you."

And they do.

Another hour passes with just the two of them. There's a little more, too. There's the rhythm of the distant waves splashing onto the private beach beyond the small yard. And there's the hushed rustle of the dune grasses. All of it beneath the lazy moon hanging out there, too. His and Celia's voices are soft. Their touches, easy and many. Kisses, intimate—missing each other, already.

⌒

After Celia leaves, Shane sits on the half-wall on his back porch. He looks out to the table and four old chairs and long white serving bench in the yard. All the lanterns are still lit, their flames flickering. The few lanterns clustered on the bench glimmer on the now-empty white enamel lobster pot. The paper lanterns looped between the propped oars cast a faint light on the table—where dishes remain.

Where forks are strewn across them.

Where residues of wine streak crystal glasses.

Where purple hydrangea blossoms wither in a white pitcher.

Where cloth napkins are crumpled.

Where whispers echo, and silhouettes waver—if he looks just right.

Shane breathes in the salt air and sits there alone, leaning against a porch post on that half-wall. It's a night he didn't want to end.

⌒

It starts right away. Right when Jason drops off Maris at their gabled house on the bluff, then actually leaves beneath the train trestle. In the dark of night, the stone walls of that tunnel feel like they're closing in on him. The feeling remains while he drives on Shore Road, and still does when picking up the highway.

But it's not the stone walls closing in. It's something else. While driving back to Ted Sullivan's cottage, that feeling presses close. It has Jason perspiring. Gets him opening the SUV window and sucking in the outside air.

When he finally parks in Ted's driveway and goes inside the cottage, Jason knows damn well what's causing the feeling. It's his own *life* closing in. His doubts. His worries about being away from Maris for weeks now.

Maybe he'll walk the anxiety off. Shake it off. So he leashes Maddy—still freshly groomed—and heads out through the back slider, then onto the beach.

Unlike Stony Point, Sea Spray is a straightaway beach— open to the winds, the surf. A stiff breeze blowing there lifts his hair. Ripples the fabric of his button-down shirt. The German shepherd beside him snorts and sniffs the salty air. Whines, too. But Jason keeps her close, on-leash. Together, they walk to the water's edge. Waves splash onto the sand. The crescent moon drops golden light on the choppy water.

Jason looks out over the Sound. "Shit. You there?" he quietly asks.

And waits.

Neil doesn't often show up at Sea Spray. Jason's listened these past few weeks here. Turned off the central air in the cottage and left windows open to the breeze—which can carry whispers of his brother's voice, his spirit. It's why Jason often works outside on the deck. Because that's where he can tip his head and listen closely to the splash of the waves, the cry of the gulls, for the inflection of Neil's words. Most of the time, Neil doesn't show. Most. But *sometimes*, he does.

Waiting still, Jason pulls Maddy closer. The dog's not used to being leashed on these night walks, and whines again.

"Come on, guy," Jason says into the wind. "You hear me?"

No response. Nothing.

Not until he starts moving with the dog. He and Maddy walk the packed sand just below the driftline. Waves break close by.

What's happening?

Jason barely makes out the words in the *hiss* of one of those sloshing waves. The sound gets him to stop and close his eyes.

Talk to me, Jay.

Jason drags a hand through his windblown hair. "Don't know how much longer I can wait for my marriage," he admits.

A passing boat motors by far out on the water. *What do you mean?* sounds in its frothy wake.

"I mean, Maris and I can't work? Look at what Shane and Celia are doing—making a go of a *really* complicated situation." Jason walks a few steps on the packed sand. "And then there's Cliff—trying like *hell* with Elsa. Kyle and Lauren, too. They actually celebrated and *owned* the hard road they've been on the past decade."

Everyone's fighting for something. Or someone, Jason hears as Maddy gives a shake and jangles her collar.

"Yeah." Jason blows out a breath and says nothing more. Minutes pass and there's only the waves breaking. The wind brushing his face, his hair. But no sound of his brother. Finally, Jason turns and walks the dog across the sand toward the cottage. When they near the dune grasses before it, he could swear there's a slight shove to his shoulder. "What the hell's that for?" he asks, glancing behind him to the dark beach.

He stops moving, too. Right there, near the dunes. In the breezy salt air, those sweeping grasses whisper.

So does someone else. *Get moving, Jay. Somehow, someway. A soldier's always on the move.* Neil's words are fading now. Or else the wind's dying down, stilling those wild grasses. *Too much time's passing ... getting away from you,* Jason barely hears. Or the grasses sway. Or a wave hisses.

"*What's* getting away, guy?" Jason asks. Time? His marriage? After a quiet moment, though, he tugs Maddy and crosses the deck to go inside.

Closes up the slider, too. And the windows. No sense in listening anymore. In waiting. Instead, Jason pours a splash of whiskey into a glass and downs a mouthful. He thought the walk might help that closing-in feeling. That it might help to unkink seaside. He glances out a window toward the beach.

Maybe it did help. Maybe Neil was warning him. Hurry up. Get moving—*now.*

So Jason does the only thing he can. He goes upstairs to the guest bedroom and packs another few boxes. Shoves in all the clothes that'll fit, leaving out just enough outfits and shoes to get by. Basic shit he can wear—and wear again. When he carries the last of the packed boxes downstairs, he nearly trips on one of Maddy's knotted-rope dog bones.

"Celia and Shane are going the distance—three hundred miles apart," he gripes while picking up that chewed ropy bone *and* holding the carton. "And I can't make it home to Maris *twenty* miles down the goddamn coast?"

He carries that box and the big roped bone into the kitchen. Maddy follows behind him. The dog's tail is low but lightly wagging. After setting the taped-and-packed carton on the counter with the mountain of others, Jason tosses the knotted rope across the kitchen floor to the dog.

"Chew it, Maddy," he says, then reaches for that whiskey glass and tosses back what's left in it. "Rip it to fucking shreds."

three

FRIDAY MORNING, THE FLAME CATCHES at the first strike of the match. Maris lowers it to the wick and gets a tarnished lantern glimmering. Even though it's early and pale sunlight streams into the old shingled shack, the lantern sets the atmosphere. Grabbing a lacy cardigan from the chairback, Maris settles in at her laptop. The sun just crested the bluff, and she's anxious to make progress on the novel before the construction racket begins. Which gives her about an hour of quiet. It's enough time, though, to type this one scene. Oh, how life works its way into her writing—even in little ways. This time, it's the intimate lobster dinner with Shane and Celia last night that does it. That very private dinner at that tiny table against the beach grasses.

A tiny table she brings to *Driftline* …

There's a secret at the table. And it's a dangerous secret, no doubt. One unspoken and almost too big for the little faded table where they sit. The table's tucked in the corner of the bedroom—a spot meant for reading a book. Or for jotting a note. A table beside the window so you can look out at the sea. Wouldn't he like to do that right now? Sit there and watch the waves crashing in. He can't, though. Not with the plywood nailed over that window. Plywood being pummeled with driving rain. It's coming down so hard, the steady drum of it against the cottage sounds like rolling thunder.

But nothing drowns out the secret at the table. A secret too big for the plain white envelope that holds it. An envelope between the two of them now. An envelope upon which a lone flickering candle casts eerie pale light. Problem is, everything's eerie, and frightening, about that damn secret—whether by candlelight or in the bright light of day.

"I said, you've got some explaining to do." As his interrogator talks, he nudges the envelope across the table. Sits back, then, and folds his arms across his chest.

In the ensuing silence, it's obvious what the gesture means. They're going nowhere. Neither one of them. Not until that secret's hashed out, dissected and resolved. But he tries to sidestep it. "What are you doing in my room, anyway? And going through my things?"

"I saw your girlfriend rush out—"

"She's not my girlfriend."

"She's someone. When she flew out, I came in to see what got her spooked. Assuming it's that," he says with a nod to the envelope. The secret. The ticking bomb in the room.

As they talk, the wind outside kicks up. Its whistle grows to a howl. He squints across the table at his interrogator then. Might as well be in a court of law getting cross-examined, what with the directness of the questions. The comments.

But he's not in a courtroom. He's in an old, rambling cottage

22

THE GOODBYE

getting the shit pelted out of it by some nasty hurricane.

A cottage—not a courtroom. Which means he's God damn free to leave.

So he snatches up that envelope, stands and lifts his hooded sweatshirt from a nail on the closet door. After slipping on the sweatshirt, he heads toward the hallway.

But a sound stops him. The sound of a chair flipping over as the interrogator abruptly stands and rushes across the room. In the dim candlelight, he looks like a shadow bolting to the door and laying a fist against it.

"Where do you think you're going?"

"Out. Out of here. Out of this cottage. Out of this beach town. Out of my fuckin' mind, okay? I'm gone, man."

The interrogator looks long at him. Stares through the darkness. And drops his outstretched arm that blocked the door. "We're not done here," he says, then steps back and moves aside.

So pulling that hoodie up around his neck, he turns into the hallway and flies down the stairs. Does more, too. He nearly knocks down the flickering candles on the cabinet there. But he catches those burnt-down candles. Rights them, too.

If only he could do the same to his life.

⁓

Maris sits back with a long breath. Studying the last two lines of the passage, she whispers, *"Don't we all."*

⁓

Jason wakes up with an arm tossed over his eyes.

"Not today," he whispers while shifting his residual limb.

23

Slivers of pain have been shooting up it, which doesn't surprise him. It happens. Sometimes the weather causes the sensation; more often, it's stress manifesting itself in the limb.

This time, he doesn't fight it. Doesn't ignore it and roll right out of bed to get to the day.

Instead, wearing his pajama shorts and a loose tee, he rolls right into his exercise routine. Lord knows, it's fallen by the wayside here at Ted's cottage—and now he's damn well paying the price. But the exercise repetitions are memorized. He can get through them with no thought.

So he begins, bending his amputated limb up to his chest, even with his hip. His hands reach around—grabbing that upper left leg from behind. With the thigh firmly clasped and supported, he unbends his knee and extends the leg straight up until feeling the stretch in the muscle.

As he does, his voice begins the count. It also gets Maddy running up the stairs. *"Four, five, six,"* Jason says while flat on his back on the mattress. And he keeps counting now, even with Maddy pacing beside the bed.

"Seventeen, eighteen, nineteen," Jason goes on, holding the stretch. It's not easy. The muscles are stiff today. But he knows better. If his leg bothers him, everything else will, too. All day. So he keeps counting. *"Twenty-nine, and thirty."*

That done, he tackles the remaining repetitions. Still counts out the holds, too. It's a mantra for him—rotely saying the numbers aloud. The words keep his thoughts at bay. Or one thought. The one that brought on his distress. The thought of Shane and Celia wrangling a relationship facing all odds *and* hundreds of miles of distance.

And Jason can't manage a marriage twenty miles away.

On top of it all, he'll be up and down the Connecticut coast today—starting with some Fenwick filming, then off to the White Sands shotgun cottage. The *last* thing he needs is to be slowed down by his leg. So he finishes the exercises, sits up and reaches for his forearm crutches beside the bed. As he crosses the room to the Shaker-style dresser, Maddy's at him. Nipping at the crutches. Bowing down playfully. Jason maneuvers his way around her, then lifts his clothing bag off the dresser and hooks it onto the crutches. "No work for you today, Maddy. Too much going on," he says, filling the bag with a fresh change of clothes. "Time for a custody swap, actually."

Easy enough to arrange. Jason crosses the room again to where his cell phone leans against the green-glass lamp on the nightstand. Sitting on the unmade bed, he takes the phone and texts Maris.

～〜

Two hours later, Jason's parked curbside at his own gabled house in Stony Point. The morning sun casts a golden hue on the old shingles. Thin white clouds streak the blue sky above. After tapping the horn, he waits for Maris to come to the front door—since he's banished from going inside. Waiting in his vehicle, Jason notices how tall and shaggy the shrubs in the side yard have gotten. They need some attention.

"*Another time*," he says to himself when Maris opens the door to the house. That's his cue to lean over and open the SUV's passenger door. "Out you go," he tells Maddy—

who bounds across the front lawn to the porch.

Wearing a cardigan and frayed denim cutoffs, Maris stands at the top step. "Maddy!" she calls while bent and patting her legs. "Come here, girl!"

Jason watches for a few seconds. Just until Maris gives a wave. He waves back, reaches for that open passenger door and pulls it shut before driving away.

four

So ANYWAY," SHANE SAYS FROM his stool. Weathered buoys hang like pendant lights over the Dockside Diner's counter. "I would've been here earlier if the Stony Point security cruiser didn't slow me down."

"No shit." Kyle, wearing a chef apron over his black tee and pants, sets a loaded breakfast plate on Shane's paper placemat. "What was going on?"

Shane eyes his meal—two sunny-side-up eggs, hash browns, several slices of crispy bacon, two pieces of toast. He salts and peppers the eggs while telling Kyle, "You won't believe it." Behind Shane, there's the hum of customer voices, the clinking of flatware on dishes. Lauren's buzzing around, too. She's wearing her waitress half-apron, seating folks, taking orders.

"Oh, I'd believe *anything* about that beach," Kyle assures him. "Seen it all."

"Okay." Shane slices into his perfectly cooked eggs and

27

downs a mouthful. "So I was driving down Hillcrest Road and got slowed down by this car in front of me."

"The security car," Kyle says, pouring himself and Shane a mug of hot coffee.

Shane nods. "Nick was driving."

"How could you tell?" Kyle asks, then leans back against a rear counter and sips his coffee.

"Cliff gave it away. He was in the front *passenger* seat, and—" Shane bites off half a bacon slice and points to the far counter. "Here. Give me that paper towel roll and I'll demonstrate."

Kyle hands him the nearly empty roll. "This oughta be good."

Shane laughs. "While Nick *slowly* cruised along, Cliff had his megaphone. His window was rolled down as he made his announcement through it. Went something like this," Shane says, then brings that cardboard roll to his mouth.

"Oh, man." Kyle grabs a cruller from the pastry case. "Lay it on me."

Shane muffles his voice and begins talking into the paper towel roll. "*Attention Hillcrest Road residents. Please report to the pavilion this morning. It's pick-up day for your Hurricane Emergency Plan. Bring proof of residency in form of parking sticker or piece of mail. Detailed emergency brochures will be distributed. Complimentary wind-up radio with built-in flashlight and phone charger included.*"

Kyle points his partially eaten cruller Shane's way. "*Right.* I read something about that in Cliff's special-edition newsletter."

"And that radio's not a bad gadget to have in an emergency," Shane says, setting aside the cardboard roll.

"So what'd Nick do?" Kyle asks, backing up to let Lauren by with a full tray of food. "Drive up and down the whole street?"

"Yeah. I had to tap the horn for him to pull over so I could pass." Shane forks off another slice of egg. "I'd still be there otherwise, stuck behind them while they made their slow-mo drive-by announcement."

Kyle dunks that cruller into his coffee and takes a soggy bite. "Wait. *Wait*," he insists, mid-chew. "Did Cliff do Bayside Road yet?"

"Don't know." Shane folds a piece of toast in half and scoops it through his runny egg yolk. "I was only on Hillcrest."

Kyle looks around, whispering, "*Shit*." When Lauren approaches again, he stops her. "Hey, doll. Did we already get our hurricane kit?"

"No," she tells him, then rips several papers from her pad and clips them on Jerry's order carousel. "You can pick them up anytime, can't you?" she asks over her shoulder.

"Oh, no. No, no," Shane says while pouring ketchup on his hash browns, then scooping up a forkful. "The commish is *very* methodical, believe me. It's street by street *only*—with designated pick-up times—*at* the pavilion."

"Well that's ridiculous. How about if someone can't make it then?" Lauren takes two plates of French toast from Jerry's cooking station. Tabs of melted butter cover the bread. Powdered sugar is sprinkled over it all. "I'm sure Cliff will make an exception and let Kyle pick ours up at his convenience," she says, setting the breakfast plates in front of customers seated at the counter.

"Cliff?" Kyle asks around another mouthful of coffee-drenched cruller. "Make an *exception?*"

"How soon you forget," Shane reminds Lauren.

"Forget what?" With a stack of folded Dockside Diner tees in her arms now, Lauren heads over to the T-shirt shelf. Beneath it, vintage anchors lean against the wall.

"The *rules* ... are the *rules*." With that, Shane raises his coffee cup in a toast.

And Kyle raises his cup back.

And Lauren shakes her head.

Jerry pulls a few orders from his carousel.

Two more customers grab empty stools beside Shane, who drags a forkful of hash browns through ketchup and egg yolk while bullshitting with his brother this fine Friday morning.

⁓

Elsa waves over Carol and Mitch. They're just emerging onto the inn grounds from the secret sandy beach path. That's not all they're doing. They're also carrying a wire cart across the inn's lawn to the front yard.

"I'm really glad I could help out with an extra flower cart," Carol says as she and Mitch set it in place.

"Except now it'll be a tomato cart." Elsa steps back and eyes it closely. The yellow wire cart is perfect. It has two mesh shelves lined with small wire hearts. Its two large wheels are also made of yellow wire, as are the curlicue cart handles. "When I got the idea to sell tomatoes here, you were the first person I thought of for supplies, Carol. What with your flower business and all."

"We had one last cart stored beneath the cottage

30

pilings," Mitch says, tucking his sunglasses into the pocket of his loose button-down. "Had to clear out that space for the reno, and now we have a place to *put* this cart. Right here."

"Let me give you some pointers." Wearing a fitted midriff top over shorts and scuffed ankle boots, Carol steps closer. She bends, too, showing Elsa how to put on the cart's brake. And how to pull out the extra mesh shelf for her cashbox.

"Oh! I got one ready." Elsa turns and picks up a rectangular tin box from the lawn, as well as a few baskets of tomatoes. She arranges them on the charming garden cart. "With the inn's opening paused, I have tons of extra tomatoes in my garden. Tomatoes intended for guests who won't be here now."

"Well, I really dig your plan, Elsa," Mitch muses, drawing a hand down his goatee'd chin. "Us Stony Pointers will benefit from the misfortune, so *some* good comes from it all."

"Just keep the sun off the veggies," Carol tells her, opening a striped beach umbrella attached to the cart. "And the tomatoes won't wilt in the heat."

"I'll do that. Lord knows, that September sun is burning hot this year," Elsa remarks, adjusting a straw visor over her eyes. "And thank you both for delivering the cart. And … well … So goodbye now!" she says, picking up a painted tomato sign she'd tacked onto a garden stake. "I don't want to keep you."

"No problem at all, Elsa," Mitch says. He takes that garden-stake sign from her and presses it into the lawn near the tomato cart. "I've just got some grading to do back at the cottage. Early essays from my students. In between a little filming that'll be happening for *Castaway Cottage*."

"And I'm hightailing it *out* of there for the filming," Carol adds. "Hitting up the community garden for some late-summer weeding."

Elsa, well, she tips up her visor and peeks out at the bright sun, then glances to Mitch and Carol. "This was very neighborly of you both," she tells them. "Thank you again."

"Much obliged. I'll check in later to see how your tomato sales went." As he says it, Mitch takes Elsa's hand, bends and lightly kisses her.

"Dad!" Carol lifts her wire-framed sunglasses and glares at her father. "Jeez!"

"Well, Carol." Mitch pauses, holding Elsa's hand still. "Elsa and I *have* been seeing each other a little bit ... for more than business. Guess you'd be finding out sooner or later."

When Carol looks from Mitch to Elsa, Elsa nods. "Oh, Carol." She gives her a small smile, but can't find any words. So instead? Instead Elsa gently swats Mitch's arm.

With an easy shrug, Mitch tells her, "You enjoy this beautiful day now, you hear?"

"Oh, I surely will," Elsa says.

Tipping his safari hat then, Mitch heads back to the beach path with Carol.

Carol—no doubt with a litany of questions—leans into her father while pointing a finger at him.

And Elsa briefly watches before turning to her snazzy new tomato cart. *This isn't half bad*, she thinks, *this little side business here*. She arranges a few of the tomatoes and adjusts the angle of the beach umbrella, tilting it so the shade falls fully on her wares.

⌒

Every minute counts out at sea. If the crew isn't hauling pots and banding lobsters, they're swabbing the deck, breaking winter ice off the rigging. Something. Always doing something—bagging bait, coiling rope.

So it's just like being on the Atlantic, the way Shane's busy here at Stony Point, too. Valuable time spent with his brother over breakfast this morning. Then back to the cottage, where he returned last night's paper lanterns and old oars to the shed. Swept the porch's painted-wood floor, too. Dragged a soapy squeegee over the cottage's rear windows. Any breeze carries the salt from the Sound right to those glass panes. Hell, he might as well be on the boat cleaning salt off the wheelhouse windows.

Once everything's spit-shined, he pours himself a second coffee and sits on the porch's half-wall facing the water. The sun is warm; the salt air, a gentle touch. It's in these pauses that Shane knows. He *has* to be efficient with his time here—before it ends with one unannounced message from the captain. Then it's back to the boat.

Problem is, there are *still* fences to mend here, and bridges to cross.

"*So sue me*," Shane says to himself as he goes to the kitchen for his cell phone. "Got to make every damn minute count on land, too."

When he's back on the porch, phone in hand, he takes his perch on the half-wall. Breathes in that salt air that cures what ails him. Then makes a call.

"Jason. Hey man, it's Shane. I know you're working. But can you free up a couple of hours this afternoon?"

"Depends. Could move a meeting to tomorrow," Jason tells him. "Why? What do you have in mind?"

five

SOME THINGS YOU CAN'T EVEN imagine.

Driving down this four-lane stretch of turnpike an hour
later, Shane takes in the view—the warehouse stores, the
gas stations, the fast-food restaurants. There are no green
lawns. No trees. Just hot pavement and traffic lights and
cars. Trucks, too.

The thing is, it's the street where Neil died. And no way
in hell can Shane imagine, for the life of him, how Jason
feels when he cruises this pavement.

Today, he's meeting Jason here.

Shane's actually following a few car lengths behind his
SUV. They took two vehicles because Jason is headed to
Sullivan's cottage at Sea Spray afterward. He won't be back
at Stony Point until fishing tonight.

And maybe it's better this way, arriving separately.
Maybe Barlow needed the space.

Traffic's busy this Friday noontime, making it difficult

for Shane to keep an eye on him. But about a mile before Hartford, that SUV stops on the road's shoulder. Shane eventually pulls off the road behind it—right as Jason gets out, pockets his keys and waits on the scrubby roadside grass. Shoves up the sleeves of his linen blazer, too.

After Shane's truck jostles to a stop, he quickly looks around. Across the street to the left, a large cemetery covers a sloping hill. Beside him on the right—beyond a parking lot—a discount store, grocery store and small shops fill a strip mall. And up ahead, Jason's walking toward him. Approaching, he holds up a hand for Shane to wait in his truck.

Shane nods and opens his driver-side window.

"Before you get out," Jason calls to him, "got a question for you."

"What's up?" Shane leans an arm on the open window.

Jason slows, stopping before reaching the pickup. A dump truck rumbling past behind him gets him to glance at it, then turn to Shane. "Why today?" Jason yells over the traffic noise.

"You mean, to come here?"

"Yeah. Because I'm still not sure what's driving you— *and* if I want to rehash my life."

Shane looks through the windshield out at the stretch of busy pavement. "Captain will be calling any day, any *minute*. So ... my time's limited."

Jason walks closer to the pickup. Dried grass snaps beneath his step. He lowers his voice, too. "That's fucking bullshit, guy. Your captain's going to call, so you're taking a field trip?"

"That, and okay, I've got some demons I need to visit."

"Demons?"

"Damn straight," Shane says, looking Jason dead-on now. "My past. Things on my mind. Hell, my own behavior—including toward you."

"Me."

"No joke we've had some bad blood between us, guy. Especially these past few weeks."

Jason nods. "I thought it was water under the bridge. Said our piece and were done with it."

Shane gives a short laugh. "A few wisecracks at my brother's vow renewal? Friendly shoves? No. I want to *legit* fix things. Not just brush it. Partly because of what *you* said last night after dinner," he adds, pointing at Jason from the driver's seat. "When we all got to talking at the table."

"About Neil?"

"Yep. And how you never *dreamt* on that one day that your brother would be stone-cold dead in only hours. Made me realize it's now or never to right the ship."

Jason drags a hand through his hair. "*Here?*" he asks as a few tractor-trailers behind him blast by.

"Listen." Still talking from his pickup, Shane raises his voice over the traffic noise. "Any of us could be gone, anytime. With the risks on the boats on the Atlantic? I'm *lucky* to have made it through twenty years of lobstering. Things happen on the sea with no warning. No sixth sense."

"That was *my* day ten years ago. As innocuous as can be. A hot August day, nothing doin'," Jason's saying as he leans against the side of the pickup now, crosses his arms and looks at the turnpike. "Got a bike part with Neil, then ..."
He pauses, motioning further down the street, past the next

traffic light. "Then we were headed to grab lunch at The Elm Café."

"And all I *know* about that day is hearsay—from the outside. Elsa. My brother. And hell, I really don't want to be on the outside anymore."

"I get it."

"Good. Because let me tell you. When I got to Stony Point a few weeks ago and found out Neil was dead? Well. I've been carrying that loss around with me. I did *not* just shrug it off. So come on, man." Shane reaches for his newsboy cap on the dash, opens his truck door and gets out of the pickup. Fast-moving traffic on the thoroughfare kicks up a hot breeze that hits his face. "Take me down the darkest road you've ever been on."

Jason turns up his hands. Says nothing. Looks like he's swallowing some knot in his throat, too. "Let me lose the jacket, it's pretty warm," he finally manages, taking off the gray linen blazer he's got on over a loose white tee and jeans.

"Wear it filming?" Shane asks when Jason tosses it into his SUV.

"Yeah. At Mitch's place this morning." He closes the SUV door, lifts his sunglasses to the top of his head and turns to Shane. "All right. Let's do this," he tells him, walking curbside down the dirty pavement.

～

Jason turns back when Shane says nothing. When he doesn't move. Shane just stands there wearing a dark black tee over olive cargo shorts. His leather boat shoes are scuffed to shit; tattoos snake down his arms; his expression is serious. So Jason turns up his hands again.

"Hold on," Shane says. "Just ... you know. Pulling myself together."

Jason nods and waits for him to catch up. "You're only the third person I've come here with. In all these years."

"Seriously? Who else?" Shane asks.

"My father, weeks after the crash. I was freshly amputated and in the thick of hell then. We were looking for these." Jason tugs the gray chain from beneath his tee and holds up his father's Vietnam War dog tags. "My father couldn't find them and thought Neil was wearing them that day, and ... you know. Maybe in the crash—"

Shane stops him. "Oh, man," he says. In his pause, a radio blares from a car speeding past. "You found them *here?*"

"No. We didn't." Jason resumes walking curbside. Dry, stubby grass grows from cracks in the pavement. He remembers the hot day he and his father scoured the road. They were looking for gray tags on a gray chain on the gray pavement. They were looking for the impossible. The invisible. Jason was on one leg and crutches; his father was desperate. It was one of Jason's lowest days after the accident. "It was the second person I brought here who found the dog tags." He looks at Shane beside him. "Maris. She found them in Foley's, of all places."

Shane gives a nod. They walk in silence for a bit, then. There's only the sound of their gritty footsteps. The sound of car engines roaring by. The vehicles are so close, the passing wind blows Jason's hair.

"Doing this for you, too," Shane's voice says beside him.

39

It's the tone that gets Jason to look at him.

"You know," Shane continues as they walk beneath the glaring midday sun. "Because where you're at in life? Where you're coming from? It's all tied to this." He motions to the street as they approach a traffic light.

"Funny, because that's the exact place the impact occurred."

"You shittin' me?"

"No, I'm not."

Shane shakes his head. Standing there, he crosses his arms over his chest and studies the street. "Give me a minute, Barlow. Got to take this in."

Jason does.

Eventually, Shane looks over at him. "Tell me something about it. Tell me something I'm *not* seeing here."

"Okay." Jason drags a knuckle down his jaw. "Picture … a stopped clock. Because man, we were out of time that day. The good Lord didn't give us a second. Not one damn second. My brother and I went from seeing the car coming up behind us in the mirror—to impact. Like that," Jason says, snapping his fingers. "Done. No time to ditch the bike. No time to run for cover."

"*Jesus Christ.*"

"Yeah. Could've used His help that day. My life went from that car's reflection to Neil going airborne."

After a quiet second, Shane asks, "You, too?"

"No. My jeans, they got hung up on the bike. Snagged on something at impact. So when that smashed Harley spun across the pavement, so did I, man—right along with it. Twisted up my leg but good. And I knew it. *Felt* it. Pain so burning, it was like fire. Until everything stopped. Sight.

Sound. Nothing but silent spinning until I got flung off, somehow."

"God's hands," Shane says. No hesitation.

Jason falters some with that. He turns, then, and points to the scrubby roadside grass. "Landed right there. Looked up at the blue sky—I remember that—and then, nothing. Next time I was conscious, I was in the hospital, minus a leg. And a brother."

Shane says nothing. He just listens, looking from the road, to the brush beyond the curb, to Jason.

"When I woke up in that hospital, I knew it was bad. Could tell by the way my father looked at me. I had road burns everywhere. Lacerations across my face." He touches the raised scar on his jaw. "Unrecognizable, I'm sure."

Shane waves him off and steps away.

Jason holds back and watches as Shane walks closer to that traffic light where the impact occurred. He stops roadside there, looks at the pavement. At the guardrails. At the weedy grasses. Finally, he takes off that newsboy cap he's wearing, holds it over his heart and bows his head.

And Jason knows. Shane lost a brother, too. Neil—his beach brother. The sting, for him, is fresh. So Jason walks to the guardrail and sits on it, leaning his elbows on his knees.

Shane turns after a long minute, draws a hand down his face, rubs his eyes, then puts his cap back on. "Neil, man," he says when he walks to Jason. "I mean, right there—"

"I know, it's tough."

Shane glances back at the road, then to Jason again. "I never got to say goodbye," Shane goes on. "And for the past ten years, when I didn't know *this* ... that he'd died," he adds, motioning to the road, "he'd been *alive* in my head."

"Hey, it's all right—"

"No. It's *not*, Jason. It's seriously not."

And there they are, those demons Shane's paying a visit: Regret. Guilt. Longing. Jason sees they're all at him.

Shane keeps struggling, too. "And I came here today thinking ... I'd *see* something," he persists. "Some evidence of the crash. But it's wiped clean. No indication of the violence. Of a death. Nothing."

"Come here," Jason says, standing then. "Take a look at this."

Shane follows him along the length of the guardrail. The hum of traffic is constant behind them.

"See it?" Jason points to an old, dried-out cross.

"Sure do. What's the story there?"

"Your brother made that."

"*Kyle* did?"

"From Stony Point driftwood. First he propped that cross in the dirt. But after the accident, new guardrails went in. So he must've been by here and rigged this up." A small wooden stake is screwed to one of the guardrail posts. Kyle's driftwood cross is nailed to it. "Been here ten years now. There's your evidence."

"Wow." Shane crouches and touches the cross. Snaps a quick picture of it, too. "Wish I brought something. Flowers. A photo." He stands, then. "I got nothing."

Jason looks at him, takes his hand and clasps it. "You brought yourself." Jason sees, too, how Shane doesn't fight the tears filling his eyes. He just shakes his head and swipes at them.

"Funny," Shane says, "but I never had a chance to say goodbye to Neil, and I couldn't do it today, either. Thought I would." Shane looks out to the road. "But I just can't."

"That makes two of us, Shane. I never had a chance to say goodbye, either. And I never have." Some weedy flowers grow in the scrubby roadside grass. Jason picks a handful of them, then waits while traffic flies by. "Flung some of Neil's drumsticks into the sea once. That's the closest I came," he says, tossing the flowers onto the pavement when there's a break in traffic. "And I really stumbled this summer, with my brother gone ten years now."

Shane nods, then looks down the turnpike toward Hartford. "That Elm Café still around?"

"Sure is. Down the road a mile."

"You ever been? Since the crash?"

"Nah. Not once."

"Come on. Let's go there." Shane puts an arm around Jason's shoulder and starts walking back toward their vehicles. The sun beats hot—just like that day. A truck roars past. "We'll break bread together, you know?"

Jason stops, steps back and squints through the glare of sunshine at Shane. "You're not talking about just a meal, are you?"

"No, brother. I'm talking about forgiveness."

six

BEING OUT ON THE FENWICK cottage deck Friday evening feels a little like this: like being out on a boat. The cottage is elevated on stilts, with the deck even more elevated. Maris looks beyond the railings to Long Island Sound just a stone's throw away. All that height makes her feel as though she's *on* that water. That it's flowing right beneath her. An optical illusion for sure, but a great one.

"Maris, hello! I'm so glad you agreed to this meeting," Mitch says when he comes outside through the kitchen slider. "And you're looking very nautical there." He nods to the outfit she wore for their meeting: a flouncy black tank top tucked into high-waisted white *sailor* shorts—with gold buttons lining the front pockets.

Maris laughs easily. "Feels very appropriate, standing here on deck." She motions to the Sound. "It's as if I'm on a ship!"

Mitch joins her at the railing. The twilight air is still

warm, and misty, too. They lean there and look out to sea while catching up some. Maris fills him in on her novel's progress. Mitch mentions that Jason was there this morning.

"Did some filming outdoors today." Mitch points down to the beach.

"Nothing inside?" Maris asks.

"No. Jason circled the cottage *exterior* to point out its significant geometric shape. And let me tell you, Maris, it was something to see—the way he went into full-on architect mode."

"Really."

Mitch motions to the sand below. "As he circled the cottage, Jason explained to viewers how the structure's angular corners deflect powerful winds—which actually *saved* the cottage from many storms. Guess they're going to run Jason's spiel side by side with one of his blueprints illustrating the boxy structure of the cottage."

"Is that why you invited me here, then?" Maris asks right as Carol carries a plate of food out to the deck. "Something about filming?"

"No." Mitch turns and motions for Maris to sit at the patio table—where Carol is now slicing what looks like a strawberry cheesecake. She sets a plate at Maris' seat, and one at her father's, then leans against a nearby railing. Mitch sits and takes one bite of that cheesecake amply drizzled with strawberry sauce, leans back and wastes no time. "I asked you here, Maris, to talk more about your novel. *Much more.*"

"*Driftline?*"

"That's right. I have a proposition for you," Mitch begins.

"A proposition? This sounds serious."

"It is. Very much so." As he says it, Mitch glances to Matt on the beach. He's jogging past, fishing pole in hand, and headed to the nearby rocky outcropping. "Listen, Maris," Mitch goes on, turning back to her. "The English language is what I do. It's who I am. I'm a *professor* of it, and live and breathe it daily. My personal library is quite extensive ... as is my editing experience."

"Editing." Maris drops a fork through her cheesecake slice. "I had no idea you edited."

"I do. I've edited university press books from time to time. But only books that whet my curiosity, or my thinking." He lifts another forkful of cheesecake while saying, "I *only* take on passion projects."

"Oh my God." Maris sets down her fork. "Are you offering to be my editor?"

Mitch leans back and steeples his hands together while squinting across the table at her. "That I am."

"So *Driftline* would be a passion project for you?"

Mitch nods, then digs into his strawberry cheesecake again. "I've been toying with the idea ever since you *mentioned* the book to me," he says around the food. "And I have good reason, too." He motions for her to wait, steps inside and quickly returns with a framed photograph—which he gives to Maris. "I knew Neil."

"Jason *told* me." Maris takes the photograph of Neil. Holding a leather journal, he's standing on this very deck. He's got on faded jeans and a tee; a sea breeze ruffles his moppy hair.

"I actually *talked* to Neil about his book—the one you're finishing, Maris," Mitch says, his voice quiet as she still looks at the old photo. "He's been *here*, in this cottage. Toured it. Took notes."

"And he'd be all *over* your offer." Maris looks from Mitch then, to Carol still standing close by at the railing, and back to Mitch. Her eyes fill with tears. "Mitch. I could never even dare to *dream* something like this," she says.

"Dad." Carol leans forward and nudges Mitch's shoulder. "I think she's saying yes."

"Are you?" Mitch asks.

"Yes, definitely yes! But what will this entail? Because I'm not done writing the book yet."

Mitch waves her off. "We'll talk more next time. This was enough for now. I just wanted to take this first step today. And now I'll leave room in my teaching schedule for it."

"But you have to know something." Maris drops her voice. "I'm not sure how I'll even *publish* the book."

"Doesn't matter how. The manuscript still needs fresh eyes. And editing. Every book does."

Maris looks at him across the table. Mitch's fading blond hair is pulled back into a tiny ponytail. He wears a two-strand rawhide choker that shows beneath the collar of his linen button-down shirt. And he holds her gaze with his own determined look.

So she stands and walks to the far deck railing facing the expanse of blue water. The early setting sun casts a golden hue on it; the horizon is streaked with orange. Oh, she can just picture Neil *here*, right now. How *stoked* he'd be, too. She briefly drops her eyes closed before finally turning back toward Mitch still sitting at the patio table.

"Shall we shake on it?" In the low evening light, he

extends a hand in her direction.

Maris smiles, just smiles, before rushing to the table and clasping his hand with both of hers. "You've got a deal, Dr. Fenwick," she tells him.

"Well, I declare," Mitch says, squeezing her hand back. "This here's the start of something good."

Carol's right there, too. And ready. She snaps a picture with her cell phone. "Caught the moment for posterity."

Finishing up their cheesecake slices, they make plans to talk again soon. Details will be discussed. The process ironed out. When Maris finally stands to leave, Mitch nods to the rocky ledge just past his cottage. Shane and Nick are approaching there from a sandy path off Champion Road. "Guys like to perch out on the rocks, I've noticed," Mitch says to Maris. "Kind of a weekly thing?"

Maris takes a look. She sees Jason and Kyle there, too, setting up their gear. "Oh, yes. Friday night fishing. It's certainly in session," she explains while heading out. But while descending the deck stairs to get back home, Mitch stops her.

"Maris! Why don't you take the rest of that cheesecake with you?" he calls down from the deck. "We can pack it up and you'll enjoy it for the next day or two."

"Thanks, Mitch. I'm tempted, but have a better idea." Maris glances at the fishing starting up on the rocks. "If you bring it over *there*, you'll be in the guys' good graces for a long time."

Mitch looks quickly from those guys casting their lines, to Carol just sitting at the patio table. "Carol, think I'm going to mosey over and say hello to the boys on the rocks," Mitch tells her. "Could you pack up that cheesecake with some paper plates and plastic forks?"

~

Anything riding on the catch tonight?
Nah, you losers won't even snag a nibble.
Betcha I will, punk.
What? A wager, now?
Damn straight, I'll bet on that.
What are we betting?
Last one to hook a fish loses.
And then what?
Next time we're at The Sand Bar, loser buys a round.

And Jason clearly sees. It's not the potential free drink that does it. It's the goddamn competition. It's the one-upmanship on the line. It's the *status* that comes with bragging rights. The way the guys' fishing lines *whizz* out over the Sound, and the way some are reeled right back and recast to a better spot, and the way Nick shoves Kyle over to get to a perfect casting rock, and the way Shane double-baits his hook? Hell, it's game on.

After the initial rivalry, though, there's just quiet.

Which is when their Friday night fishing gets crashed and all heads turn. Some harsh *shushing* happens, too.

Mitch Fenwick smiles and holds up a hand as he works his way over to Jason leaning against a large boulder. Kyle's not far beyond him, and gives a wave.

"Hey, Mitch," Jason says.

"What's going on here?" Mitch asks with a look over his shoulder.

"Little fishing competition. Gets intense sometimes."

"I can see that." Mitch sets down a plastic container and tips up the safari hat he's wearing with a loose button-down and rolled-cuff khakis. "Anything biting?"

"Stripers." Jason casts his line out over the water. "Albies, too."

"Albacore? Pretty big fish, no?" Mitch asks.

"In deep waters, yeah," Kyle explains. Resets his *Gone Fishing* cap on his head, too. "Near shore, here? Five, six pounds, maybe."

"Not bad." Mitch nods, stepping closer. "Listen, Jason. I was out on my deck earlier, with Maris."

"Is that right?" Jason asks, watching his slack line. The quarter moon rises over the Sound and drops silver light on the water.

"Talking some business with that book of hers," Mitch explains.

"Business? About what?"

"About my editing it. I've got plenty of experience and would consider it an honor."

"All right, Professor!" Kyle tosses over while reeling in his line. "Mighty generous of you."

"She take you up on it?" Jason asks.

"Well, now." Mitch sits on a flat boulder beside Jason's. He pulls up a knee and draws his hand along his goatee. "I did surprise her with the offer. And I must say, she seemed floored. But *totally* on board."

Jason, Mitch and Kyle all look further out on the rocks to Shane—declaring he's got a nibble. He toys with his catch, reeling it in some, then letting the fish take out the line.

"Mitch," Jason says then, switching his fishing pole to his left hand and reaching out to shake Mitch's. "I'm sure it really means a lot to Maris—you editing the book. It does to me, too. Especially since you and my brother knew each other."

"I appreciate that, Jason," Mitch says with a nod. "Really dig that I get to be part of the project, and wanted to walk over and clue you in. *And* say hello to the rest of the fishermen. Deliver some strawberry cheesecake, too, if someone would allow me to cast their line."

"You got it, Professor." Kyle hurries closer and hands over his fishing pole. "Maybe you'll have better luck than me—and a round of drinks is riding on it," he says. "So you fish. And I'll divvy up the chow."

⌒

Shane has to laugh. At the word *chow*, all fishing gets timed out—just like on the boats. When that dinner bell rings, the lobsters in the sea are spared an hour or two. And here, the same goes for the fish. All the guys circle around Kyle on the rocks now. One by one, he hands each a paper plate loaded down with cheesecake.

"What happened to your catch?" Kyle asks, giving Shane a plate, too.

"Eh." Shane takes a fork and digs right in, then finds a good-sized boulder to settle on. "The one that got away."

"Oh, man. Who *made* this?" Nick asks around a mouthful. He's standing there in his fishing vest—every pocket stuffed with tiny tackle boxes, leaders, a mini flashlight, lures. Tapping the dessert with his fork, he asks, "You the cook, Mitch?"

"No, no." Mitch steps to some lower, more level rocks and casts Kyle's fishing line. "My daughter, Carol, this time."

"Tell her she won our hearts," Nick goes on. "Sweet dessert going on here."

The satisfied groans all agree. Everyone's digging in while nodding.

The ruckus is enough to get Mitch to squint back at them from beneath that safari hat he wears. He scopes out the whole crowd of them. "Y'all single tonight, boys?"

Matt nods while chewing. "Friday nights? We're always stag."

"Nick, though," Kyle mentions, hitching his head to him. "He's perma-stag."

Nick shoves Kyle enough to get him to catch his footing. Forks another hunk of cheesecake, too. "How about you, Professor?" Nick asks, jabbing his laden fork in Mitch's direction. "You seeing anyone these days?"

"Matter of fact, I am." Standing there on the lower rocks, seawater swirls in a tide pool at his feet. Mitch shifts his fishing rod and glances back at the guys. "Really been enjoying Elsa DeLuca's company."

Shane raises an eyebrow at that one—at both Mitch's comment *and* the momentary silence that follows. There's a random throat clearing, too.

Until Kyle jumps in. "That right?" he asks.

"Yeah, here and there." As Mitch talks, a fish gets his line ripping out. "Things kind of took off the past couple of weeks," he says while slowly reeling the line back in. The reel clicks and hums; the rod bends with the pressure—fish versus man. "With Elsa? Situation went in a way kind of unexpected ... but a *good* way."

"Little bit like a rogue wave?" Shane asks, then bites into another forkful of that cheesecake. "The way they swamp you sometimes?"

"You got that right," Mitch vaguely agrees while reeling in more of that line.

Jason motions for Kyle to add another cheesecake slice to his plate. "Things serious with Elsa, Mitch?" he asks while Kyle serves.

"Too soon to tell, Jason. But I'm fixin' to get it there." Mitch's line is still taut with a hooked fish. "Let me think a moment," he muses while pulling back on that arched rod. The fish randomly splashes the water's surface. "What was it Elsa told me?" Another tug on the fishing rod, then, "Some Italian phrase. *Avanti ... Avanti ...*"

"*Tutta*," Jason finishes.

"That's right! *Avanti tutta.* Full speed ahead. And that's what I intend to do with Elsa." He turns and carefully gives his bent-and-reeling fishing pole to Kyle. "I'm going full speed ahead, boys," Mitch says as he tips his safari hat and heads off the rocks.

The problem—a problem that keeps the guys silent—is that Mitch pulls out his cell phone while he walks. Shane watches this with mild amusement, especially once Mitch starts talking on that phone. Shane's not sure he's ever seen this rowdy fishing group more quiet.

"*Elsa*," Mitch's voice carries on the still, misty air. He idles nearby on the sandy beach. "Meant to ask you something this morning, when I delivered your tomato cart. You free this weekend?"

While this is all going down, Shane crosses the rocks to what's left of the cheesecake and snags another slice.

Standing near Jason, he still listens to that phone talk, too. "Hmm. Saturday won't work for you?" Mitch asks, looking out over the night Sound. "How about Sunday, then?" In the pause while Elsa must be talking, he slowly heads down the beach toward his cottage. The farther away he gets, the more his voice fades. "You know, darlin'? I've had, uh, such a *hankerin'* for pancakes. So how about breakfast with a view? Big farm I pass by does it up nice." Another pause, then. "Okay. Okay, I'll swing by early Sunday morning and pick you up. Bring your appetite!"

It's the last thing they all hear. Mitch is finally out of earshot. As he walks down the beach and talks more to Elsa, they only see his silhouette.

Which is when all hell breaks loose.

Shit, the raucous noise gets Shane to turn back to the guys. He can't tell who's saying what, but it's a mile a minute, that's for damn sure.

Did you hear that?
They're a couple now?
What about Cliff?
What about him?
I thought Elsa was with him. Going on a year, no?
Or going by the wayside!
Wait. I saw Mitch and Elsa driving in under the trestle a few days back. Semi-together!
Need some clarification, dude!

The guys calm somewhat as they get back to their fishing. Lines are cast out into the Sound. The Gull Island Lighthouse flashes in the distance. The seawater's small waves ripple beneath the pale moonlight. And the wager is back on as no one wants to be last to hook a fish.

"Got it," Kyle announces, reeling in and finally netting the fish Mitch snagged just minutes ago.

"Wait a minute," Matt says. "Didn't *Mitch* catch that one?"

"Disqualified," Nick calls out, casting his line beneath the moonlight.

"No way." Kyle holds up the catch for all to see. "Caught with *my* gear, makes it *my* fish." He unhooks the decent-sized albie and sets it swimming in the water. "So keep at it. Last guy in buys."

They gripe somewhat, but the rivalry is heated. When Jason picks up his fishing pole and gets it rebaited, Shane does, too.

But everyone stops and looks toward the beach when they hear a new arrival. It's Cliff, holding his fishing rod and walking over the rocks.

"Sorry I'm late, fellas," he calls into the shadows. "I miss anything?"

seven

BACK AT SEA SPRAY AFTER fishing wound down, Jason doesn't feel much like going inside the cottage. Doesn't feel like sitting alone there. Putting on the TV. Checking his phone. Opening the fridge to find something to eat.

It's been a long, long day—from sunup to sundown.

From that ache in his limb waking him, to the shave he skipped looking in the bathroom mirror.

From dropping off the dog with Maris, to working the rest of the morning.

From getting Shane's call, to revisiting the crash site.

From forgiving an old friend, to casting off with others.

From putting more miles between Stony Point and himself, to facing another night here alone.

Well, now. Jason might not *mind* going inside Sullivan's cottage—if he had something to believe in.

Instead he walks around the place and climbs the stairs

to the deck. There, he heads to the far railing facing Long Island Sound. Except for pale moonlight falling on the water, the beach is dark this September night. Even the dune grasses are nothing more than shadows. Waves break onshore. A wind lifts off the water.

Jason just leans on that railing and breathes the pungent salt air. Everything's stronger here on this straightaway beach—the currents, the breezes, the breaking waves. The salt air, too. So Jason takes a full dose of it. One deep breath after the other as he stands alone on the dark deck.

But it's not working, the salt air. Not curing what ails him. It didn't while fishing tonight, either.

Okay, so maybe the salt air was his brother's salvation. His father's, too—when the salt air at China Beach gave him a reprieve from the grit of fighting in 'Nam.

But … but maybe the salt air isn't Jason's salvation.

Actually, he's sure of it as he stands there in the night. The waves are rhythmic in their splashing on the distant sand. The dune grasses rustle in that sea breeze.

No, Jason knows what his salvation is. Tonight, especially, he's feeling the distance separating him from it.

His salvation is situated on a seaside bluff back at Stony Point.

His salvation is close to the stone bench his father built on that bluff.

His family's old shingled cottage sits on the hill there, too. He can see it now, in his mind, as though he's looking right at it. Oftentimes, sunlight glances off the cottage's weathered shingles—giving them a golden hue. He can visualize the faded trim around the paned windows and gabled roofline. Can picture the rickety picket fence running along the edge of the yard. The cottage stands solitary there behind it. Imposing against the coastal elements.

But his salvation? It's not the land. Not the salt air. Not the cottage.

Jason knows it as he still stands at Sullivan's deck railing. The breezy sea air feels damp on the skin of his face; it tousles his hair.

His salvation is behind the door of his family's old home.

It's Maris. Only Maris.

eight

EARLY SATURDAY MORNING, MARIS KNOWS something. Well, she's known since Thursday night's lobster dinner with Shane and Celia. It wasn't easy having her marriage come under their friends' scrutiny there. They saw the fissure between her and Jason. Jason got quiet, too, when she walked the beach with him later.

So Maris knows. Things need righting.

Or—as she likes to think—the stars need help aligning. And soon.

Which has her put on a loose, wide-striped black-and-white tank top over red twill shorts. A gold chain and a long beaded necklace. Easy. Clothes that move. That swing. Because she's got work to do, aligning those stars. Starting first with rushing across her backyard to the barn studio. She's on a mission today, and okay, only *one* thing can stop her.

Cody arriving with his construction crew.

"Working double duty," he tells Maris from his pickup in the driveway. "Crew's on overtime to start on the stonework around the stove. Installing your quartz countertops, too—everything except the island top. Still waiting on that slab."

Maris, her arms filled with coffee and a canvas tote and a leash clipped to the dog, backs across the yard. "Okay, Cody. I'll be in the barn if you need me," she tells him, then turns and hurries along.

It helps that *some* of her stars are aligning. She's getting a new kitchen.

Star one.

Inside the barn, she unleashes Maddy. She also stops to breathe in the faint scent of barnwood. Oh, this is so Jason's space. His father's, too—the old masonry barn now renovated into a coastal architect's studio. Markers and an architectural scale are on Jason's drafting table. Two sketches are askew there, too. Dimensions denoted with tiny numbers written by Jason's hand edge the straight black lines.

All of it—work unfinished. Work disrupted by their separation.

So quickly, Maris takes her coffee and tote up the loft stairs. For luck, she manages to pat the mounted moose head halfway up, too. Because, heck, she needs all the luck she can get shifting the stars of their lives into order.

And another star *did* come into alignment last evening. Her novel's *really* happening. Because she has an editor now. And an *esteemed* editor, at that. Mitch Fenwick.

Star two.

There's one last star that needs nudging today. "*I got it,*" she whispers while setting her tote and coffee cup on her planked worktable. She and Jason are overdue for another date. Just the two of them. She'll call him later to set something up.

Star three.

But first? Her special Saturday project. Before she gets to work on it, though, she has to do *one* more thing—text Cliff. Today's the day he'll propose to Elsa, after all. So Maris pulls her cell phone from her tote.

Good luck tonight at bandshell, she types. *Make sure you wear that outfit EXACTLY how we planned!*

With Cliff's text sent, Maris is ready and focused. Standing in her old denim-design loft, she sets aside her phone and pulls some of Neil's threadbare bandanas from her tote. Jason keeps a stack of them in his dresser and certainly won't miss a few. So shoving aside a random bolt of denim fabric, she then lays flat the bandanas on her notched-and-nicked worktable. As she does, Maddy scrambles up the stairs to the loft. She paces around the workspace first, sniffs at two mannequins left over from Maris' design days, then settles at the railing overlooking Jason's studio. The dog lies there and pokes her muzzle beneath that railing—watching below as if Jason will walk in *any* minute now.

Maris pays her no mind while she works. Morning sunlight streams in through the stained-glass wave window nearby. Dust particles shimmer in the sunshine. There's a muffled quiet in the big barn that keeps her in the creative zone. After lowering the built-in ironing board from the wall, she runs a hand over each of the faded bandanas— two blue, one red. Random threads on them need trimming. When she doesn't see her scissors anywhere with her fabric supplies, she hurries down the stairs to check Jason's big L-shaped desk. Her scissors are right there in his top drawer—he must've needed them for something.

"*Ach*," she says upon also seeing a half-full pack of cigarettes. "You are *not* starting those again." Taking them with her, she returns to her loft studio and tosses the cigarette pack in her tote.

Now, back to her project. First, the prep. She trims the bandanas' wayward threads. Lifts up one of the bandanas for a better look. Irons the faded fabric. Gently, each fold is steamed out. Each curled edge, flattened.

When she's done, she lays out the bandanas on the long table again. And considers them for this project. When riding his motorcycle, Neil wore the bandanas rolled and tied around his head. Jason said it was a signature look of his brother's, keeping Neil's dark unruly hair somewhat tamed. Even as a teen, back in the day, he'd have a bandana tucked into a jeans pocket or tied to a belt loop.

Stepping closer, Maris touches the bandana fabric as she thinks out her idea. She turns the bandanas this way, and that. With a finger to her chin, she looks at a bare stretch of wall in her design studio, but imagines a wall in her new kitchen. Finally, she arranges those scissors, a flat screwdriver and wide masking tape on the worktable.

And gets to it.

⌒﹏

This is when things hang in the balance.

Late Saturday morning, Jason stands in front of the

partially demo'd shotgun cottage at White Sands. While waiting for his clients, he eyes the empty structure. Its brown shingled siding is tinged black from the sea damp. Exposed wood shows through fading paint on the window trim. A shutter hangs loose, too. And until the blueprints are finalized, the interior demo's been paused—all due to a last-minute phone call from the homeowners.

So the whole project hangs in the balance, pending this meeting with them today.

"Thanks for coming out on the weekend," Jason says minutes later. "Sorry I had to reschedule yesterday." They talk in the front yard. The sun shines warm as they consider the cottage.

"No problem," the husband, Austin, replies. "We get how busy you are hosting *Castaway Cottage*, and are just glad you could fit us in."

"Happy to," Jason tells him.

"Okay, good," Austin says. "Because we actually reviewed your plans *again* last night, did a lot of thinking and came up with something."

"Lay it on me."

"Well," Austin's wife, Nina, begins then. "Your designs are spot-on. They have *just* the coastal aesthetic we're seeking. But we want to incorporate even more. So we'd like to change the exterior cedar shingles to vinyl siding— a deep navy with wide white trim."

"Got it," Jason says, nodding for them to continue.

"And we want to make a structural adjustment," Nina goes on. "The portico you designed over the front door? We'd like to expand that to a full front porch."

"A porch? Now we've talked about this before," Jason

reminds them. He pulls up a design sketch on his tablet. The added portico extends over the door and has scrolled braces, with a fish-scale trim along the eave. "Previously your budget couldn't take the hit for a full porch." He shows them the portico design. It might as well be a photograph, the way he's got it in full color, with the surrounding landscape sketched in as well.

The couple looks at his tablet screen, then to Jason. "We're actually going to cash out some of our investments and put that money into the cottage," Austin explains. "We look at it as just shifting the investment from one avenue to another."

"Ah, wise move." Jason draws a hand down his scarred jaw and considers the beat-up little cottage on the scrubby yard. "You're investing in your *life*. Spend summer evenings sitting here on the porch? You'll have sweet hours together, for sure. Making your life all the richer."

"We think so, too," Nina tells him. "So it's not too late to adjust the blueprints?"

"No. Now's the time, actually. Just tell me what you're specifically after, then I'll grab some photographs and get to work on it for our next meetup."

But they don't get far explaining before Jason's cell phone rings. A quick look clues him in that it's Maris. So he excuses himself, crosses the yard and answers.

"Maris," he says into the phone.

"Jason! Oh, I'm glad I caught you. I *really* need to ask you something."

"What's up?" Jason asks as he looks toward White Sands Beach just down the block.

"Well, *so* much is going on, we have to catch up. I want

to hear about *Castaway Cottage* filming. And I have things to tell you, too. So I was thinking maybe we could go on a little afternoon date?"

"Today?"

"Yes. After lunch."

"Maris." Jason takes a breath. And drags a hand through his hair. Glances back at the waiting homeowners, too. "I'm actually going to skip this one."

"What? Wait, where are you?"

"Working at White Sands right now. And later I've got my first meet-and-greet at some local fair a few towns over. You know, in the CT-TV tent. Trent's got these gigs booked all fall."

"Oh, that's right. You're promoting the show."

"I am."

"Well … I can meet you there for a fair date afterward! We'll ride the Ferris wheel. Play some games. Share a bag of kettle corn."

Jason's quiet for a long second. "I don't think so," he finally says into the phone.

"No?"

"No."

"But *Jason*. This was your idea. We're supposed to go on fun dates together—to get to know each other again."

"I understand. And maybe it was a mistake."

"What?"

Jason walks a few steps further from his clients standing outside the old cottage. "I just didn't count on something, Maris."

"What is it, babe?" she asks.

Hell, wouldn't it be easy to simply blow past this. To let

it go and see Maris later at the fair. To have something to eat together, talk, lean close on the Tilt-A-Whirl. Be with her. He *could*, after all.

"Listen," he says instead. Lets out a long breath, too. And presses the phone really close. "When we date," he goes on, "it does something I didn't see coming."

Maris' voice drops now. "What does?"

"The end of the night. It leaves me pretty down, actually. Every time I say goodbye to you. And I can't do it anymore."

There's just a muffled quiet from the phone as Maris says nothing. "Well," she finally presses, "maybe a date at the *fair* would be different. It might—"

"It won't," he says, cutting her off.

"Jason. I'm not sure what to do then," Maris goes on. "Because this isn't ... well—"

"Maris. I have to go," he tells her with a quick glance back at his clients. "I'm working right now. People are waiting for me here."

"Oh, I didn't realize ..." A pause—this one a noticeably longer silence. "*Okay, then,*" she finally just about whispers. "I'll let you go."

Jason nods without saying more. He disconnects, too, and waits there in the cottage yard. A minute passes. Eventually, he pockets his phone, turns and gets back to work. But he knows something, too, as he walks over to the little shotgun cottage again—with its dried-out and exposed laths and rafters inside. With its old, weather-beaten shingles and half-hanging window shutter.

He knows something, damn straight. And it scares him.

This reno project isn't the only thing in his life that's hanging in the balance.

nine

SOMETIMES IT TAKES YEARS FOR something to
make sense. A decision. An experience. A conversation.
Years of living might put the right perspective on a
moment. On a look, even.

On Saturday evening, doesn't Cliff know it.

All it takes is opening the closet in this flat-roofed,
modular trailer he calls home to fully understand. Going
into the closet, he'd only meant to get Elsa's diamond ring
off the back shelf. But he sees something else as he's
brushing past hangers of jackets and sweatshirts. There, on
the pegs up above. They hold his *Commissioner* caps and an
assortment of baseball caps.

And on the very last peg, *way* in the back, hangs one
blue-and-white sailor cap.

He lifts it off now and runs a hand over the fifty-year-
old fabric. It's *his* very own sailor cap, the one he religiously
wore when he was seven years old. Oh, yes. He *was* the little

lost Sailor everybody went searching for in that hurricane.

Funny, it may have taken fifty years, but for the first time? Cliff doesn't feel lost anymore.

Not at all.

In fact, he feels happy.

Because this is where *being* little lost Sailor led him. This is where that awful hurricane tragedy steered him through the years. All these decades later, it brought him back to Stony Point—with the intention of keeping folks safe as their beach commissioner.

Hanging up that sailor cap again, he knows it *also* brought him to the love of his life. To Elsa DeLuca.

At long last, his winding journey here makes sense. Cliff reaches for and opens the black velvet box now. On the ring inside, an emerald-cut diamond is flanked by diamond baguettes. After a moment, he closes and pockets the velvet box. There's really no time to spare. In the next few hours, his whole life could change.

But first, he *uses* some of those minutes to stop at the mirror in the trailer's tiny bathroom. There, he musses his newly textured hair. That done, he tucks his navy silk pocket square into his beige linen blazer. Tightens the laces on his mesh oxford shoes. Rolls the thinnest cuffs on his white jeans, too. With a final look, he remembers Maris telling him to pull up the collar of his cream button-down. So he does.

Oh, there's a swagger in his step as he flies around the trailer. He scoops up his keys and lucky domino from the tanker desk, opens the metal front door and finally goes down the four metal stairs.

This is it. A big day in his life. He's about to propose to the woman he loves.

Heading across the potholed parking area to his car, Cliff does one more thing.

He takes that scuffed-up domino and gives the talisman a lucky flip.

⁓

Well, this should be fun, Elsa thinks after Cliff picks her up. They're in his car and cruising the sandy beach roads. The Saturday evening couldn't be more gorgeous. A pink sunset sky, wispy clouds. The air is warm and crystal clear. Just right, actually. She's going to go with it—the night. She's not going to think, not going to fret. Not going to raise one hand in her mind for Mitch, the other for Cliff. She's *tossing* that scale for the evening—lest she not even enjoy it. So as Cliff stops at the stone train trestle, she digs in her purse for a lipstick.

"Looking *swank*, you two. Dressed to the nines," Nick says, bending low and peering in through Cliff's open window. "Going somewhere special?"

"Bandshell concert in Niantic," Cliff tells him. "It's big-band night, and they'll be playing all the old standards."

"Sweet," Nick says with a slow nod.

"Plan on having a food-truck dinner and a dance with my lady," Cliff says, looking to Elsa—then leaning over to give her a kiss.

"*Uh-uh-uh*, mister. Just my cheek, I'm doing my makeup." But Elsa smiles as she leans to him—head tipped for his kiss—then turns down her visor and adjusts the mirror there. She's wearing a fitted black sleeveless sheath that shimmers with sequins on the top and sways with a beaded-fringe skirt. "It's the last concert of the season," she says to Nick while dabbing on a sheer lipstick.

"Well, kids. Make it a good one," Nick tells them, slapping the roof of Cliff's car before backing away.

Elsa waves out to Nick, right before putting on her sunglasses. As she does, Cliff drives beneath the stone trestle and turns onto Shore Road. Late-day sunlight there makes the evening almost a fairy tale. The September marsh grasses are sweeping; lone rowboats are moored in still saltwater inlets. And everything is cast in a golden glow.

"You're looking very dapper, Mr. Raines," Elsa remarks, touching Cliff's beige jacket.

"Thank you, Elsa." He gives her hand a squeeze. "It felt like an event meant for dressing up. And you're looking pretty chic yourself."

Elsa nods and straightens in her seat. Shadows fall long across the road. Traffic is sparse. The evening is a little hushed, a little magical. It has her roll down her car window to let some of that magical air come through. As the miles go by, she checks her watch before turning to Cliff. "I think we might be fashionably late. Didn't the concert start already?"

"It may have," Cliff says as he stops at a traffic light. "But you don't have to miss anything. The local radio station is live broadcasting the show." He tunes the car radio to the station.

Right away, a familiar song gets Elsa's fingers snapping. She sways, too, as a male voice croons, "*Yes, sir, that's my baby.*"

"Oh, I *love* this song!" Elsa declares. "Turn it up, Cliff." When he does, Elsa extends an arm out her open window and cups the salt air. She belts out a few lines, too. *"No, sir, don't mean maybe,"* she sings. *"Yes, sir, that's my baby now."* Heck, she even manages to shimmy in her fringed black dress. It's just wonderful, the way the fun's already begun. "Come on, Cliff," she calls out while nudging his shoulder. "Join in!"

And he does.

When Elsa leans in his direction, Cliff leans into her while driving. With one hand on the steering wheel, he snaps his fingers with the *other* and sings along.

"Yes, ma'am, we've decided," Cliff sings. *"No, ma'am, we won't hide it … Yes, ma'am, you're invited now."*

Still swaying side to side, *and* snapping her fingers, Elsa belts out a few more lines with the radio. As she does, they drive past a block of tiny cottages-turned-boutiques. A canopied restaurant, too. Cliff cruises through a green traffic light—all while rocking out with Elsa.

"By the way," Cliff accompanies Elsa and the blasting radio—right as he turns into the concert parking area. *"By the way … When we reach the preacher, I'll say …"*

"Oh! There it is!" Elsa points to the bandshell at the base of a gently sloping lawn. The orchestra is all set up. The vocalist stands center stage. He wears a black suit and holds that microphone stand while singing. Stage lights shimmer on the performance. The low setting sun casts the bandshell in a ring of gold.

"Yes, sir, that's my baby," the singer serenades the audience watching from the lush green lawn. *"No, sir, don't mean maybe … Yes, sir, that's my baby now."*

After parking, Cliff hurries around the car and opens the passenger door. "Mrs. DeLuca," he says, taking her hand.

"Why thank you," Elsa tells him, stepping a sandaled foot onto the pavement. Once she's out, Cliff lifts two folding chairs from the trunk. Meanwhile, the music still plays and Elsa straightens the black beaded fringe on the lower half of her dress. As she loops an arm through Cliff's, those beads swing just so while they cross the parking lot toward the illuminated stage. Cars are still pulling in; families and couples mill about; the moon is rising in the twilight sky. Oh, the air is just electric tonight.

Elsa's so excited to get to the lawn and dance to the big-band tunes, she snaps her fingers to the music while they walk. Gives Cliff's free hand a squeeze, too. And what that does is this. It gets Cliff to stop, set down those two chairs and give Elsa an impromptu twirl—right there in the parking lot—before they head out into the enchanted night.

ten

SHANE WAITED UNTIL AFTER DARK.

He's safer this way. Safe from any prying eyes noticing him as he walks the shadows of the sandy beach roads. He even dressed innocuously—wearing a long-sleeve denim shirt loose over a white tee and black jeans. A soft cooler is hooked on one arm. While walking, he glances both ways. Over his shoulder, too—just to be sure he's not seen.

Once he gets to Celia's gingerbread cottage, though, he stops looking around. Instead he hurries across the front yard and circles around back—right as the door of her screened-in porch there swings open.

"You made it!" Celia says when he climbs the steps. "Don't worry. Elsa's long gone. I saw Cliff pick her up for the concert an hour ago."

"Okay, good." Shane walks onto the back porch and gives Celia a quick kiss.

"Hey! I *told* you no one's around," Celia says with a

wink. "So you *could* give me a kiss like you actually mean it."

"Ha, okay. Take two," he tells her while setting down his cooler. Cradling her face then, he gives her one helluva kiss. One leaving them both a little breathless.

"Much better," Celia murmurs right into it.

"Good. Because that kiss is going to have to last us," he says, pulling away and brushing a finger across her cheek. "Unfortunately? I have to get back to Maine tomorrow."

"So that was a *goodbye* kiss?"

"Afraid so," he tells her while crossing the porch to Aria in her baby swing. "Hi there, little one," he says, gently taking her hand and giving a shake. The baby's wearing a pajama onesie and coos while he talks.

"Wait. You're leaving? You mean, your captain called?" Celia asks from behind him. She takes the cooler he brought and sets it on the porch table. "Already?"

That one word, *already*, gets Shane to turn to her. Celia stands there in a lace-trimmed black camisole over cropped skinny jeans. A long string of beads hangs around her neck. A wide-stitched cardigan drapes open over it all. As beautiful as she is, he heard her disappointment. Sees it in her eyes now, too.

"No, Celia. No word from the captain." He walks to her, touches her loose side braid. "I have to get to the Maine *DMV* Monday."

"Motor Vehicle?"

Shane nods. "Apparently during my past few weeks here—while I was at vow renewals, and getting my ass kicked out of this beach, then wrangling back-and-forth trips—my truck registration came in the mail. It was sitting

74

in that drop-front desk in my living room. In a pile of mail Bruno held for me all that time. And I *wasn't* going to take care of that registration with you and Aria there."

"But we could've kept you company at the DMV!"

"Wouldn't hear of it. And technically I'm *supposed* to renew by mail. Which I didn't. So if I don't get there by Monday, my truck's unregistered and we're *never* seeing each other again."

Celia smiles. "In that case, it was nice knowing you," she says playfully, then turns to that cooler again.

"I'll be back here late Tuesday," he quietly lets on, walking up to her at the table.

"All right." Celia's lifting out wrapped Pizza Palace grinders. "But I'll still miss you."

Shane kisses her on the head and pulls the cooler over. "Likewise. Now let me get these ice-cream cups into your freezer before they melt."

"I'll do it. You sit. Relax. Aria just had her bottle, so you can keep her company," Celia says on her way to the kitchen.

Shane does just that. He sits in a painted wicker chair on the porch. A large Boston fern cascades from a wooden plant stand beside him. He turns his chair some to face the baby. Tells her, too, how he had lemonade with an old friend today. And how on his walk here, he saw a few swans paddling in the marsh. *"I'll have to show them to you sometime,"* he says, his voice low.

When Celia returns with napkins and cups, they move to a long painted table abutting the back wall. Celia lifts Aria out of the swing while Shane moves it close to the table. They set out plates then; pour soda into those cups;

unwrap grinders—Shane's Genoa, Celia's ham. They eat facing the patio outside the screened-in porch. Among clay pots brimming with late-season geraniums, and along the green lawn, solar-powered garden lights glimmer. Dune grasses edge the back of the yard—grasses keeping secret the winding, sandy path to the beach.

As Shane lifts his Genoa grinder spilling with shredded lettuce, tomatoes and provolone cheese—all if it drizzled with mayo and olive oil—he tells Celia about his day. How he took Walter up on his offer of that lemonade.

"We talked about my father, and our summers years ago when we rented Walter's place. Toured his old blue cottage, too. It was nice," his voice goes on as they sit close on the dimly lit porch.

Celia tells him how she took Aria to the beach. "I set up her little sun tent and we sat near the water. Watched the seagulls fly by. Took a walk down the beach. Looked at the ocean stars together."

And Shane loves it. He loves sitting at the big porch table like this. Loves talking with Celia and the baby here. Katydids creak outside in the darkness. Crickets slowly chirp. Salt air drifts in through the screens.

Hell, he'd be one happy man if he could just sit here like this all night.

But what he knows, sadly, is that he actually can't.

～

"Hey, I got some good news today," Shane says later when they've pushed away their crumb-covered dishes and linger at the table.

"What is it?" Celia's holding Aria in her lap now. The baby clutches Celia's necklace and is gnawing on the beads.

"Good news I can always use."

"Wait." Shane hitches his head to the baby. "You do realize Aria's gumming your pretty necklace?"

Celia laughs and strokes the baby's fine dark hair. Bends and kisses her head, too. "It's a teething necklace," Celia explains. "The beads are silicone and massage her gums when she chews on them."

"How do you like that?" Shane leans over and touches the beads, then pats Aria's arm. "Okay, then. So. My good news now." He pulls his wallet from his jeans pocket and slides out the Scoop Shop punch card—which he flashes to her. "Two punches to go, then a freebie."

"Shane!" She swats his arm. "*That's* your news?"

"Hell, yeah. And won't you be glad when that day comes?" he goes on while tucking away the card. "Speaking of which, I'll go get our ice cream from the freezer." Standing then, he puts his wallet back in his pocket.

"While you do that," Celia says, standing too, "I'll put Aria to bed."

"Goodnight, little one." Shane steps closer and bends to the baby. He strokes a hooked finger along her cheek. "Happy dreams." He brings their dishes and grinder wrappings into the kitchen then. Wipes the porch table with a damp cloth and gets their ice-cream cups from the freezer. As he does, Shane hears the tinkling tune of Aria's music box from the baby's bedroom. Hears Celia's soft voice talking, too. He stands there, ice-cream cups in hand, and listens. Just for a moment. Just until he notices some papers on Celia's kitchen counter. He walks closer and skims them briefly before heading out to the porch.

"Saw your papers on the kitchen counter," Shane says minutes later, when Celia's back and they're spooning ice cream. "An application of some sort? Is that for the inn's zoning issue?"

"No." Celia lifts a hefty spoonful of butter crunch ice cream. "That pile's actually my life plan."

"Well now." Shane digs into his own fudge-swirled coffee ice cream. "You once said," he says around a mouthful, "that you don't believe in dreams coming true." He looks at her sitting beside him. "Those papers maybe a dream in progress?"

Celia shakes her head, sets down her ice cream and walks to the kitchen. When she returns, she's holding the few papers he'd seen on the counter. "*This* wasn't the dream, teaching a home-staging class for Stony Point Adult Ed," she explains, setting the papers on the table before sitting again. "My *dream* was the Ocean Star Inn. To help manage a beautiful seaside haven for all. Which, no, did not come true." She pulls over her ice-cream cup and scoops up a mouthful. "Elsa says that *zoning* put the kibosh on the inn. But I beg to differ."

"How so?"

"I'd say Elsa put the kibosh on everything herself. Including my dream."

"You really think that?"

Celia nods. "Absolutely."

"But why?"

"Guess her heart wasn't in it, after all." Celia lifts a spoonful of her butter crunch for Shane to taste. "But my heart was, Shane. All the way."

"Yeah. I can see that."

"And Elsa knew if she approached me about the zoning issue, we'd have conflicting opinions. As the assistant innkeeper, *I'd* have told her to open the inn anyway."

"She could have?"

"Yes! Screw the rowboat rides in the marsh already! Let them go until we square things with zoning."

Shane lifts a spoonful of his ice cream. "Instead she let *everything* go?"

"She did. Our beautiful plans."

"Have you guys talked?"

"Here and there." Celia gives a wave of her hand. "And we worked *so* hard this past year getting the inn ready," she explains. "The complete renovation. *Castaway Cottage* filming. Decorating. Menu planning. Booking reservations. It was going to be … *grand*. My days would be filled and I'd earn an income."

Shane looks at her. "And now?"

"Now I'm piecing together adult-ed classes to teach. And have to talk to Eva about doing some staging for her real-estate business. I'm taking on singing gigs at The Sand Bar, too. Some dream, huh?"

"Celia." Shane gives her a spoonful of his fudge-laced coffee ice cream. "I don't know. Maybe Elsa just wasn't ready. She lost her son—who was supposed to be a part of the inn, no?"

Celia looks at Shane and whispers, "*I lost him, too.* You know that."

"I do. So you and Elsa are both coming to the inn from a difficult—but *different*—place. And I *get* that, because it's what happened when my father died."

"With you and Kyle."

"Right. We were both grieving, but not seeing eye to eye. And I don't want what happened to me and my brother happening to you and Elsa. You can't lose her from your life."

Celia pushes away her ice-cream cup and stands. She walks to the screen door and looks out onto the night. Doesn't turn to Shane. Doesn't talk. Just stands there with her arms crossed.

"Celia. Look at me."

Celia turns, but doesn't leave her post at the door.

"I know what you're doing." When she turns back to the screen door, Shane pushes on. "If you make a rift with Elsa ..." he quietly says. Still, Celia doesn't turn to him. But he continues. "I can see where this is headed. If you make a rift with Elsa, it'll be *easier* to one day choose me. And I *won't* have it."

Celia whips around then. "No. You listen to *me*," she insists through clenched teeth. "I'm standing here unemployed, with a new baby and a *boatload* of responsibilities. And Elsa's out dancing? With no worries, she's *living it up* at some bandshell concert. Like she doesn't have a care in the world!"

Shane stands and walks to that screen door, too. "I'm not sure that's the case, Celia. Elsa's going to have her way of handling things. And maybe that way is more roundabout than yours. Maybe she's processing this last year differently than you." He tries to turn Celia from where she's looking out onto the dark night again. She resists for a second, but gives in. Turns. Looks at him standing there inches away. *"Give Elsa some time,"* Shane whispers.

Celia turns away—again. Stamps her sandaled foot, too. Her posture is rigid. "And meanwhile, it's dally with Cliff here. And Mitch, there."

Shane steps behind Celia. Gently, he wraps his arms around her waist. Pulls her close as he talks softly over her shoulder. "Well, one good thing with all that dallying," he says, brushing a few wisps of hair fallen from her side braid. "It lets me be here with you."

eleven

AFTER HIS MEET-AND-GREET GIG AT a local fair, Jason takes the long way back to Ted Sullivan's cottage. He picks up Shore Road to get to the highway. This way he can stop at The Sand Bar and grab some triple-decker sandwich to-go for dinner. As he cruises his SUV down the winding pavement, the street is dark; shadows, long. Stands of trees loom roadside. Pale silver light falls from the moon onto a nearby saltwater marsh. Except for a few take-out joints and ice-cream stands, most of the businesses are shuttered for the day.

Finally, he turns into The Sand Bar's parking lot. *This* place is jumping on a Saturday night, so he drives through the packed lot until coming to an empty space. Swinging in and parking there, he also surprisingly recognizes a nearby car.

It's Cliff's.

Well, that went one of two ways, Jason thinks while walking to the bar's entrance. The door's propped open; the jukebox inside is cranking; rowdy voices reach out to the night.

And he knows. Either Cliff's celebrating with Elsa inside—with cheers all around.

Or his night went belly-up.

"Only one way to find out," Jason tells himself as he steps into the dark bar.

⌒

It doesn't take long, either.

As Jason approaches the long bar, Cliff glances over his shoulder from the stool where he sits alone. He's got on a beige linen blazer—sleeves shoved back—over white jeans. Gray mesh oxfords, too. And Jason can't miss that navy pocket square in his jacket. The commish is dressed to impress.

"I see you coming, Jason," Cliff says. "And you can just turn around and scram. I'd appreciate some space."

Jason keeps walking—straight to the bar. He sits on the empty stool beside Cliff's. "That doesn't sound like a yes."

"It isn't."

"You mean, Elsa said *no*?"

"No." Cliff swirls the liquor in his glass. "The proposal never even happened."

"*Shit.*" Jason settles on his barstool. "Yo, Patrick," he calls to the passing bartender. "Fill 'er up," he says, motioning for a draft beer.

"Mr. Barlow." Patrick sets down the frothy brew. "To what do we owe the pleasure?" he asks.

Jason takes a long swallow of the draft. "Need some

takeout, guy. I'm on my way home. How about a hefty sandwich? Smoked turkey on ciabatta. All the fillings. Tomato, spinach, provolone. The works."

"You got it," Patrick tells him, turning away with an easy nod.

While Jason waits, he gives his stool a slow spin—three hundred sixty degrees around. Takes in the entire bar, scans all the faces. "So where *is* Elsa?" he asks Cliff then.

"She's back at the inn. I dropped her off after the concert."

"The concert where your proposal was *supposed* to happen."

Cliff only nods.

"She aware of that?" Jason presses.

"No."

"Of *anything*?"

"Nothing."

"You get cold feet?"

"Not at all."

Jason props his elbows on the bar. Takes a swallow of his beer. Turns to Cliff. "So what the hell happened?"

Cliff, nursing some potent drink, throws Jason a look. "Kyle Bradford happened."

"What?"

Cliff just faces the bar. Slowly, he spins his glass. "Don't get me wrong. Kyle's a good guy, but with *real* bad timing tonight."

Jason waits for Cliff to explain. Behind them, the jukebox is quiet now. But a few mounted big-screen TVs are tuned to a late-season ballgame. Voices rise from the billiard room, too, where someone gave their cue a hard shot—ricocheting the balls.

But nothing out of Cliff, so Jason keeps at him. "Come on, guy. What's Kyle got to do with *any* of this?"

"Everything. Apparently he and Lauren were having a date night. You know ... cruising around in his shiny new truck. And the big-band concert was their destination." Cliff takes a swig of his drink. "Spotted us there and pulled up their quilt right next to us on the lawn."

"Oh, man," Jason says, clapping his forehead as he does.

"That's right," Cliff goes on. "They had a bottle of wine and a brimming picnic basket. Yep, those two kept me and Elsa fed the whole time. And when I danced with Elsa to a certain slow number—thinking, hell, I might get my nerve up alone with her like that—Kyle cut in and swept her away from me."

"Still, Cliff. There must've been a way—"

"No. *No* way. In my mind, I had the proposal all planned out—just so. The wooing. The dancing beneath the stars. The romancing, okay? And the vibe got killed. The plan, thwarted. So that ring's haunting my pocket now." As he says it, Cliff pulls out the small velvet box and flashes it to Jason at the bar.

"Well what about afterward? Driving Elsa home?" Jason asks. "You could've proposed then."

"No." Cliff sips his drink. "Wasn't in me, Jason. The way my big night was derailed? Took the wind right out of my sails."

"But your *threads*," Jason says, flicking the shoulder of Cliff's slick blazer.

"Gone to waste."

And Jason knows. Cliff's shot. Psyched himself up for the big moment—and the moment never came. "What about tomorrow? Knock on her door, man. Bring Elsa an egg sandwich and the ring, for God's sake." Jason gives him a slight shove. "Propose at that marble island of hers."

"No. Not going to happen." Cliff sits there, arms on the bartop. Watches some hitter bat a line drive on the TV screen. "Got to think about this," he says, his eyes not leaving the TV. "I just don't know now."

Patrick approaches with Jason's bag of takeout then. "Here you go, Barlow," he says, dropping it and the bill on the bar.

Jason pulls out his wallet, pays his tab and takes one last swallow of his beer. "How long you sticking around here, Commish?" he asks while Patrick gets him his change.

"Nursing this one drink, then I'll hit the road." Cliff looks directly at him now. His face is tired. His clothes, a little wilted. "I'm fine, Jason. You can go."

"You sure?" Jason asks right as Patrick leaves a few bills on the bar before drawing several draft beers for a nearby waitress.

"Yeah." Cliff takes a long breath. "I won't be getting myself into trouble. That's the last thing I need." He pauses, then half-waves Jason away. "Just want to sit here alone for a while."

So Jason stands, claps Cliff on the shoulder, grabs up his take-out dinner and walks away. Manages one look back at Cliff as he heads out the door, too.

Halfway up the stairs on her way to bed, Maris turns around.

Turns and walks back down the stairs, down the paneled hallway to the dark kitchen. There, she flicks on the light. Her secret reno is paused, midway through. The new floor's been installed. Cabinets, too—though their handles haven't been attached. The pendant lights aren't installed yet, either. And the masonry work around the stove is unfinished. But the appliances are in, so she'll do what she intended—make a cup of tea. Maybe the warm brew will help her sleep. Turning to the mess of her dining room, she finds the kettle, fills it with water at her new sink and sets it on her new stainless-steel stove. She stands there, then, in her olive jogger pajama pants with slouchy, short-sleeve olive top. She wears no slippers. The hardwood floor is cool beneath her bare feet.

A minute later, she walks back to the dining room in search of a teabag on the painted farm table. She rummages around granola boxes and pasta boxes and bags of organic potato chips. There are stacks of paper plates and cups. A pile of napkins. A heap of unopened mail. She finally finds the box of teabags and takes one out. Finds a clean mug on the sideboard, too. After blowing any dust from the cup, she drops in the teabag and returns to the kitchen. A few seconds later, Maris turns off the stove, sets down her cup and walks to the closed-and-locked slider. Standing there, she runs her fingers through her hair, then flicks on the outside deck light.

Well. By now, Maddy must think they're going out for a walk. The German shepherd steps out of her big dog bed near the pantry and joins Maris at the door.

"You stay here, Maddy," she says, then opens the slider and slips out onto the deck—leaving the dog to watch from the kitchen.

But once outside, Maris isn't sure *what* she's doing. She carefully walks her bare feet across the slivery deck boards to the far railing. Standing there in the night, she clasps the railing, tips her head up to the starlit sky and breathes. The air is salty, but still. In the distance, waves slosh at the bluff. She can feel the sea damp on her skin. Hear the katydids creaking in the trees. She closes her eyes for a long moment, too, before turning and going inside again.

Back in the kitchen, Maris shuts off the deck light, locks up the slider and checks that the stove is off. Giving one last look at her handle-less cabinets, she then shuts off the kitchen light and goes to the living room.

She can't settle down, though. The dog must sense it, because Maddy quietly trails after her. All the while, different sights make Maris sad. Or pause. Like the glimmering silver trim on the old Foley's jukebox tucked into the alcove. She lightly traces her fingers along that jukebox. In the living room next, she paces. Walks past Jason's upholstered chair to the mantel. There, she picks up her conch shell and holds it while circling the shadowy room.

She wonders if she should call Jason then, but decides against it. Not after their strained phone call that afternoon. Even *that* talk makes her sad—the way he felt they shouldn't date anymore.

So instead of calling him, she clutches that conch shell, skips the tea and goes back upstairs to bed.

Sets the conch shell on the nightstand.

Gets under the covers.

Shuts off the bedside lamp and lies there in the dark.

Punches her pillow, turns on the light and reaches for

some manuscript pages on the nightstand.

Sitting up now, she tries to read a few lines—but can't focus. Maybe if she trails her fingers along the paper while whispering the words, it'll help.

It doesn't.

So she gets out of bed and opens the windows all the way. She pauses there, too, trying to feel the cooler night air waft in. When she turns away, instead of getting back into bed, she scoops that conch shell off her nightstand and brings the shell back downstairs.

Jason gave her that conch shell three years ago—her first summer back in Stony Point. The old shell is faded white; its inside, whorls of pale pink. As she sets it on the mantel again, Maris sees her and Jason's wedding picture there, too. In it, the two of them dance on the sand that beautiful night. Jason holds her close; his black tux jacket is draped over her shoulders.

When Maris turns away, she notices the framed photograph of Neil on the mantel, too. His smile is wide, his thick hair blowing in some sea breeze, no doubt.

"*Neil,*" she whispers, touching the glass over his image. She's writing his novel. Feels so connected to him. But unlike Jason, she never hears his whispered words.

"*What am I doing?*" Maris asks herself, dragging both hands back through her hair.

She hurries to the kitchen again, too. Swats at the wall switch to flick on the light. Squints around the room— from the half-done stonework near the stove to the denim-blue island base to the unfinished cabinets. Right away, she spins to the dining room, stops at the farm table and lifts a package of brown paper lunch bags. She whips one out and stands right there at the table. All her cabinet handle choices are laid out on it: polished-nickel bar pulls and bronze cup pulls and nautical boat-cleat pulls. There are silver knobs, and black-painted knobs.

Maris opens that brown paper bag and drops in each cabinet handle sample. From behind tears, her hand blindly reaches for one at a time—before just sweeping the whole lot of them right into that paper bag.

twelve

THE KITCHEN IS STILL AT Sullivan's cottage.

From the planked hardwood ceiling, only the recessed lights glow. Even those, Jason had set to dim. So the cream cabinets and gray-swirled marble island are all just silhouettes in the low light. He sits alone at the round table in the kitchen nook. He finished his meal from The Sand Bar, and the wrappings are moved aside on the tabletop. There's a newspaper there, too, untouched. And a remote for a nearby mounted TV.

Jason reaches for that remote, fidgets with it and sets it back down. The paned windows around him are all opened. The night drifts in through the screens. Here at Sea Spray, he makes out the waves breaking on the distant beach. And some buzzing night bugs. The neighbor's cottage is lit up, and folks are hanging out on the deck this Saturday night. Their low, chattering voices carry over. The sound gets Jason to look out the window. Though some solar lights glimmer outside on the deck, Long Island Sound further beyond the dune grasses is black. It's actually hard to distinguish the water from the dark sky. But he looks longer and notices the string of lights on a barge being towed across the shipping lanes. There's always something, some sight, some sound, giving the sea away.

After shoving his dinner wrappings into their bag, Jason reaches for his forearm crutches, gets up and clears the table. Tosses out the bag. Maneuvers across the kitchen and sets a shot glass on the table in the nook. A bottle of Ted's whiskey, too.

When he sits again, Jason faces the night sea. He fills his shot glass with the amber liquor and takes a swallow. The warm salt air from outside feels good on his face. He drags a hand along his whiskered jaw. Closes his eyes and draws his hand down his whole face, then. With his eyes still closed, and head dropped, and hand pressed to his forehead, he just breathes in that salt air in the dimly lit kitchen. The house is quiet. It's just him and the night.

In a minute, or five—it doesn't matter, really—he reaches for the bottle of whiskey and adds a splash more to his glass.

～

When Maris turns her car onto the sandy road, she feels almost winded. It's as though it was a race to get here. And maybe it was. A race against time. Against fate. Against her doubt.

She drives slowly now, looking out at the seaside homes lining the street. But only one in particular matters. When it comes into view, she turns into the driveway. Brass wall lanterns cast soft light on the cottage's golden cedar shingles. There's lamplight inside the cottage, too. A few paned windows are illuminated. Sitting there in her parked car, she looks out for a few seconds. Time, time.

Well, she won't waste any more, and so grabs the paper bag on the passenger seat, steps out of the car and quietly—*so quietly*—closes her door.

Before approaching the cottage, she smoothes out her ripped jeans and the fisherman sweater she threw on before coming here. Takes a deep breath of that salt air, too, then walks up the stairs to the front door and reaches out to knock.

But she stops herself—right as her knuckles are about to rap on the door.

Instead, she lowers her hand, tips her head and listens. Not a sound comes from inside. She only hears waves splashing onto the beach. So she looks at the cottage door and reaches for the doorknob. Tries it, too. And it turns easily. It's not locked. Silently, she walks inside.

After carefully closing the door behind her, Maris stops in the foyer and looks toward the dimly lit rooms. Takes a few cautious steps, too. When she gets to the living room, a table lamp is on there. She sees the driftwood-gray sofa, and coffee table, and upholstered chairs. But the room is empty, so she walks on toward the kitchen.

And slows her step.

Listens.

There's no noise from a TV. No kitchen sounds, either. Nothing. No running water. No dishwasher sloshing. She's not even sure if Jason's there, or asleep upstairs.

So she keeps walking in the shadows.

Just before the kitchen, she spots him sitting in the windowed nook. The sight of him has her freeze in the darkness right outside the room. From this side view, she can see his drawn face, and the shadows on it. He's not happy. He's wearing an old, threadbare tee with cargo shorts. His face is unshaven and covered with stubble. His hand is holding a glass tumbler filled with some liquor. His forearm crutches lean against a nearby chair.

And her heart drops. It's everything—*everything*—written on his face that does it. Sadness. Loneliness, maybe. Regret, too. Oh, it's all there as he sits alone near the windows open to the sea.

"*Jason*," she quietly says, almost without realizing it.

⌒

Jason looks to Maris in the kitchen doorway. At first, he thinks he's imagined her. She wears a loose fisherman sweater over some ripped skinny jeans. Her hair is down and tucked behind an ear. A paper bag is clutched in her hand.

And she doesn't move.

His eyes stop on her face, which is fighting some emotion as she only looks at him. And then she speaks.

"The door was open," she says, glancing over her shoulder toward the front foyer. "So I let myself in." She takes a step closer, only one. "I know it's late, but I ..." She raises that crumpled paper bag, reaches in and pulls out a handful of some hardware. "I don't know if you knew this, but I've been renovating the kitchen these past few weeks. I wanted to surprise you."

Still Jason doesn't talk. Doesn't move.

But he watches as Maris raises a hand and swipes a tear from her face.

"And I couldn't sleep tonight. I'm not sure why. But I have to decide on drawer pulls for Cody. I've got knobs, and nautical handles, and ..." Her voice drops to a whisper. "*I didn't know what you'd like.*" Again, she takes a few steps— but stops in the middle of the kitchen, halfway to him. Silent tears run down her face now. "*I just didn't know.*"

Still sitting in the kitchen nook, Jason looks at her in the shadowy silence. Neither of them moves for several seconds.

Not until he tells her, his voice husky with its own emotion, "Come here, beautiful."

She takes a quick step, before stopping suddenly. In one blur then, she rushes to him—landing on the chair beside him. She scoots it close. So close. Tears line her face. Her hair is mussed. Her hand is clenching that paper bag of cabinet hardware. He takes it from her, gently, and sets it aside. She's still crying, too.

"*I just didn't know,*" Maris whispers again.

"It's okay," Jason says, brushing a tear from her face.

"Jason." She barely smiles, and shakes her head. "Jason," she says again, touching his hair now, and his face. He feels it. Feels every emotion, every fear *he's* been feeling, all in the tremble of her fingers against his skin.

So he takes her arm, wraps both his hands around it, one above the other—and lowers her trembling hand to his chest. He simply presses her hand close—right to his heart. They watch each other, saying nothing. But they know. They both do; he can tell. It's over, this separation. It's just over. Holding her hand to his chest like that, they sit quiet for a long moment until he slowly lets go. But he doesn't stop touching her as he raises his hands to her shoulders and manages a hug. It isn't easy, seated at the kitchen table. But he's on one leg, and won't lose a second because of that. So he pulls her close, his arms wrapped fully around her, and encloses her. There's no room for her to even move, to turn to him. His face presses to the side of her head. Her dark, silky hair is soft against his skin. His mouth. There is only touch now. Just touch. All their feelings are there in it.

"*Come home,*" Maris whispers near his ear. She slightly gasps, too.

"*Shhh,*" Jason tells her, moving his face against her hair, feeling Maris in his arms. Feeling her breathe against him.

"No." She shakes her head—he feels that, too. "No, no, no. *Just come home.*" The words, whispered into their embrace, get him to squeeze his eyes shut as his face is pressed to her hair. "*Now.*"

Jason pulls back and watches her. "Maris."

Quickly, she shakes her head again. Shakes off whatever he might say that she doesn't want to hear. She stands, too, and paces the kitchen. Takes a deep breath. Walks around the island. Along the counters. Her fingers alight on them as she moves—moves away from whatever he might say.

But he persists. "It's late, Maris," he tells her from where he still sits at the table. "Tomorrow, maybe tomorrow." As he says it, he gets his crutches and stands.

Maris freezes. "No."

"But you can stay *here,* it's all right. Spend the night and we'll take off first thing."

"No." Her eyes don't leave his now. "You're not spending one more night away from home, Jason. *Home.*"

To that, he says nothing. He simply walks to her—the only sound being his crutches on the floor with each step. When he reaches her, he manages to lift an arm to cup her neck. And there it is again—the warmth of her skin, the silkiness of her hair. From that raised arm, his forearm crutch hangs as he keeps his other crutch to the floor—maintaining his balance without his prosthesis.

"Okay, sweetheart," he finally says, dropping that raised arm down low around her waist and holding her close in a one-arm hug—the other crutch still keeping him standing steady.

"*We'll come back together tomorrow,*" she whispers into a kiss as he stands there on that one crutch, the other arm around her. "I'll help you pack everything then."

When he nods, Maris presses her face to his shoulder and leans into him. She sobs, too. It's quiet, and faint as she fights it, but he feels that sob. So he doesn't move. He just holds her there, his arm still wrapped around her waist.

In a few moments, Maris nods and backs up a step, carefully. Smoothes her hair. Breathes. Jason gets his balance on his both crutches then. When he does, she tenderly brushes his face.

"We'll take my car tonight," she says. "Let's go."

thirteen

ON THE RIDE HOME, NOT much is said.

What can you say in the dark of night when a prayer you didn't dare utter, think, send to the skies—to God, to the universe—is answered?

Jason sits back in the passenger seat as Maris drives her car down the highway. The tires hum on the pavement. Light comes and fades with each passing streetlamp. In the light, he sometimes reaches over and touches her shoulder, her face. She takes that hand and briefly squeezes it. And in the dark moments, he lets his eyes drop closed. His body gives in to the rest that comes easy now.

Time passes muffled, somehow. A few hushed words are spoken. Hushed touches happen. Hushed silences. Finally, Stony Point is just around the bend. Maris takes the turnoff from Shore Road and cruises beneath the stone train trestle. When she emerges on the other side, they drive the dark beach roads toward the bluff. It's late. They pass bungalows and shingled cottages. Some front porches are illuminated as people linger with the misty night. As summer holds on.

Then? Jason can barely believe it. It's really happening. He's home.

Maris drives up their long, twig-strewn driveway and parks behind the house. "Wait here," she tells him, leaning over to kiss his cheek. "Let me go up and put on the lights."

As if he can wait.

Once she goes ahead, Jason gets out, too.

By the time Maris hurries up the deck stairs to the slider, he's getting his forearm crutches on.

And by the time Maddy bolts *down* the deck stairs, Jason's closing the car door. There's enough moonlight to see.

Hell, he has his homeland memorized, anyway.

So he crosses the dark driveway, walks around a large dumpster, and nears those stone steps—right when Maris switches on the deck lights. At the bottom of the stairs, Jason orders Maddy up first. Behind her, he lifts his crutches to each step and goes up, too. The dog waits on the deck but can't stop circling him when he gets there. She nudges a hand holding a crutch; presses into him.

But it's Maris that Jason watches. She's standing at the open slider.

"Welcome home, Jason," she says.

"*Maris.*" He gives a disbelieving shake of his head, kisses her, then follows her inside.

Actually walks into their home for the first time in weeks.

Right away, Maris is pointing out the half-finished kitchen.

The pale gray Shaker cabinets. The stonework around the stove. The stainless-steel appliances.

If he were a different man, Jason might fight the tears at seeing it all.

At seeing Maris in their home.

But he doesn't. Instead, he swipes at an escaped tear and turns away from the kitchen and its refurbished glory. Stands there in his old tee and shorts and leans on his crutches.

"It's beautiful, the kitchen," he quietly says to Maris. "But what's more beautiful is seeing you in it."

⁓

There's more, though.

Jason doesn't fully realize it, doesn't get the scope of what he's feeling until he's in their bedroom again. It happens after he takes his wallet and keys out of his shorts pockets and sets them on the dresser. *His* dresser.

After he walks to the bed and hears the comforting creak of the mattress when he sits on it.

After he sets his crutches against the bedside chair there.

Who knew familiarity, God damn familiarity, could be this much a relief?

Maris is talking while she moves around the room. While she glances out the windows open to the September night. While she takes off her earrings and sets them on her dresser. While she turns off the ceiling light, leaving on only one bedside lamp. She's rambling a little bit, actually. Sitting on the bed, Jason listens to the words and phrases and thoughts she appears to say right as they come to her.

Words apologizing for taking so long to do this. To bring him home. To fix things. Her words just keep bubbling up like water bubbling along a stony brook. Flowing and turning and moving along.

"Why didn't I do this a week ago?" she asks when she sits beside him on the bed. "Why didn't I listen to you?"

"Don't worry, sweetheart," Jason tells her. "It'll be all right now."

"I know. But we lost so much time. We could've done all—"

Jason raises his hands and cradles her face. Which stops her monologue. He brushes a thumb over her lips and slowly shakes his head.

Maris drops her eyes closed with his touch. Then smiles.

He feels that smile beneath his thumb on her lips. "*No more talking*," he whispers, then leans in and kisses her.

"*None?*" she manages into the kiss.

He pulls back. "No. None."

As he says it, his hands drop to her fisherman sweater, which he lifts off over her head. They drop again then, his hands, and glide along the skin of her sides, her hips, to her jeans. This gets Maris to stand and face him as he's sitting on the edge of the bed. She stands really close and waits there, wearing only a black bra and jeans—and saying nothing. So he unzips that zipper and slips her jeans down over her hips. When he tugs those jeans lower, she steps out of them— leaving her wearing only that black bra and panties now.

The lamplight is low in the room. Sea air drifts in the windows.

And talking is forbidden, so Jason hitches his head for her to join him in bed.

Maris does. Fully. When he settles back against his pillow, she straddles him on the mattress. Oh, the night is finally as right as can be. She bends to his face, letting her long brown hair fall forward as she kisses him. Her mouth opens to his. He feels her lips. Her tongue. She kisses him longer, still—moving her kiss to his face, to his neck as she drops lower. Her fingers reach for the bottom of his tee and lift it off over his head. They don't stop there, though. Next, her fingers are unbuckling his belt, and sliding off his shorts. When he hears those shorts and belt buckle hit the floor, Jason reaches over and turns off the light.

The night is just about touch, then. Not about words. Or whispers. Not about sight, even.

Touch only.

And he lets Maris know it with his. In the shadows, he lays her down now. His hands touch everywhere. Tenderly. They slip off her bra and stroke her breasts. There are kisses, too, trailing his hands, moving along her skin.

But no words.

Sometimes it's his hands touching her body, and sometimes it's only his mouth. In places thrilling to her, too. He knows by her sighs in the dark. By her back subtly arching in the night. By her hands toying with his hair, his shoulders, as he does.

And he keeps going. In that darkness, his fingers trace along her belly. His mouth does, too, until his hands—touching, stroking—slip beneath her silky panties. When he slides them lower, and off, there is still only touch, and more touch. Now though, it's not just his hands, his mouth. He moves *entirely* over her and feels every bit of her body against all of his own. Feels more as he slips a hand behind her back. Feels her raise her legs around his hips as he kisses her once, then deeper. Feels her hands reach for him. They stroke his arms, his scarred back. Her fingers trace over his road burns there, then slide down his sides.

Yet not a word is spoken.

There is only touch. And sighs. Murmurs and grunts and gasps. Sharp intakes of breath. All else is quiet. Everything. The house. The night itself. There's a scant sea breeze whispering in past the curtains. But no words come between them as they make love in their big old home on the bluff.

~

Afterward, the sheets are tangled around them.

They shift on the bed and lie still on their backs. They catch their breath. They calm. Jason lightly raises Maris' hand to his mouth and presses the softest kiss there. Minutes pass. And more. In time, Maris only feels the misty salt air drifting in through the open windows. That sea air cools her perspiring skin. Nothing else moves in the night except for the distant waves breaking on the bluff. She hears that faint sloshing sound, over and over, now that there is no rustle of sheets. No noise of their bodies moving together. Even Jason isn't moving now.

Maris doesn't, either. She only breathes. Her breathing slows as she drifts in and out of light sleep.

Something wakes her, though. The sound—Jason's voice—has her open her eyes in the shadowed room. She senses him lying beside her, but still unmoving, as his words come to her now.

"*I love you*," he whispers into the darkness.

His voice is so quiet, Maris can't even be sure if it's a dream, or real.

"*I really missed you*," he only says then, his voice low. And she knows. This is no dream. He's saying all the words that he didn't say only minutes ago. A moment passes. Jason doesn't move, though, except to voice the words.

"*You're everything to me.*"

Between his phrases, those distant waves break rhythmically, like the second hands on a clock ticking time, until he speaks again. Which he does—apparently making up for lost time. And Maris loves just lying there, listening to his litany of words. Words about her making his life matter. And about how he'll never be apart from her again. Words of promise. Of affection.

In the darkness, he turns his head to Maris now. Strokes her hair. She feels it and drops her eyes closed.

"*You're beautiful, sweetheart*," he whispers. "*Thank you.*"

And he says nothing else. He just goes quiet again as she lies there beside him on the bed.

A minute later, she touches him. A feather touch grazing his jaw. Her fingers move to his damp hair—lightly, so lightly—as she twirls her fingers in it. But not a word from her. She's silent.

Jason shifts onto his side and watches her in the night. "What's the matter?" he asks.

"*Nothing*," she whispers, then leaves a long, tender kiss on his mouth. "*Not anymore.*"

fourteen

JASON GOT IT BACK.

Paradise.

Sunday morning, he's in it. The windows were open all night and now the seagulls wake him up. As they feed out over the bluff, he listens to their every squawk, every whistle, every repeating wail. There's the sound of waves sloshing on the bluff, too. And a breeze whispers in through the window screens. That salt air touching his skin makes it hard to open his eyes and start the day. He could lie here like this all morning.

And he does—for a while longer, anyway. His eyes stay closed. His breathing comes easy. His world, righted. If the clock could be stopped, he'd stop it right here. Right now. He'd stretch out this moment for as long as possible. And he does, actually, by drifting back to sleep. The sea air brushes his face, his chest. The seagulls' song lulls him. Dozing feels so right.

In time, he does open his eyes. Maris is still sleeping. Her back is to him as she lies beneath the sheet. But her long brown hair spreads out on her pillow. So Jason reaches over and touches it. Lifts it. Lightly pulls it through his fingers. Loosely twists wide strands of it. Eventually, she reaches back for his hand, pulls it close around her and kisses it before giving in to his, okay, his guilty pleasure.

Oh, she damn well knows it's his pleasure, too. Because wearing only a sapphire-blue silky nightshirt, she shifts on the bed. As she does, Jason props himself up on his pillow and watches. He crooks an arm behind his head as she turns on her back and lies *sideways* across the bed so that her head rests right on his belly. First, though, she lifts her hair and fans it out behind her. That done, she settles in and looks up at him.

"*Good morning*," Maris whispers, lounging there with a knee crooked.

"Oh, it *is* good, sweetheart," Jason tells her. Reaching a hand for her hair then, he takes some and drapes it forward, over her shoulder. Strokes it. When he opens his fingers and combs them back through her brown tresses, her eyes drop closed with that tugging touch. It gets him to sit up more, shifting her higher on him as his touch continues. Her face rests on his chest now, and he presses a kiss to her head. Still, her eyes are closed. It seems she's enjoying each stroke of her hair as much as he is. Every soft, silky strand feels luxurious beneath his fingers.

"*Will you do something for me, babe?*" Maris murmurs.

"Anything you want."

"Good. Because what I want … is for you not to move." She sits up then, presses him back on his pillow and kneels over him—one leg on either side of his belly. Her arms, they're extended straight so that it's like she's on all fours—on her hands and knees. But not touching him. Not until she lifts her hands and takes one of his wrists in each. Locking him in place, flat on his back, she raises his arms and presses them into the mattress above his head.

"*Now don't move, Jason,*" she reminds him, her voice low as she straddles him.

"I'm not," he says, only watching her.

She bends then, and sweeps her hair—every silky strand of it—across his chest. Slowly turning her head, she keeps that long brown hair brushing his skin. Just barely, at times. When she releases his hands, she shifts lower, too, so that all her hair skims the skin of his shoulders first, then his chest again, and down his belly. The sensation of its trailing touch is almost more than he can take.

And Maris knows she's turning him on. Because, still on her hands and knees, she lifts that blue nightshirt off, tosses it aside and lowers her body onto his. First her hair, her hips, her breasts. She kisses him then, too. Making damn sure he has all the paradise he wants this Sunday morning.

~

Maris is used to her turned-upside-down, partially renovated kitchen.

Jason is not. She can tell later, after showering and getting dressed. As he feeds the dog, and she gets the coffeepot going, they keep bumping into each other.

Not that she minds. She'd bump into him anytime rather than the alternative. Rather than being here alone.

"You don't want to go to the diner?" Jason asks while lifting a powdered-sugar doughnut from a half-filled box. "Kyle would cook us up a great spread."

"No. Oh, no, Jason." Maris gets the coffee percolating before turning to him. "If we go to the diner, your being back home will go through the Stony Point pipeline like *wildfire*."

Standing there in his black tee over camo shorts, Jason nods. Well. Sort of nods as he bites into that powdered doughnut.

"And then?" Maris continues as she rinses blueberries at the sink. "Then we won't have a *minute* to ourselves. Everyone will be coming by, knocking on the door, wanting to see you here with their own eyes." She turns to him standing at the kitchen island that's still missing its quartz countertop. "So let's make a pact," she goes on. "You and me, right now. For a few days, no one knows you're home."

"Days?"

Maris opens a drawer and gets out a loaf of cinnamon bread. "Yes," she insists. "It'll be like a … second honeymoon. With no one around." She drops two slices into the toaster. "Just us."

"All right. I can keep things on the down low." He walks to Maris at the toaster and turns her to him. "I almost lost you," he says, tipping her chin up and kissing her, too. "So yeah. I'm in."

~

Now that he's home, Jason's got to square away one pressing issue. So he heads outside to the deck and gets right to it.

THE GOODBYE

"Cody," he says into his cell phone. "I'm in a pinch and need your help."

"Name it, guy," his contractor tells him.

"What's left on Maris' kitchen reno?"

"Finish trim. You know, toe molding, some crown. Cabinet hardware."

"That's it?"

"Hell, no. Get the wood ceiling beams in. Island countertop installed. Finish some painting. Hang light fixtures."

"Okay, well listen. I need the job to kick into high gear tomorrow. Whatever it takes, whatever it costs."

"Money's not the problem, Barlow. It's manpower. Got a limited crew."

"Not anymore. Folks at the shotgun cottage adjusted the design—considerably. I've got to rework plans, then we have to get materials ordered. So if you pull your crew off that job, when can you finish my place?"

"Hm. Tuesday? Might be late, though."

"Work some miracles, would you?"

"Throw in pizza for the crew, it'll keep them happy."

"Just place the order and bill me, okay?"

"Will do."

"All right. Later, man," Jason tells him, disconnecting right as Maris comes out with their breakfast.

"So what did Cody say?" Maris sets down the buttered cinnamon toast and bowl of fruit. "Can he get the job done?"

"Tuesday. Late." Jason stands and opens the patio umbrella.

"Really?"

"I lit a fire under the project. Because I need the crews out of here while we have this time alone. So," he says, sitting again and filling their glasses with orange juice, "it'll be busy around here. Until Tuesday night." He takes a long swallow of the juice. "Then the place is totally ours."

Maris sits across from him and lifts a slice of toast. Spoons some berries onto her plate. Onto his, too.

Jason just sits back and watches her. She's dressed so simply—in a fitted white tee half-tucked into her cuffed jeans. Wide leather belt, too. Her gold star pendant hangs from her neck. Her hair is pulled back in a low twist. Beautiful, beautiful as ever.

And they talk. About how it feels for him to be home again. About the dog, too, and how happy Maddy is now that Jason's back.

"I hope Cliff's feeling happy today, too," Maris adds.

"About that ..." Jason stands, telling her, "Hang on. Let me get our coffees." When he returns with two steaming mugs, he sits again. "Cliff," he goes on. "Oh, man."

"What?" Maris lifts her coffee for a sip.

"He never proposed to Elsa last night."

Well, Maris almost sputters on her mouthful of coffee. "Are you *kidding* me?"

"No. I stopped in at The Sand Bar for some take-out supper. You know, after the fair gig yesterday? Found Cliff alone at the bar."

"No way! What the hell happened?" Maris asks. "He was so *stoked* for that proposal."

"Yeah. And he got Elsa to the bandshell, all good. But his plan was waylaid when Kyle and Lauren rolled in— unannounced." Jason explains how they were having a date

110

night and made it a double date with Cliff and Elsa. How Kyle had a cooler of food and wine; how they pulled their blanket up to Cliff and Elsa's chairs; how Kyle cut in on Cliff's dance. "And that was it. The commish didn't have it in him to ask Elsa to marry him, not with the Bradfords watching."

"Oh, poor Cliff. He'll try again, I'm sure."

"Don't know. He was pretty defeated," Jason says, snagging another piece of toast.

As they eat, and talk, a salty breeze lifts off Long Island Sound. It rustles the leaves in the big maple tree in the yard. The sun rises higher, too. Birdsong floats through the late-summer air. And he and Maris linger there on the deck with a second cup of coffee.

"We should get ready," she eventually says.

Jason leans back in his chair. "For what?"

"We have to get back to Ted's this morning. Get you packed and the place cleaned."

"All right, we will." Jason sips his coffee and glances out toward the bluff. "In a little bit."

"You have to leave his place in *better* condition than you found it, Jason. I mean, that Ted. What he did for you was immense."

Jason nods. It *was* immense. In many ways, Ted broke his fall this summer. "But first, Maris? We have to settle on something."

"Like what?"

"Hold on. I'll show you." Jason gets up, goes into the kitchen and returns holding Maris' heavy, crumpled paper bag from the night before. "It's crunch time now," he explains. "We've got to make our decision for Cody." As he says it, he tips the bag and empties all the cabinet hardware samples on the patio table.

Maris pulls in her chair and lines up each piece. Each pull and knob. Each finish—brushed nickel and black-painted and polished chrome and copper. There are classic and modern and whimsical styles.

"Oh, this is *so* much easier than making decisions by myself," Maris says. She gets up then, too, and walks around the table. Sits right in Jason's lap and gives him a lazy kiss, then wraps her arms around his shoulders. "I am so glad you're home."

"Me too, sweetheart," he says, nuzzling her neck before giving her backside a little swat.

"Jason!" But her feigned huff fades fast. She's smiling while getting up, then brushing her fingers down his whiskered jaw. "Now you go first," she explains on the way back to her seat. "Pick one handle that you *don't* like and remove it. We'll go back and forth until there's only one left."

They do. As they sip their coffee, and as some robin serenades them, and as the sun rises higher, they reach to the table and remove round knobs and cup pulls and bar pulls. And get distracted by their talking. And stop to fill the dog's water bowl. And split another of those powdered doughnuts.

But still, they keep removing handles and their choices slowly dwindle.

To one.

"Boat-cleat pulls, it is," Maris finally says.

fifteen

CONTEMPLATION IS IN SERIOUS ORDER. And pronto. Elsa figures she can get that done in one of two places. Church, or her Sea Garden.

Early Sunday morning, she opts for the second. Behind the garden's white picket fence, her thoughts wind this way and that—just like the towering sunflowers and wayward tomato vines winding through the fence pickets. The rising sun casts misty light on her weeding and vegetable plucking. It's not too warm yet, either. She's comfortable in her cropped jeans and tee. There's a garden apron around her waist, too, and garden clogs on her feet.

Peace surrounds her here. In the dawn's stillness, there's the whisper of waves lapping on the distant beach. A seagull cries as it swoops low near the garden. And there's nothing else.

Nothing but her thoughts, anyway.

Thoughts that she's contemplating in garden solitude this morning.

Ripe tomatoes dangle from tall, staked plants. Elsa pulls the red tomatoes from the vines and places each in a long, wide basket. She's got enough fresh-plucked inventory to amply stock her tomato cart in front of the inn. As she moves among the plants, she also tugs out an occasional weed. Finds a stray cucumber or two. Crouches to deadhead the yellow-and-red marigolds ringing her garden.

And thinks.

Thinks of Cliff. And of the wonderful time she had dancing with him under the stars last night. The evening was ... *sublime*. They waltzed, and shimmied, and spun around. Foot-stomped with Kyle and Lauren, too. As the band played on, Cliff swept her off her feet.

Standing to toss the spent marigold blossoms in a pile of weeds, Elsa glances over her shoulder. Problem is, she thinks as she turns back to her garden, then there's Mitch.

"*Wait*," she says under her breath, all while spinning around again. Yes, there's Mitch, all right. *Here*. He's got on a tan windbreaker jacket over a cream tee and light khaki pants. Beyond him, his safari-style vehicle is parked at the inn's curb. But Mitch? He's crossing the lawn and—*damn it*—heading her way!

"Hey, Elsa," he calls out. "You ready for some pancakes?"

"What?" Elsa presses the back of her arm to her perspiring forehead. "Pancakes?"

"Why, sure. When no one answered my knock at the door, thought I might find you tending something or other out here." He looks at her basket of tomatoes, and hand rake, and pile of discarded weeds. Then he looks to her, turning up his hands in question as he does.

114

"*Oh, right,*" she whispers as her eyes momentarily drop closed. "*Breakfast.*"

"With a view?" Mitch reminds her.

"Yes, of course!" Elsa looks past him to the inn, then to her garden detritus. "It's just that I needed tomatoes for my cart, and then …"

Mitch walks closer, opening the picket gate and stepping into the garden area.

So Elsa takes a quick breath and finishes her thought. "I'm sorry. It's one of those things, that … Well, it plumb slipped my mind, Mitch."

He watches her while running a hand down his goatee. "Seems like something's *on* your mind?"

"Yes." Something *is* on her mind. It's visions of dancing with Cliff, and tipping her head to the starlit sky while laughing and twirling in her black tassel dress. Visions of sipping wine in their folding chairs. Of a magical time the night before. She doesn't mention any of this, though. "Yes, something is on my mind," she admits, tucking an escaped wisp of hair beneath her rolled bandana. "But I can't get into it with you," she says instead.

"Well, Elsa. I surely understand." Mitch looks at his watch. "But *you* surely can have a hearty breakfast after all this morning gardening. Sun's not even fully in the sky yet."

Elsa glances down at her tee; glances down further to her dirt-stained jeans; and down further to her soil-caked shoes.

"You look *fine,*" Mitch tells her. "It's just a farm breakfast, you know? And all you have to bring is your appetite."

"No, no." Elsa brushes her dusty hands together. "I

115

have dirt under my nails. And ... *garden* clogs on." She looks at Mitch standing there near her tomato patch. And sees his spiffy vehicle out on the street. "Okay. Okay, we did make a date, after all. Give me ten minutes to freshen up?"

"Absolutely," Mitch says with a nod, then turns to the garden gate and starts crossing the lawn. "I'll be waiting out front," he calls back.

"Actually ... Why don't you go on ahead and save a table?" Elsa picks up her hand rake and follows behind him. "I'll just meet you there. At the farm. Bailey's Berry Farm," she adds, veering off to her stone garden shed. She also gives a decisive wave of her hand—*quickly*—right before she tears open the shed door and hurries inside. *Fast.* Before Mitch can even counter her suggestion.

Oh, and when she closes that door, she leans the weight of her body against it as she recoups her grace. And dignity. And shakes off the embarrassment of not only forgetting their date, but getting caught red-handed doing so. In her *garden* clothes! Moments later, she peeks outside and sees it's all clear. Mitch is getting into his vehicle. So she hightails it to the inn's side door and keeps moving straight to her bedroom—in seconds flat.

Ah, but the clock's *ticking*—with much to be done! To start, a quick wash-up, followed by a vigorous flip-and-brushing of her hair. After that, a closet scan accomplishes what felt impossible mere minutes ago.

Yes, Elsa DeLuca transforms herself.

Completely.

Right down to the long, slubbed-satin beige tank top over black cropped pants—in lieu of her soiled garden tee and dusty jeans. Gone are her canvas multi-pocket apron and muddy floral-print rubber clogs—replaced with layers of gold chain necklaces and a pair of pointed-toe pumps. Every last detail makes up for the pathetic sight Mitch last glimpsed of her with her plants.

Before heading out, she also slips on a sand-colored cardigan over her tank top and tailored black pants. Ties a paisley scarf to her purse strap, too, for a little pizzazz.

After grabbing her cat-eye sunglasses and car keys off the kitchen island then, she stops.

And *breathes*.

Finally, with a determined step, she marches down the inn's hallway—and out the front door she goes.

～

And at the bottom of the porch steps, Elsa stops again.

"*Mitch?*" she asks. He's leaning against the passenger door of his vehicle—now parked at the end of her driveway! "I thought I was meeting you at the farm." Elsa tosses up her hands and walks slowly in his direction.

"Elsa. I am *not* going to have you drive. You're distracted this morning, and well … we don't need another tap-and-go incident. So," he says, opening the passenger door of that safari vehicle, "hop in. And enjoy the ride."

Elsa stops halfway to his vehicle—until Mitch motions her closer. So she does it. She walks to that passenger seat.

"Looking downright smashing, I might add," Mitch says when she gets there, leaving a hint of a kiss on her cheek.

Climbing in then, Elsa looks back and tells him, "Why, thank you." Though whether for the kiss *or* compliment—she's not sure.

Mitch nods and walks around to the driver's side, all while Elsa puts on her big sunglasses.

Does something else, too, from behind those shades. She takes in the sight of Mitch Fenwick beside her as he drives off down the beach roads. And while tying that paisley scarf around her blowing hair then, she has one particular thought. It happens as she steals another look at Mitch's beaded necklace showing around his tee collar, and at his slicked-back tiny ponytail, *and* his easy nod in her direction.

Oh, mercy me, she thinks when she straightens in the seat and reaches for the hand-grip over her door. *Wait till Concetta hears this one!*

It's hard to wake up to disappointment.

But Sunday morning, Cliff does. Because he *thought* he'd have a fiancée today. Instead? He's got nothing but that disappointment.

He tries to shake it off, though. Heck, it's not like Elsa turned down his proposal. It's just that there *was* no proposal. So with his hair damp from a shower, he puts on jeans and a polo shirt before giving his shoulders a good shake. That done, he proceeds to rattle around his tin-can residence.

Sure, he could blame things on Kyle and Lauren's concert-crashing. But who's he kidding? There were plenty of chances to pop the question—driving back to Stony Point, or even while walking Elsa to her door at the night's end.

"But no, oh, no," Cliff gripes. Maybe he's disappointed today mostly because he straight-up … chickened out.

At the very least, Elsa didn't seem to notice his disappointment. What with the distractions of the Bradfords and food and music and dancing.

Maybe if Cliff just gets back to his regular routine, life will seem normal again. Normal was good enough a week ago, so why not now?

"All right, then," he says to himself, lifting the plastic decanter from his mini juicer and filling a glass with fresh-squeezed orange juice. After taking a sip, he drops two bagel halves into the toaster. While he waits for the toaster to pop, though, something catches his eye.

Something he'd rather not mull over.

It's the beige blazer from his bandshell date with Elsa. When he got home last night, he'd tossed that blazer—with its leather buttons and snazzy pocket square—right over the back of a bistro chair. Now it hangs there, limp. A little deflated.

Well. No sense in looking at any reminders of his epic failure of a night. So he grabs that blazer and hangs it on the rolling clothes rack behind his nearby room divider. Might as well empty the blazer pockets while he's at it. He pulls out a folded program from the concert. A hanky, too. Both of those he sets on a small chest of drawers there.

But when his fingers reach into the *other* blazer pocket, they pull out one more thing—his lucky domino.

"Lot of good you did me," he whispers as he shoves the worn, scuffed-up domino into a kitchenette drawer—right as his toasted bagel pops.

sixteen

SHANE STANDS ON THE OPEN-AIR back porch of his cottage. It's going to be a beautiful day, the way the sun's rising out over the water. The sky's clear, too; the sea breeze, slight.

"*Good day for driving, anyway,*" he whispers while pulling his cell phone from his pocket. His rented cottage is all locked up before his drive home to Maine. At least it'll be a quick trip. One renewed truck registration, a few errands, and he'll be on the highway here again.

But there's one last thing to do before he hits that highway. He sits on the half-wall and sends a quick text to Celia.

Leaving in 10 minutes. Can you and Aria steal away on a walk? I'll find you.

Before she even responds, he pockets his phone, lifts the packed duffel from the painted porch floor and walks out to his pickup. By the time he tosses the duffel on the front passenger seat, he's got Celia's return message.

So he cruises down Sea View Road. The landscape changes in September, somehow. Beyond the coastal cottages, Long Island Sound seems a darker shade of blue. Beach grasses are more golden than green.

Giving Celia some time, he turns onto Hillcrest Road next. It's quiet for a Sunday morning. Shingled bungalows sit in the shade of tall oak trees. A lighthouse statue stands sentry in a roadside rock garden. He follows Hillcrest to the end, then circles back and drives a few more streets, slowing when he spots Celia and Aria ahead. Celia's pushing the baby in her stroller near the marsh. Wispy grasses sway beyond them, the tall grass winding through pools of rippling water.

"There you are," Shane says, pulling alongside them.

Celia wheels the stroller to his driver's door. She's got on her denim-shorts overalls over a black bandeau bikini top. White sneakers are on her feet; her auburn hair is down. And he can't miss that she's a little teary today.

"Hey." Shane reaches through the open window and brushes her cheek. "It's not a big goodbye. I'm back Tuesday."

Celia gives a sad nod and briefly squeezes his hand. "Unless the captain calls." Bending then, she lifts Aria from her stroller and settles the baby in her arms. "And if he does, I don't know when you'll be back."

"Don't think like that. Right now, as it is," Shane says, giving Aria's tiny hand a shake, "I'm back Tuesday."

"*Okay,*" Celia whispers.

Shane watches her. He tips up his newsboy cap, too. "So what are you two ladies up to today?"

"Stopping by Lauren's for a coffee and a visit after this.

She wants to see the baby," Celia says, bending to Aria in her arms and kissing her head. "I might set up her shade tent later on. Sit with her on the sand as she naps. Maybe walk the beach afterward. Dip her toes in."

"Sounds nice." Shane glances in his rearview mirror as his truck's idled roadside. "Glad I got to see you before hitting the road home."

"Me, too."

He resettles his cap on his head. "Listen. You enjoy your Sunday," he says, reaching out and squeezing Celia's hand. "Really got to go."

Celia nods. Glances right and left, too. Still holding Aria, she leans in and kisses him then.

"You're living dangerously, Cee," he warns with a smile *and* a pointed finger.

"I'll take my chances," she says, then settles Aria back in her stroller. When she straightens, Celia steals one more kiss. "*Safe travels*," she whispers, brushing his tattooed arm with her fingers before backing away.

Shane nods, puts his truck in gear and drives off. Slowly. He glances at his rearview mirror too, all while noticing something. Celia wouldn't say goodbye. They're hard for her, and she said anything but.

Before he reaches a bend in the road, he catches another glimpse of Celia and the baby in the mirror.

And that's it—the last he sees of them.

Up ahead now, the train trestle comes into view. He slows and drives beneath it—feeling like today, maybe that imposing brown-stoned trestle does a little *taketh away*.

With a tip of his cap at it, Shane turns onto Shore Road and begins driving the three hundred miles back to Maine.

seventeen

JASON BARLOW! THIS IS WHAT you've been eating?"
Maris backs out of the refrigerator at Ted Sullivan's cottage
later Sunday morning. She's also waving a cardboard box.
"*TV dinners?*"

"Little bit," Jason says as he wipes a damp sponge over
the countertops.

"Do you know how bad these are for you? With all that
salt, and ... and *processing*?"

Jason stops his counter-wiping, crosses the kitchen and
stands at the open freezer door. "Well, I had TV dinners,
and ..." He points to a Dockside Diner bag. "Kyle's
dinners some nights. Then," he goes on, moving aside
some frozen packages, "Eva's dinners. Oh, and Elsa's,
too." As he says it, he lifts a plastic container filled with
turkey meatballs.

Maris whips around to him. "*Eva* was here? And Elsa,
too?"

"Yep. Worried about me, I guess," he says with a wink. "Keeping me well fed."

Maris squints suspiciously at him. "Well, I hope you at least had a *salad* with the TV dinners," she says, then looks over his shoulder at the spray bottle of cleaner on the countertop. "And you shouldn't be wiping down counters now. Why aren't you packing?"

"Already did. Been packed for days."

"What?"

"All my boxes are over there," Jason says, pointing to the stacked cardboard cartons near the slider. "There's more in the living room, too. In the corner."

"I don't believe you." Maris closes the fridge and walks to the living room. When she returns to the kitchen, she stops—hands on her hips—in the doorway. "When did this happen?" she asks.

Jason shrugs. "I wanted to be ready at a moment's notice," he says, watching her stand there in her half-tucked tee and cuffed jeans and black high-top sneakers. A wisp of hair's fallen from her low twist as she's been scouring the kitchen with him. "You know," he continues, "for whenever you came calling."

"*Oh, Jason,*" Maris whispers as she walks to him and wraps her arms around his waist. "It's really over."

"It is." He presses his lips to her forehead before tucking that wayward strand of hair behind an ear. "I'll bring all the boxes out," he says then. "Fill up both vehicles—the SUV and your car. Then? All that's left is the cleaning."

An hour later, that's exactly what they're doing.

Cleaning.

And as Jason vacuums; and Maris dusts; and Jason wipes down windowsills; and Maris shines the stovetop; and as Jason double-checks that his dresser drawers are empty; and as Maris damp-mops the kitchen floor—Jason thinks one thought the whole time.

Thinks this. *You would never know.*

Nobody would. Not from the ordered and cleaned and tended look of the cottage now.

You would never know that he violently fell out of bed here weeks ago—the morning after his second wedding anniversary came and went.

Would never know the private conversations that went down behind these walls.

The confession to his sister, Paige, when he thought he was losing Maris for good.

The concerned pizza dinner with Celia and the baby.

Kyle dropping off meals, and staying for a beer.

No one would ever guess the sadness trapped inside this cottage the past few weeks.

That the ten-year marker of Neil's death felt as raw now as it did then.

Nobody would ever realize the panic attack that took hold of Jason on the beach here. His father's tactical breathing saved him that frightening night.

You would never know arguments happened in these weeks, too.

On the phone, with Maris.

And with Shane, on the deck. Shane telling him, *Don't fuckin' blow it.*

No one would ever think there's been loneliness here.

Missing Neil. Missing Maris.

Worry, too.

Sleepless nights.

All of it—every last hint, memory—is being cleaned up today.

Washed down.

Swept away.

It's all behind them now.

When they're done polishing and dusting and straightening, Jason finds Maris in the living room. She's closing and locking the paned windows there.

"I'm going to take one last walk on the beach," he says from the doorway. "Come with me."

Maris shakes her head. "No. You go," she tells him, then walks over, presses her hands on his chest and gives him a kiss.

And as he walks out the slider to the deck minutes later, he knows. Maris is letting him privately say goodbye to everything—*everything*—that held him down this past summer.

~

Here at Sea Spray, Maris takes her final walk through Ted Sullivan's cottage. Every room is in order. Everything in place. Baskets dusted. Dish stacks straightened behind glass cabinet doors. Chairs pushed close to tables. Linens washed and folded. Couch cushions plumped. Carved swan centered on the mantel. Ted's brand-new gray moccasin slippers set near the sofa. Cotton throws shaken out.

Decorative white starfish aligned on shelves.

When she goes upstairs, Maris turns into the loft. A gorgeous wall of windows there faces the sea. Nothing but blue sky and blue water fill the view.

But it's the center stained-glass window that she approaches. The window's image is of a great white egret standing in shallow blue water. Reeds of marsh grass rise around the bird. The stained-glass window itself is tall and narrow, with the bird's pure white feathers distinct in separate leadlines holding together the glass pieces. Sun is shining through them now, bringing the blues and greens of the sea right into the room of this coastal cottage. That stained-glass window is a stunning sight, and she completely understands why Jason installed it here. It was his tip of the hat to Neil—who spent countless hours at the water's edge. Observing. Note-taking. A part of the seascape, just like the egret.

Maris moves aside now and looks out the clear windows to the long beach beyond the dune grasses. Jason's down there—she notices him walking along the packed sand below the tideline. A stiff sea breeze off the water blows his hair. Ripples his tee fabric. The waves break stronger here than at Stony Point. They splash up onto the sand in a silver froth as Jason walks the beach.

Maris gives a quick shake of her head. "Wait!" she urgently says, spinning around and hurrying downstairs. Her sneakered feet thud on the hardwood floors; she feels a little desperate in her rush through the cottage rooms. In the kitchen, she runs to the slider, opens the screen and dashes outside onto the deck—stopping only to kick off her sneakers. Barefoot then, she rushes through the dune grasses and onto the sandy beach.

"Jason! *Wait!*" she calls into the wind. His back is to her, though, and he doesn't hear her voice. It's getting lost in that sea breeze.

So she runs.

Her bare feet hit the sand; her breath comes in short gasps; her twisted-back hair falls loose.

Finally, *finally* she comes up behind him. "Jason!" she calls again.

He turns, and she slips an arm around his waist. When Jason just pulls her closer, and leaves a kiss on her head, she hooks her thumb through one of his belt loops.

Catches her breath.

Leans into him.

And they walk the beach together.

eighteen

LATER THAT AFTERNOON, SHANE'S BACK in Maine
and pulling into a gas station in Rockport. He's tired; traffic
north was a beast; shadows grow long now. The *last* thing he
wants to do after that eternal drive is stop here, but his tank's
practically empty. So he tops it off and goes inside the station
to pay and grab the local paper. Wouldn't mind catching up on
what's happening in these parts as he eats some take-out
dinner. While walking out the gas station door *and* reading the
paper's headlines, he almost bumps into someone coming in.

"Hey, watch it, bub," the guy warns, giving him a
friendly shove.

Shane sidesteps him with a laugh. "Shiloh. What's up?"
he asks, folding the newspaper and walking backward
toward his truck. A cool sea breeze blows, nearly lifting his
cap from his head.

"Haven't seen you around." Shiloh follows after him
and stops outside the door. "Where you been?"

"With Celia a few days. Back in Connecticut."

"Oh, man."

"Oh, man—what?"

"Gonna need eyes in the back of my head now, you lovesick dog."

"What're you talkin' about?"

"You're officially a liability on the boat, pining for your lady," Shiloh explains. "I'm watching you." He points two fingers to his own eyes, then to Shane's. "So don't slip up and sink the boat now, you hear?"

"If we ever get *back* on the damn boat." Shane motions his friend to follow him to his truck, where he tosses the newspaper into the front seat. "I miss anything here? Any updates from the captain?"

"Ayuh. Saw him this morning at the boatyard. He filled me in some. Got a few minutes?"

"Not really." Shane checks his watch and glances at his duffel in the truck. "Just came off a five-hour drive. I'm beat. Picking up a pizza and going home to crash."

"I get it. Some other time, then."

"Hold up!" Shane yells as Shiloh's turning away. "It's a large pizza. Get a six-pack and bring it to my place." Shane climbs into his truck and rolls down the window. "We'll eat outside and you can tell me the latest."

Shiloh salutes him and heads into the gas station. "Meet you there," he calls over his shoulder.

⌒〜

Shane has just enough time to unpack his duffel before Shiloh's at the door.

"Pizza's on the deck, guy," Shane says, letting him in. "Bring the beer out there. I'll be out in a sec."

Shiloh does. From the kitchen, Shane sees him open the patio umbrella and snap two cans of beer off the six-pack he brought. Meanwhile, Shane's grabbing napkins, paper plates and potato chips off the kitchen counter.

"What do you want?" he calls through the screen door. "Salt and vinegar chips, or barbecue?"

"Salt and vinegar," Shiloh calls back.

At the same time, Shane hears a clacking sound coming from down the hallway, but can't place what it is. There's no rhythm to it. It's just a soft *clicking* and *clacking* noise. It starts up, then randomly stops.

"You sticking around now, or what?" Shiloh's voice carries from outside through the screen.

"Stopping at DMV tomorrow," Shane calls back from the kitchen. "Doing some shopping at MaineStay, too."

"The outdoor gear place?"

"You got it." Shane shoulders open the screen door—which a stiff sea breeze slams against the shingled house. So he latches the door and walks to the table. "Need some fall threads for out on the boats. My stuff's pretty shot." As he says it, he sets down the dinner things and a MaineStay store flyer. "That came in the newspaper."

"Looks like they're having a wicked sale." Shiloh pulls over the flyer as Shane sits. "Man, you got a coupon, too," Shiloh says, turning the page and fishing out change from his pocket. "Here's a penny. Scratch it."

Shane first snaps open his beer and takes a long swallow while Shiloh looks at pictures of fishing bibs and insulated winter jackets.

"Memba when I was a greenhorn and showed up in a *ski* bib? Jeezum Crow, the boys gave me hell," Shiloh's saying as he turns the flyer pages. "Got lots of sideways looks that trip."

"Yeah. Plenty of trash talk sent your way, too," Shane adds. "Come a long way in five years. What were you, twenty, twenty-one then?"

"Ayuh. Twenty-one."

"Well, Shiloh? You're an old salt now." Shane raises his penny in a toast, then scratches off his coupon.

"Wow!" Shiloh sets aside the flyer and leans over the table. "You got *thirty* percent."

"That I did." When another salty breeze lifts the pages of the store flyer, Shane grabs at it and anchors it on the table with the rest of the six-pack. "Welcome to meet me there tomorrow, Shiloh. I'll text you once I get the hell out of DMV. We can grab our gear together."

"Okay, bub," Shiloh tells him as he lifts a cheesy pizza slice. "Hey, this looks friggin' awesome. What's on it?"

"Sausage. Mushroom. Onion. Little eggplant." Shane swigs his beer and helps himself to a slice, too. Digs right in with a double bite.

"Good stuff. And believe me, guy," Shiloh tells him, nodding to his beer can. "You're going to *need* that beer when you hear what I heard from the captain. Man, he's still in a wicked bad mood."

"No shit," Shane says around the food. "What happened now?"

"Wrong part came in for the fuel pump. A *big* mix-up. That effin' repair's leaving us high and dry for too long."

Shane groans as he sits back in his chair. "Captain's not too happy?"

"'Tain't likely." Shiloh motions for him to wait while chewing a mouthful of pizza. "Plans to work us to the bone when we get back out there," Shiloh says then, chasing the food down with a swallow of beer. "Warned me we'll never be back for suppah most days. So catch your rest now, my friend."

Shane nods, right as he hears that *clacking* noise from somewhere inside the house again—right as that sea breeze kicks up. It's a familiar sound, and a pleasant kind of *clacking* and *clicking*. He turns and listens closely. "*Ach*," he says, shaking his head when he suddenly realizes exactly what's making the sound.

"What's wrong, bub?"

Shane waves him off. "Just thought of something," he says, then tosses a few potato chips in his mouth. "It's nothing."

"You sure?"

"Yeah. So what're you buying tomorrow at MaineStay?" As he asks, Shane slides over the flyer, holding down the wind-fluttered pages as he takes a look.

"A bib, for starters. The *right* kind. Boots, too."

But the whole time Shiloh talks, Shane knows that the clacking noise inside wasn't *nothing*. It was a pretty significant *something*, actually. But he doesn't say anything while he downs a couple of beers and puts away a few more pizza slices.

～

Once Shiloh takes off an hour later, Shane checks out the source of that clacking, rattling noise.

133

"*Nothing, like hell*," he whispers once he's in the spare bedroom. He stands at the window he must've left open this last trip to Stony Point. That clacking sound he heard earlier is as far from *nothing* as can be. And that sea breeze that's been blowing since he got home is causing the sound. He lifts a hand now and clatters the shells on Aria's seashell wind chime hanging from the curtain rod. Smiles with the sound, too. Celia must've forgotten to take the wind chime when they packed up last week.

Shane looks out the window toward the distant harbor. That salty breeze still lifts off the water. A bell buoy clangs. The twilight sky is growing dark.

And when the seashells *click* and *rattle* again, Shane looks at them. In the evening's shadows, he touches a few of the thin, clattering shells, too, before closing the window for the night.

nineteen

DRESS UP," JASON SAYS.

"Dress up?" Maris asks back, walking into their bedroom. After getting home from Ted's and helping Jason unpack, she'd just taken a quick shower and blow-dried her hair. "Why?"

Jason stands at her dresser mirror. He's putting his father's dog-tag chain on over his head. "I made reservations," he tells her reflection as Maris comes up behind him in her robe.

"*Bella's?*" she whispers.

He nods, slipping the dog tags beneath the collar of his chambray shirt. "You helped put away all my stuff, so I want to take you out to dinner. Thought Bella's would be nice."

"Oh, it'll be *beautiful.* But what'll I wear?" Maris asks—mostly herself—as she hurries to the bedroom closet.

Jason straightens his button-down shirt, cuffs the

sleeves and slips a belt through his dark jeans. Grabbing his tan blazer off the bedside chair, he walks out of the room. "I'll wait downstairs for you," he tells Maris.

She doesn't take long. As soon as he feeds the dog and brings her out in the yard for a bit, Maris is dressed to the nines and breezing into the kitchen.

"I brought down your tie," she says, her stiletto booties clicking on the floor as she crosses the room to him. "You know, because we're going out on the town, right?"

When she reaches up to lift his collar, Jason stops her. "*Wait*. Wait, wait, wait, Maris."

"What's wrong?"

He steps back, palm to his whiskered jaw, and looks at her standing there in a black lace cocktail dress. From its narrow V neckline to the lace three-quarter sleeves, the dress is fitted in all the right places. Sequins are scattered on the black fabric. Her brown hair is down. A gold cuff loops around her wrist. Her gold star pendant hangs around her neck. "What's *wrong*?" Jason asks, taking her hand now and pulling her close. "Nothing could be more right, sweetheart," he says, cradling her face and lightly kissing her.

"*I think so, too*," she murmurs into his kiss. "Now come on. Let me finish with this." She stands very close and lifts his collar again, then slides on his black skinny tie. "After all that moving today, you dress up pretty nice yourself," she says while perfectly knotting that tie. "Very nice, indeed, Mr. Barlow."

It is said that familiarity breeds contempt.

Maris would *beg* to differ. Because in her world? Familiarity breeds *comfort*. That comfort washes over her like a gentle wave of the sea now. It soothes. And relieves. And buoys her, that comfort.

She feels all of that as Jason drives them through Hartford's Little Italy late that Sunday afternoon. What a whirlwind day it's been. They'd finished cleaning Ted Sullivan's cottage and returned home with Jason's belongings. Got everything unpacked and put away, too. All his things—his clothes and razor and toothbrush and belts and what have you. Work things, too. His architectural T-square and scale ruler and compass and pens and calculator and measuring tape and tracing paper. Everything. His studio is stocked and in order, as is the house.

Now? Their lives. Maris knew it all day. She knew they still had to talk. *Seriously* talk. The past three weeks of separation can't just end with no apparent resolution. With no analyzing the whys and therefores. And now that the initial bustle of Jason being back home is done, they can get to the long-awaited conversation.

Of course, the talk would have to happen in *their* place. At Bella's Ristorante.

In the city, late-day sunlight shines golden on the passing brick-front bakeries, and boutiques, and pizzerias. Mom-and-pop markets sell fresh produce and homemade sausages. It's a warm September day, and beneath sloping canopies, people dine at sidewalk tables outside small cafés.

But nothing comforts like the *familiarity* of the cool, dark interior of Bella's. With its dim lighting and aroma of fresh tomato sauce, the restaurant just feels like home. They're seated at their regular padded booth. On the tabletop, a candle flame flickers low in a red-glass globe. A crystal vase holds a small bouquet of silk flowers. After they order their meals, the waiter delivers a carafe of wine and Jason fills their goblets.

Maris sips the wine, then reaches across the table and takes Jason's hands in hers. She smiles, too. Maybe it's a sad smile, but with reason. They have to begin the hard talk. Her thumb idly strokes Jason's hands.

"Did I tell you already how absolutely stunning you look this evening?" he asks.

Maris nods, still holding his hands. "Two times now."

"Well, you do. So that makes it three," he says, raising his wineglass to hers.

She lightly clinks his glass. "It's because I'm happy, Jason. Really happy. And I have so much to tell you! About the kitchen. And my novel. About Mitch being my editor. I mean, I have an *editor*!"

"I want to hear all about it, too."

"You will. But first, we have to talk about us." She sits back and sips her wine again. "Just us." As she says it, she notices the whiskers on Jason's face, the shadows beneath his eyes. Their separation hasn't been easy on him.

They're interrupted, though, by the waiter setting down a basket of warm rolls and foil-wrapped butter tabs. When Jason unfolds the red-and-white checked cloth covering the rolls, Maris goes on.

"I want to sort through the past three weeks. To explain where I'm coming from, Jason, and hear where *you're* coming from. We have a few hours to kill at this table," she says as he sets a roll on her bread plate. "So we can rehash some things and be sure we're in a *really* good place."

Jason's sitting back now and shaking his head.

"*No?*" Maris whispers.

He hesitates, then leans forward and takes *her* hands on the table. In the shadows of the restaurant, he lowers his voice. "Sweetheart," he begins. "You don't have to wonder anything, like if we're in a good place now. We don't have to apologize, either. Or sort through what we did. None of it. Who's to blame. Who did what. And I need to tell you why."

"But Jason—"

"No," he interrupts. "No, you just butter one of those heavenly rolls—one for me, too—while I explain something. Okay?"

Maris cautiously nods and watches him as she unwraps the foil from a butter tab.

"We *are* in a good place," he begins, pushing up the sleeves of his tan blazer as he does.

"But don't you think we should talk about what we went through?" Maris asks while spreading butter on a roll. "What pushed us apart? And our feelings about it all?"

"We *did* all that, while we were separated. While we dated." Jason pauses and sips his wine. "Look. For many years, you lost your sister—"

"Eva?"

"Yeah. Thirty *years* gone. Your entire childhood and a lot of your adult life? You didn't even *know* you were sisters. And I lost my brother. Neil. He's gone and *never* coming back. And let me tell you, never's a long time."

"What are you saying?" Maris asks while setting a buttered roll on his plate.

"I'm saying ..." Jason draws a knuckle down his scarred jaw. "I'm saying that we lost a few *weeks*. That's it. Twenty or so days. So in the scope of it all, we're damn lucky. And *that's* all we need to understand. The rest we can let go."

"Just like that?"

"Just like that."

Maris, well, she smiles with a small laugh. Looks at Jason across the table from her, too. His chambray shirtsleeves are cuffed beneath those shoved-up blazer sleeves. His tie hangs just so. His dark eyes watch hers. And okay, in her fitted, sequined black cocktail dress, she does it. She half stands, leans right up over that table, cradles his face and kisses him. Quietly tells him she loves him, too.

Yes, just like that.

And they *do* kill those hours at the table.

While lingering with Caesar salads. While swapping tastes of their meals. Jason cuts a slab of his three-cheese meat lasagna and sets it on her dish. Maris forks off some of her breaded eggplant drizzled in mozzarella cheese and lifts that loaded fork right over the table. He takes her wrist and guides the food to his mouth. Drops his eyes closed with the flavor, too. They savor the carafe of wine. Lean close. He loosely holds her hand on the table. She nods at little things he says. His thumb strokes the soft skin of her wrist.

The lighting in Bella's is dim. Paintings of piazzas and olive orchards hang on the restaurant's gold walls. The candle in its red globe flickers between them.

And Lord, do they talk.

Maris tells him about the stonework she had done around the stove in their renovated kitchen. How the stones are her nod to his father's masonry. Jason tells her about the latest segment filmed for *Castaway Cottage*. How he talked about the design of the Fenwick cottage, and explained its angled walls' protective nature in deflecting hurricane winds.

Maris turns her wineglass on the table.

Jason drags a hunk of buttered roll through sauce on his plate.

They talk more. Jason tells Maris how much he's missed her. Maris' eyes fill with tears. She tells him it's the saddest feeling, missing someone.

They talk of the mundane—the weather. Of the walks on the beach they'll take with Maddy. Maris mentions Cliff's hurricane safety package—and that they'll have to pick up theirs at the pavilion when he announces their street. Jason tells her about the CT-TV meet-and-greet at the fair yesterday. And how a sheep got loose from the farm exhibit there. The little sheep was up and down the midway, loitering at the concession stands. Maris says her car needs tires before the winter, and she made an appointment to have it done.

She touches his hand.

Jason tucks her hair behind an ear. His fingers brush her gold hoop earrings. Her star necklace glimmers against her sequined black dress.

Dinner plates are cleared for dessert. Their waiter wheels out a cart of delicacies—Jason chooses the toppling tiramisu; Maris, the chocolate torte. Wineglasses are swapped for coffee mugs.

And time is finally sweet ... these few hours sitting together in their Italian restaurant.

twenty

OKAY, IT MIGHT AS WELL be Sunday morning—with the way Jason's just dozing in bed. Beneath the sheets, he's got on a loose tee over his pajama shorts and is utterly relaxed. The soft breeze drifting in the open bedroom windows is a little cooler today. There's some autumn in that air. But just the same, it carries the cry of the seagulls feeding on the bluff. Pale sunlight crests the distant horizon. And Jason dozes there, relishing all of it.

Just like his Sunday paradise mornings.

Except here's the difference. It's Monday.

Monday, and his itinerary is chock-full—mostly with extensive *Castaway Cottage* filming, followed by design work in his barn studio, all while scheduling two new-client meetings. If he doesn't get going now, he'll never get it all done. So he runs a hand through his hair, folds back the sheet and starts to sit up.

Until Maris stops him. She reaches over and slips an arm

143

around his waist. Pulls herself close, too, nestling against his shoulder.

"*Maris*," he whispers. "I *really* have to get up," he says, kissing the top of her head.

"*Stay*," she whispers back, dragging her fingers down his arm.

"Can't. Trent will kill me if I'm late."

Maris is quiet for a few seconds of tracing on his skin. "I called in sick for you."

"What?" Jason reaches beneath her chin and tips up her face.

"Yesterday. When you were in the shower after we unpacked everything? Before we left for Bella's? I was on the phone."

"With Trent?"

Maris nods. "You're out sick today."

Jason props himself up on his elbows. "Are you *serious*?"

"Absolutely."

"Well, that's not good, Maris. I mean, you and I are back together now." Jason groans and falls back onto the bed. "And we're supposed to *consult* with each other on things like this."

"You're right." As she says it, Maris' tracing fingers reach to his pajama shorts and tug them off. "*So listen, Jason*," she whispers.

"Oh, I'm listening," he answers. "Believe me, you've got my full attention now, darling." Beneath the sheet, he turns on his side. Slowly, he moves the delicate spaghetti straps on Maris' black silky pajamas—and slips the lace-trimmed top right off her shoulders *while* he listens.

"You see? We *are* consulting," Maris murmurs, pressing

close and kissing his mouth then. "I'm giving you a *private* consultation … right now."

⌒

I have so many important things to tell you, Elsa's fingers type on her laptop. *Ah! Where to begin?*

She pauses then, and adjusts her leopard-print reading glasses on her nose. She's sitting up in bed with her pillow propped behind her. It's very early Monday morning, with sunlight just edging her window blinds. A biscotti and fresh coffee are on her nightstand. For some reason, it felt more appropriate to send this email here, in the privacy of her bedroom, than at her kitchen island. Her thoughts seem more personal here. It's easier to get down to the nitty-gritty of her life predicaments. That's right—*predicaments.* Plural! And oh, how those situations are mounting. Her madly typing fingers tell all to her friend across the ocean in Milan.

The current in my sea of troubles is pulling me under, Concetta, Elsa types. She reaches for her cappuccino biscotti dotted with chocolate chips. After taking a nibble and wiping away a few crumbs, she types again. *What is a woman to do?*

Before writing more, Elsa adjusts her turquoise caftan while remembering Saturday night. She types the details to Concetta. *Dancing beneath the stars with Cliff was magical. And then there was that moon in the sky, and Cliff's arms twirling me, holding me close. And the music!*

"*Yes, sir, that's my baby,*" Elsa whisper-sings now.

But she doesn't sing for long, Oh, no. There's too much to tell Concetta.

And then? Elsa continues typing. *In all that romance I got swept up in with Cliff? I forgot I had a farm-breakfast date Sunday morning—with Mitch!*

If you'd call it a breakfast, Elsa thinks now. It was sinfully gluttonous.

The food, Concetta. What a feast! Heaps of pancakes with homemade whipped cream and the most decadent blueberry topping. Fluffy, buttered muffins, too. And the yogurt parfait? With farm-fresh raspberries, and more blueberries.

Elsa pauses her typing to dunk that biscotti into her coffee and have another bite. She has to—just to calm herself down. Because far more than the *food* did her in yesterday morning. She sips her coffee, then types on.

Mitch and I were seated on a large outdoor porch overlooking the sweeping farm fields. The sun was coming up over the river valley. Birds were singing. Bulb lights dangled from the ceiling beams. Lush plants—ferns and flowers—hung from the porch rafters.

Elsa has to stop. It's time to be honest. *After* finishing that sweet cappuccino biscotti and wiping her fingertips with her napkin.

But mostly, there was Mitch. With his hair in a tiny ponytail. And his goatee. And a beaded choker. And that twinkle in his eyes as he leaned close, or leaned back with an easy laugh in the warm sunshine.

Elsa quickly lifts her fingers off the laptop as though the keyboard is on fire. Or maybe it's her own fingertips sizzling. She takes that napkin and fans herself before typing the rest of her friend's email.

Oh, Marone. Part of me says this just isn't right. But another part of me is really enjoying it all. And I know I can't keep this up. Mitch, Cliff. Cliff, Mitch. Actually? I might even be going to hell!

But first? Well, first I'm off to my fancy new vegetable stand to sell my surplus tomatoes.

Ciao,
Elsa

∼

The sound of a diesel boat engine out in the harbor wakes up Shane. Lying in bed, he knows—it's Monday and he *should* be working. Damn, captain must be seething.

"*Oh, man,*" Shane says, tossing an arm over his closed eyes as he listens to that boat chug through the harbor. Listens to it head out lobstering. His days of leisure are numbered, no denying it. It's just a matter of time before *Shane* will be on a boat chugging out before the crack of dawn.

"*But not yet,*" he says—right as his alarm clock buzzes. Reaching to the nightstand to shut it off, his fingers land on a piece of paper. He half sits up for a look, and sees it's a folded note tucked beneath the tarnished brass crab beside the lamp. Carefully, he tugs the paper loose and lies back in bed again. This time, he runs his fingers over the one word written on the folded note: *Shane.*

Which gets him smiling. He knows Celia's handwriting from the notes they've been sending each other up and down the coast. She must've left this for him when she was here last week. For a moment, he listens to that now-fading diesel engine. A light breeze comes in the open window, rustling the long curtains held back with jute rope. He glances toward that window, then opens the note. Reads it, too.

147

Shane,

There's something important you need to know ... I love you, too. Have for a while now.

Yours,
Celia

His hand that's holding the note drops on the bed. And still he smiles. Can't shake it from his face, actually. He raises the note and reads it once more—just to be sure. Then he reaches for his cell phone on the nightstand and calls Celia.

"Where are you?" he asks right when she answers. "Can you talk?"

"Shane?" Celia asks back. "Is everything okay?"

"Yes. Where are you?"

"Well, I'm in my kitchen. Warming up Aria's bottle."

Shane pictures Celia there. Imagines she's in her robe. Probably barefoot, too. Her hair, sleep-mussed at this early hour. "I just have to tell you something," he says to her.

"You sound so serious. What is it?"

"That right now? You are speaking to the happiest man in the state of Maine."

"Shane! What are you *talking* about?"

He's quiet for several seconds. There's only the two of them listening to the other being silent. "You love me," he finally says, lifting that note again and reading it while he's on the phone.

"Hey! You found my note!"

"That I did." As he says it, Aria's cries reach him. She

must be in her crib—and it's probably time for her to eat.

"*Oh, Shane,*" Celia whispers. Her voice is soft. There's some longing in it, too, as though she wants to say more. Wants to share some private thought. "I have to go," she says instead. "Aria needs her bottle."

And that's it, he knows. He'll get nothing more out of Celia about love. Or about her note. It might've taken everything in her just to write it.

Once he hangs up, Shane gets out of bed, folds that note and tucks it away in his wallet. Standing there in his long pajama bottoms, he looks around the bedroom until spotting the notepad on his wall shelf. Never has either of them written a note without a return note being delivered. So he gets that pad and sits back in bed long enough to pen a few lines back to Celia. Some surprise message she'll find in her mailbox in a few days. He'll drop the note off at the post office on his way to the DMV.

~

An hour later, Elsa cranks open the beach umbrella on her tomato stand. She's strategically setting out her latest crop for the day. Positioning the self-serve cashbox, too, when her cell phone dings. It's Concetta, emailing her back. And Elsa can only shake her head with a small laugh over this one.

Honey,

If you're going to hell, would you save me a seat at your table? Seriously, you have all the fun—and I'm living vicariously through you. Keep me posted! Wish we could chat all about it on my terrace. Autumn in Italy is beautiful, as you well know. A little vacanza at my villa? Door's always open ...

—*Concetta*

Jason contemplates shaving.

After all, his shaving strike was supposed to end once he was home again, and here he is. Home. He's standing in his bathroom and looking at his reflection in the porthole mirror—not always an easy thing to do. Not if you're not living right. Some recent days, he's turned away from any mirror.

Turned away with his father's words in mind. *You have to live in such a way that you can look yourself in the mirror,* he'd told Jason. Told him more than once. Told him both before *and* after the accident—though probably more often afterward.

Now Jason stands there in his navy polo shirt loose over cargo shorts. Stands still in front of the mirror, looks himself straight on and draws a hand along the dark stubble on his jaw. It's been a few days since his last shave, five maybe. And he *might've* shaved right now, if he didn't hear the thud of Maris' car door closing in the driveway. So he looks right into his reflected eyes for a long second, then turns and goes downstairs on his forearm crutches.

"Madison!" he scolds as the German shepherd nips at the crutches. "Stop that." The dog picked up with that crutch-nipping habit without missing a beat—now that

Jason's home again. He slowly maneuvers the stairs and turns to the living room for his prosthetic leg.

"*Babe!*" Maris calls out when she comes in through the kitchen slider. "Got us some egg sandwiches from Scoop Shop!"

Jason nearly trips on Maddy doing an about-face to Maris now. The dog scrambles out of the living room when she hears her voice. So Jason stops still until there's no wayward dog at his feet. He safely sits then in his upholstered chair and lifts his silicone liner off the end table. After shoving back the fabric of his cargo shorts, he also gives the liner a visual inspection. "Have a quick breakfast outside?" he calls back to Maris. While asking, he's leaning forward and rolling that liner onto the stump of his left leg—where it's amputated below the knee.

"*Okay,*" Maris' muffled voice comes to him. She must be getting juice or fruit out of the fridge. "I'll set up on the patio table."

Jason pulls on a sock over the liner. After smoothing it all out on his thigh, he reaches for his prosthesis leaning against the chair. "With the reno ramping up again, did you get take-out coffee, too?" he calls out.

"I did."

Then nothing except the slider screen banging closed. So Jason inserts his stump into the socket and attaches his prosthetic limb. He stands to test that all's secure before walking to the kitchen. Maris and the dog come back inside through the slider right when he stops in the doorway.

"We're all set," Maris tells him. "Ready for breakfast?"

"You bet. But there'll be a full construction crew here today. Pretty soon, too. So what's on tap for us on my sick day?"

Maris walks to him standing there. She stops right in front of him and straightens the collar of his navy polo. "What's on tap for us?" she repeats. Kisses him, then, too. Little kisses peppered in between her words. "Something very important." A kiss to his cheek. "Later." A kiss to his jaw. "After breakfast." Light kisses to his neck, his mouth. "You'll see."

twenty-one

JASON SAYS THE SEA SPEAKS to you.

His father taught him that. Said he learned it when he came home from fighting in the jungles of 'Nam. He'd sit here on the stone bench he built on the bluff and wrangle his thoughts. Relive relentless memories of skirmishes with the VC. Remember the rapid M16 gunfire while flat on his belly in the trenches. The screaming engines of overhead fighter aircraft. The successive, muffled booms of multiple bombs released from the stratosphere by B-52s. Jason's father said that sitting on that bench on the bluff *after* the war? The sound of the sea calmed him. Assured him. Cautioned him, too. Answered his gut-wrenching questions.

Maris believes it later Monday morning when she's standing out on the bluff behind their house. But she also thinks that sometimes? Sometimes the sea simply listens. Its mere presence—splashing on the rocks below or lapping at the sandy beach—gets *you* to talk. To open up in its presence. There's some safety in doing so, almost like the safety of confession.

The last time she was here on the bluff, Ted Sullivan visited her. It's been two weeks now. The sea was calm that day. It made little noise as the water ripples glistened beneath the late-August sun. They talked about Jason leaving home. Ted explained, too, how he offered him the use of his cottage as Jason worked through things in his life. With that massive sea idle beside them, Ted also told Maris a secret. She listened—as she felt the sea did, too—when Ted confessed. Privately, he revealed that in the throes of the accident ten years ago, he was very much conscious and knew. He knew what he was about to drive into during his heart attack at the wheel. Two innocent men sitting on a motorcycle idled at a traffic light.

Maris' heart broke beside the sea the day he told her.

She looks out at the expanse of blue now. Ah, the sea. The sea. Recipient of so much emotion.

Today? Today is different. Today, there is healing as Ted sits on the stone bench again—this time *with* Jason. The sea is as September-blue as the sky. The salty breeze is light, so Maris wears a thin cardigan over her white sleeveless top and frayed denim skirt. With her hands on his shoulders, she also stands close behind Jason. Maddy lies in the grass nearby. A table is set out, too, with muffins and a coffee carafe. A gray rock anchors a handful of napkins.

And behind them, construction racket comes from the house.

But here? Peace, together.

"Did you find the place all right?" Jason asks Ted.

"I was actually here with Maris a couple of weeks ago," Ted tells him. Wearing navy slacks and a short-sleeve button-down, he sits beside Jason. The sea breeze lifts Ted's silver hair.

Jason tips his head. "You were *here?*"

When Ted only nods, Jason raises a hand to Maris' hand on his shoulder and gives a squeeze.

So Maris knows that Jason gets it. He was never truly alone at Ted's. Everyone was pulling for him. Caring. Trying.

Now, while they eat muffins and sip coffee, the three of them catch up. Maris and Jason bring Ted up-to-date on their lives, their marriage. They assure him it's back on solid ground.

"And *good,*" Jason says, right as Maris—still behind him—kisses the side of his head.

Maris tells Ted about her new kitchen then, and how she'd hoped to surprise Jason with it. That she didn't move any walls, so the reno is more a facelift than a gut.

"The crew should be wrapping up tomorrow," she says with a glance behind her to the house.

Jason talks about the slippers he bought Ted after Maddy chewed his to pieces. They're the same gray-canvas moccasin pair from MaineStay. Ted leans forward, elbows on his knees, as he listens.

"I left your new pair near the sofa. And I'm sorry about that. Though you wouldn't know it now, the dog picks up on things," Jason says, nodding to the German shepherd dozing in the grass. "Tension. Worry. And her anxiety sometimes comes out that way."

"She's really tuned in to you?" Ted asks, then sits back and sips his coffee.

155

"Is she ever," Jason answers.

There's more talk. Easy words—once they got the emotional ones out of the way. Maris asks about Ted's wife, and if they have any autumn plans. More muffins are eaten. A second cup of coffee is poured all around. Ted notices the rickety, overgrown staircase descending the steep bluff. Jason tells him the old stairs lead to a secluded, sandy spot there. Eventually, Jason hands over Ted's cottage keys. But still, they stay there, facing the vast sea. It's as though it's the only place to express their gratitude to Ted for opening his cottage to Jason.

"I'll walk you to your car," Jason tells him when Ted stands to leave.

First, though, Maris hurries around the bench. With a teary smile, she stands there and opens her arms to Ted. He smiles, walks into her arms and she hugs him close.

"*Thank you*," she whispers. "*For all you've done, Ted.*"

Holding her in that hug, he starts to say something. But it's obvious that he chokes up when the words stop and all he does is nod. Just nod.

It doesn't matter, though. Because standing there by the beautiful sea, no more words are said, nor necessary.

⁓

Ted stops suddenly as he and Jason walk the narrow path from the bluff back to the yard.

"So, you're *really* okay?" Ted asks. When he squints against the sun, deep leathery wrinkles form in his face.

"I am. Maris, too." Jason motions for Ted to go ahead toward the yard. "I think you can understand. This past month's been difficult," Jason says as they walk together. "For you, too, I'm sure."

Ted nods and looks over at Jason. "But I've been more concerned about you."

"We're getting there, Maris and I," Jason tells him as they walk down the driveway. Ted's car is parked there on the street. "Things are finally looking up."

"And I'm happy about that. Happy to see the two of you together. Oh, Maris was so worried when I saw her last."

"Breaks my heart, hearing that," Jason says.

"Well, what matters now is that you're both back where you belong."

"Yeah." Jason draws a hand down his jaw. "We were in a dangerous place," he admits. "Those damn miles between us grew into *walls*, and it felt like we started going our own ways." Jason pauses and glances back to his gabled house behind him. "Scares the shit out of me still—the thought of that happening."

"I don't think your guardian angel would allow that."

Jason throws him a look. "Neil?"

"That's right. So many times these past few weeks, I've had you and your brother in my thoughts."

Jason nods as they approach Ted's car at the curb now. He gets it. He's thought of Ted, too. They were both in the same accident, after all. Same accident, different outcomes, same world tipped on edge.

"And listen, Jason. I'm going to keep checking in with you. From time to time."

"Hope so, Ted." Jason claps his shoulder. "I really do. You're a part of my life."

Before Ted leaves, they talk a little more about his cottage at Sea Spray. Ted says he and his wife will head there in a week or so and stay for a month. Jason tells him *he's* kicking work into overdrive—now that The Hammer Law's lifted.

"Work's good, Jason." Ted's standing at the car now. "For you, especially. It's who you are."

"It is, my friend." Jason stands there at the curb and crosses his arms over his chest.

But Ted steps forward and clasps Jason's arm with his hands. "Goodbye, Jason. Take care of yourself," he says, then pulls Jason into a back-slapping hug.

"See you around, Ted," Jason tells him. He watches from the yard as Ted gets in his car then. Gives a wave, too, right when Ted turns the ignition.

Before driving off, Ted meets his eye and gives a solemn salute in return.

twenty-two

SHIPSHAPE," SHANE SAYS TO HIMSELF. Later that Monday morning, he's stacking cleaned breakfast dishes on the open wooden shelf near the kitchen sink. All that's left is to dry the frying pan he'd cooked a few eggs in. He does that, then hangs the pan along with others dangling from exposed beams near the stove. There's enough time to finish a second coffee, too. So he pours out the last of the brew from his coffee maker and sits at the table with the steaming mug.

And listens.

Problem is, there's nothing much to listen to today. No seashell wind chime *clicking-and-clacking*. No gurgling baby. No Celia's voice saying sweet nothings to Aria. No sound of Celia sliding a small pan onto the stove burner. No Celia warming the baby bottle behind him. No bathroom tap water running. No dresser drawer sliding open. No footsteps coming down the hallway.

Nothing.

Nothing he *wants* to hear, anyway.

Instead come the sounds of the distant harbor. The slow clang of a bell buoy. The diesel engine of a late-starting lobster boat. The cry of seagulls, over and over and over.

But in his shingled Maine home? Nothing but the soft thud of his coffee mug as he sets it on the wooden table. Celia's note is in front of him, too. Okay, he's read it so many times, it's memorized. Still, his eyes glance at her words: *There's something important you need to know ... I love you, too. Have for a while now.* Reading her message somehow makes the house seem even quieter.

Still sipping his coffee, Shane catches sight of his happiness jar on the kitchen counter. So he tips his chair back and reaches for it. Inspects what's in it as he slowly spins it on the table. Celia's frosted sea glass pieces dot the sand. Kyle's flattened nickel from the train tracks is there, too, leaning on the glass. There's the skimming stone Shane pocketed from the Shore Road docks.

He leans back with a long breath and looks at the tangled seaweed Lauren tucked in his jar. It's all dried up, the sea lettuce. Kelp. Irish moss. *Because we're all about as tangled up as the seaweed is,* Lauren explained a month ago, when they first talked on the open porch of his rented cottage.

Shane's voice is the only sound in his kitchen now. "Well maybe I *want* the tangled mess of Stony Point—relationships, pasts, histories. Connections," he tells himself, or the jar, or a memory of Lauren.

But he also knows what that would mean. It would mean walking away from his life here in Rockport, Maine.

Walking away from his lobsterman identity. From his shingled, harborside home.

It would mean saying goodbye to it all.

He lifts Celia's note, holds it and considers folding it into the happiness jar. Instead, he stands and slips it back into his wallet. Rinses his coffee cup in the sink, too. Lifts his denim button-down off the chairback and puts it on over his tee. Grabs his keys and registration papers off the counter and heads out to the DMV.

⌒ᴗ

Elsa reknots her tie-front blouse over denim capris. "These are just *precious*," she says then, picking up a formal summer portrait of Aria. Once Celia told her they'd come in from the photographer, Elsa had a few framed for her living room nook.

Today, Celia's helping hang the pictures. She's in all black—a cropped boxy tee over frayed black shorts. Stretching up to the wall, she's also clenching a pencil in her teeth and painter's tape in her hands. Aria is cooing in her play yard behind them. Her little arms pump at the mobile slowly spinning over her head.

The morning sun shines bright through the paned windows. And on the nook wall, four rectangular outlines of painter's tape fill the space. Celia had measured each picture frame and arranged those preliminary tape-squares.

"Good?" Celia asks, backing up while looking at the taped arrangement.

"Perfect." Elsa tucks a wisp of hair behind her rolled paisley bandana before picking up a few nails and hammer off an end table. "I'm so glad you're helping me, Cee. You have such an *eye* for design."

Celia backs up and squints at an X she'd penciled on the painted wall. She nods at it, too. "Right there," she says. "Put the first picture hanger there."

Carefully, Elsa aligns the hanger on the wall and taps in one nail. As she's tapping the second, a cell phone rings.

"Wait, Elsa," Celia tells her. "Pause that hammering—I really have to take this call."

Elsa sets down the hammer as Celia hurries, phone to her ear, into the dining room. But her voice carries in the quiet inn. While half listening, Elsa lifts a portrait of Aria. In the picture, she's nestled in a basket on the sand, and wearing a lace sunbonnet with her chambray onesie.

"You are *so* cute," Elsa says to the baby beside her in the play yard. Today, Aria's wearing a dusty blue romper with a floral print. The romper legs have a wide gold cuff on the bottom, which Elsa can't miss as the baby kicks her legs and gurgles at her. But Elsa straightens and tips her head then. Celia's voice gets her attention, though she can only make out a few phrases.

First: *So when does the fall term start?*

A pause, then: *I missed the application deadline? But you'll make an exception?*

Another pause before Celia again: *Yes, there's such a demand with the real estate market being what it is.*

Quiet. Now Celia: *References? Of course, I can provide them.*

Elsa's not sure what to make of it all. She bends and lifts Aria from her play yard. Holding the baby to her shoulder, she whispers, "*And you're not telling either, are you, sweetie pie?*"

"Okay!" Celia says, breezing back into the living room

162

moments later. "Let's get hanging!"

"Celia." Elsa sits on the sofa with Aria. "I couldn't help overhearing. Are you taking a class?"

"Not exactly," Celia says, remeasuring her pencil marks on the wall. "I'll be *teaching* one. A class on home staging. I'm trying to line up some jobs for the fall," she adds while erasing and remarking one penciled X.

"I see. You mentioned last week that you needed a life plan—"

"And this is part of it. I'm putting my plan into action now. Adult-ed staging classes. I taught some when I lived in Addison, so I have the experience. Then I've got a singing gig at The Sand Bar."

Still on the sofa, Elsa sits Aria on her lap and gently strokes her dark, silky hair. "What about the baby?" she asks.

"I'm not sure yet. Taylor might be able to babysit on those nights I'm working."

"*Tsk-tsk.*"

"What?" Celia curtly asks, spinning around to Elsa.

"You'll be spending all the money you earn on *babysitting* fees."

Celia picks up another picture hanger from the end table. "Well I'm not going to impose on *you*, Elsa," she's saying. "You're busy with *your* life, and so am I. So this is best."

Elsa slightly bounces her knee where Aria sits. "You're just saying that because you're … *miffed*, I guess … about my inn decision. And honestly, you *know* I'd watch my sweet granddaughter any time you were working. And I'd never charge you."

"*Mm-hmm.*" Celia taps a hanger nail into the wall. "More of the same," she says over her shoulder. "More handouts."

"*Handouts?*" Elsa gets up and gently lays Aria in her play yard, then winds up her tinkling musical mobile. "Celia, it's not like that. And ... and this is so sudden," she says then, taking the hammer from Celia. "Just because I *paused* the inn's opening?"

Celia crosses her arms and looks directly at Elsa. "That's right."

"But the inn was only going to be open for two months anyway—until November. Just for the leaf-peeping season, then closed till spring. And now?" Elsa picks up a few nails and walks to the taped-up portrait arrangement. "Well, you've been putting up a wall ever since that vow renewal. Resisting my help. Keeping me at a distance. And it's actually starting to feel like you're just punishing me."

"For what?"

"For pausing the inn without *consulting* you. But I just didn't think we were quite ready to open, Celia. It felt more like a *go-go-go* race to the finish line," Elsa says while tapping in a picture hanger. "And right before the vow renewal, we *did* have lunch together. Which is when I *told* you about the delayed opening. So why didn't you say something then?"

"*Seriously?*" Celia steps closer, her arms still crossed in front of her. "*When?* You *threw* the news at me, then whisked yourself off to be Kyle and Lauren's justice of the peace. I had no *time* to answer—or *process*—any of it. And since then? It's all been festering, okay?"

"And I never *dreamt* you'd react this way. Going to your father's all last week. Avoiding me. Looking for another ... *job!*"

Celia's quiet for a long moment. "You're clueless then, about my life," her dropped voice finally says.

Which gets Elsa to turn to her. "So why don't you enlighten me?"

Celia reaches for the first portrait to hang and gives it to Elsa. "That's a pretty loaded question, Elsa. Because you can easily spin my answer against me."

"Trust me." Elsa raises Aria's basket portrait to the wall. "I won't."

And honestly, Elsa's glad her back is to Celia for much of the explanation. Glad that she's busy tapping in nails and hanging pictures of Aria. And one of Celia holding her infant daughter while wading in Long Island Sound. Because Elsa's anger flares, and her eyes tear up some of the time—while Celia tells all.

"I understand Sal didn't even know I was pregnant," Celia says. "*And* he believed he would survive his surgery. But the reality is that I'm now a single mother raising *his* child—alone."

Elsa turns now from hanging a framed portrait. "Celia. Of course I know that. And this past year, when you were pregnant, we took care of that. We went through *all* the legal proceedings proving Sal's paternity and seeking financial support of his child. His estate was complicated, but *is* nearly settled. When it is, you know that Aria will be well provided for."

"I do. So this is where it gets hard, Elsa. Sal's death did *not* leave *you* with a new identity. One which you had to consider, and rebuild your life around." Celia squints across the room at Elsa. "You *have* to see what I'm saying."

Elsa looks silently at Celia and waits for the rest.

Celia only takes a long breath. Her hair is in a topknot. Wisps fall from it and frame her face as she stands there in her casual black tee and shorts. And as she quietly goes on. "Yes, Sal and I were engaged, Elsa. And if—*if*—he'd lived, we would raise Aria together. Married or not." Celia sits, then, in an upholstered chair beside Aria's play yard. She leans over the top of it and touches her baby's hand. When she looks at Elsa next, Celia's face is drawn. "Instead, I'm raising her on my own. I'm a single mother now. And I do *not* expect you to do any more for me. You've graciously let me live rent-free in the guest cottage. Which works for both of us. And that's enough. *But.*"

Elsa, standing near her half-finished portrait wall, turns up her hands. "But?"

Celia nods. "But I *still* have to make a life for myself, especially being responsible for Aria. I actually have to *rebuild* my old, single life—with a new identity. I'm a mother, now. A *responsible* mother who needs to work, too. And set a good example. Which I *thought* I was doing, being your assistant innkeeper. It was my career. So I *don't* appreciate you being so tight-lipped when making big business decisions—of which I *should* be included!"

"You mean … that I decided alone to put off the inn opening? And to deal with zoning at a later time?"

"Yes! Which pulled the rug right out from my carefully constructed life. The zoning issue *never* had to be handled that way. The Ocean Star Inn could've been open—right now!" As she says it, Celia stands and sweeps her arm around the room. "We could've had a full house! Could've canned those goddamn rowboat rides and went forward, business as usual." She gives a sad laugh, then. "But it was too late for me to even give you my input. My thoughts. You left me out." Again she sinks into that chair, right as Aria starts to fuss. "You kept everything *secret* from me. Just like Sal did."

Elsa stares at Celia. "*Sal?*" she harshly asks.

"That's right." Still Aria fusses, so Celia shakes her fluffy lion rattle. "Like mother, like son," Celia goes on, looking at Elsa across the room. "Sal kept the most important things hidden away from me—his health, his intentions, his future. Guess I know where he got that secrecy from now." She looks long at Elsa, and nearly whispers as her eyes tear up. "From *you*. You're the master of it, Elsa."

"And *you* are being *very* insensitive," Elsa says, picking up a few more nails and the hammer as she does.

"No. Not insensitive." Celia touches the soft lion's mane to Aria's cheek, then straightens and looks only at Elsa. "It's the truth. And the truth is tough to hear sometimes."

Elsa abruptly puts down her hammer, looks from the few hung portraits, then to Celia. "Do you know what I've been through this past year?"

"*You?*" Celia raises her voice. "What about me?"

"*What about you?*" Elsa repeats, really quietly. "*You* got something so beautiful—a daughter."

"How dare you. And may I remind you? *You* got a beautiful granddaughter. Who I was trying to honorably care for—before you changed the game plan."

"It's *temporary*, Celia."

"Maybe it is, maybe it isn't. Regardless, you can leave Aria out of this."

"All right." Elsa nods. "We'll talk about me. I've got a

hole in my heart that *nothing* can fill, okay? Not the inn, not an inheritance. I've lost everybody dear to me—my sister, my husband and now, my son. And from the looks of it, I'm wondering if I'm going to lose you and Aria, too."

"Elsa! How can you say that?"

Elsa shrugs. "It's how I feel. No secrets. Just the truth—which you just said is tough to hear."

Celia swipes at a tear. "Well, I guess right now we can only agree that we've both been through our own version of hell these months. And we *don't* seem to handle it the same way." Celia stands then, bends over the play yard and picks up Aria. Holding the baby to her shoulder, she turns and heads to the kitchen.

"*Celia!*" Elsa follows after her. "Where are you going?" She glances back to the living room. "And what about the pictures?" When there's no answer, Elsa runs down the hallway to the kitchen. "*Celia!*"

Celia's at the side door and half outside already. "Not today, Elsa." Her voice is flat. There's no mistaking how upset she is. And the hurt in her level tone is undeniable. "I just don't feel like it." She lets the door slam behind her as she turns with Aria and walks out into the late-morning sunshine.

Elsa hurries across the kitchen. She stops in the doorway and watches Celia outside. Warm air comes in through the screen. Birdsong, too. Some oblivious, lucky bird singing a happy tune—all while Celia lowers Aria to her stroller. Without looking back then, she wheels her baby down the street toward the beach.

twenty-three

EARLY AFTERNOON SUNLIGHT STREAMS IN through the stained-glass wave window in Maris' loft. Maris thinks that seeing the rich colors of the glass illuminated is like seeing the sea itself. Like seeing a wave unfurling and rolling onto shore. Two years ago, Jason gave her the window as a wedding gift—his way of bringing the sea to her.

She glances at that stained-glass wave, then gets to work. After Ted left, she and Jason had lunch on the deck—away from the construction crew in the kitchen. Now she's back at her special bandana project. Maddy's in the barn loft, too, stationed at her regular spot. The dog's lying at the railing. Her muzzle is resting beneath it as she watches her master below.

Maris is also aware of Jason down there. He's opening and closing drawers. Shifting things around. His drafting table. A rack of blueprint rolls. He's making phone calls at his desk, too, talking to new clients. She hears his voice as she re-irons one of the faded bandanas. Since working on them Saturday, this one has a leftover crease. So she spreads the bandana on her fold-down ironing board and *pffts* the steam iron. Carefully, she keeps at the wrinkle until the faded-blue fabric is smooth.

"*Beautiful,*" she whispers.

Now, to finish the project. First, she needs to make room for the bandanas on her worktable—a table Jason actually made. It's crafted with old wood planks from this very barn. The table's dark wood is grooved and speckled with tree knots. Maris moves some things around to make space. The large picture frames from Cliff *thud* as she sets them aside. A screwdriver she'll be needing clatters to the floor. She picks it up, then picks up a roll of masking tape. After contemplating her project with a few fingers to her chin, she rips off several pieces of that thick tape and lines the pieces on the edge of the worktable.

"*What* are you doing up there?" Jason calls from his studio below.

"I can't tell you. It's a surprise for the kitchen." Maris lays out both blue bandanas and sets the red one aside. "I'll show you when it's done. And what are *you* doing down *there?*" she asks, again pressing flat the bandana fabric.

"Organizing more work stuff from Ted's. Dusting. It's such a relief being back." Jason's voice rises up to the loft as he tidies his studio. "I couldn't design on his deck much longer."

Suddenly Maddy jumps to her feet with a low growl and slinks quickly down the stairs.

"Oh, babe!" Maris calls to Jason. She hurries to the

railing and looks down at him. Sunlight streaming through skylights floods his studio. "A delivery truck must be here, out front. Can you go get the packages off the stoop?"

Jason looks up from adjusting the swing-arm lamp on his drafting table. "What's in them?"

"Just some things I ordered." She leans her elbows on the railing. "*Please?* And can you fill up Maddy's pool while you're out there? She looks hot."

As soon as Jason heads to the double sliding doors and goes out with the dog, Maris turns right back to her special project.

"*Now,*" she whispers. "*Where was I?*"

～～

Minutes later, Jason walks back into the studio. Packages spill from his arms. The faint scent of his father's old tools and wood dust fills the barn.

"Sweetheart," Jason calls up to the loft. "You ordered *some* things?"

"Yes!" Maris' voice carries down from where she's working. "Can you open them? With that nice utility knife you keep in your desk?"

He stands there, looking up to her loft railing. "All right."

"Where's the dog?"

"I put her pool right outside. She's cooling off there. Got her in my sights," Jason says, turning to the double door. "Oh," he goes on, turning back to the loft above. "I almost got busted, too."

The loft goes quiet, until suddenly Maris is at the railing.

"What do you mean?" she asks, tucking her hair back. "*Busted.*"

"Celia was walking by with the baby. I had to grab Maddy and duck behind the hedges until she passed," Jason explains, walking to his desk and setting down the packages. "So she wouldn't know I'm back."

"Did she see you?"

"No." He opens his drawer, grabs that utility knife and starts slicing open cartons and padded envelopes. "Um, Maris?" he calls out. "This is all for the *dog.*"

"I know." Her voice is distant again as she's back at her worktable. "Maddy's been traumatized by our separation, Jason. She needs extra love now," Maris calls out.

Jason just shakes his head. And to every item he lifts out of a box or package, Maris gives her reasoning. "Booties?" Jason calls up, holding a pair of rubber dog boots.

"For the slush, on rainy days," she yells back. "And we can take the booties off at the door so our new kitchen floor won't get dirty."

Jason lifts a rubbery gray mat. "A *food* mat?" he asks.

"No, a *placemat.* For Maddy's dish. It coordinates with our new hardwood floor."

"Wait. The mat has her name on it?"

"Yes, it's custom."

Jason opens a small box. "A new brush?"

"With special bristles—for her undercoat. She'll look so pretty after you brush her."

Jason glances toward the loft, then slices open a padded envelope. "Seriously, Maris?"

There's a moment's quiet before Maris' voice is closer. "What?" she asks.

Jason looks back to see her at the railing again. Her hands are crossed over it as she leans there, watching him. Her sleeveless button-down is white; her denim skirt, frayed at the hem. Green sea glass glimmers on her dangling earrings. "Maris," he says, holding up the item. "A *squall* jacket?"

She shrugs. "For the fall."

He steps in her direction. "But a *pink* jacket?"

"Jason! She's a girl, after all. And it's not pink. It's magenta."

"Listen." Still holding the dog jacket, he walks out into the studio and looks up at Maris at the railing. "Do you get *any* writing done out there in the shack?" He motions outside as he says it. "Or do you just ... shop?"

"When I need a break, I shop. A little. And anyway, Maddy was upset with you gone—chewing throw pillows, barking, escaping out the door. So she *needed* some extra loving."

Jason sits on the stool at his drafting table and spins around. "Well," he begins. "Maybe *I* need some extra loving, too. I was pretty traumatized by being away, you know."

"Is that right?"

"Afraid so."

"Hmm," Maris says. "Now *what* can we do to remedy that?"

When he looks up at Maris at the railing again, she's watching him, then coyly motions for him to come upstairs.

"But ... the workers," Jason says with a glance out the double slider.

"They're in the house. And they just text me if they have

173

questions. Because they think I'm working and don't want to bother me when I'm writing." Again, Maris shrugs—with a subtle smile, too, as she beckons him up.

So Jason leaves the magenta squall jacket on his drafting table and starts up the stairs to the loft. "But where …" he's asking, the question drifting off.

Maris moves to the stairs. She waits for him there, but glances toward her studio. "Behind my divider up here."

Jason reaches the top step and stops. "There?" he asks, looking over to the right, beyond her worktable. A tall divider stands by the wall in the rear of the studio. She'd set it up when designing denim—in case she had to try on a pair of jeans-in-progress.

Maris takes his hand and gives a tug. "We just have to be fast, Jason." Turning to him, her fingers graze his arms before dropping to his cargo shorts. She lifts his loose polo shirt fabric to get at his belt. "*Fast. Like this,*" she whispers while unbuckling—and giving him a soft kiss at the same time.

Jason eyes her. Presses back her hair, too, before getting her sleeveless blouse half unbuttoned. "Okay," he says, following her when she turns to the divider. "Fast I can do."

twenty-four

By LATE MONDAY AFTERNOON, SHANE'S winding it down. From running a few morning errands, to waiting in long lines at DMV to renew his truck registration, to shopping at MaineStay with Shiloh for new lobstering threads—his day's almost over.

Almost.

Sitting in his parked pickup, he answers Celia's text checking in with him.

Good to drive, registration's renewed, his thumbs type out on his phone. *Did some shopping with Shiloh, work stuff. New bib + boots for boat. One more thing to take care of, then headed home. Leaving for Stony Point sunup tomorrow.*

The afternoon's gotten surprisingly warm. So when he steps out of the truck, Shane also takes off the denim shirt loose over his tee—one ragged at the shoulders from the sleeves being ripped off. He leans against his truck parked at the curb, too. Leans there, crosses his arms in front of

175

him and eyes the Red Boat Tavern.

"*Yep*," he whispers, pushing off and heading inside. "*Just one more thing to do.*"

～

"Where's your mermaids?" a voice calls out when the door closes behind him. It's Landon. Wearing a maroon apron over his shirt and pants, he's watching Shane from behind the bar. "Those pretty mermaids didn't swim away, did they, tough guy?"

Shane laughs as he passes the buccaneer statue in the front alcove, veers across the tavern and grabs a stool at that bar. "Nah. Celia and the baby are in Connecticut. I'll be heading back there until I get some work news from the captain."

Landon pulls two draft beers for waiting customers, then turns to Shane. "Heard your crew's been landlocked a *week* now."

"You heard right," Shane says. "Not good. Talked to the captain earlier. He's fit to be tied."

"Ayuh. Out of commission, out of cash. Till he gets rollin' again, anyway." Landon drags a damp rag over the bar top. "Now what can I get you, matey? Beer today?"

"No, how about dinner? To go. Give me the Philly-style steak and cheese sub. Toasted. Fried onions. Salad and a side of crispy potato wedges, too."

"All right, guy. Be a few minutes," Landon tells him, sending the order to the kitchen.

"*Perfect*," Shane whispers, turning his stool to the dining area. Café-style tables line the windows overlooking the

176

harbor across the street. It's early, so only a few tables have customers. He stands and walks to those windows for a glimpse outside.

Hell, right *now* is the time to take care of this *one* last thing—and the clock's ticking, damn it. Leaning close, he scopes out the patio area. It's pretty busy *there*. Folks always like that outdoor dining. But still, he doesn't see what he's looking for. So he idly crosses the bar's dining area, winding around a few tables to a wall shelf lined with model schooners, fishing boats. Acts like he's checking them out, when he's really scoping out the rest of the bar. The back room filled with booths.

As he's standing there, he finally spots what he's looking for through the window. Mandy is outside—just leaving a customer's table. Order pad in hand, she's headed toward the door.

"*Bingo*," Shane says to himself. He moves around the boat shelf and gets to the door alcove—pronto.

"Shane!" Mandy says, coming into the tavern and nearly bumping into him, then awkwardly stepping back.

He grabs her arm to keep her balance. "Hey, Mandy," he says, moving closer. She's got on her barmaid uniform—fitted maroon tank top with black denim skirt. In a pause then, he steps even closer—still holding her arm. "Just who I wanted to see."

"*Really?*" She flashes him a smile. "Well, then. What can I do for you, pirate?"

He backs her up past the buccaneer statue there. The bearded swashbuckler has on a black skull-and-crossbones hat and wears a black patch over one eye. Wood-carved knives and a pistol are strapped over his black coat; one arm is hooked. Shane gently—but insistently—gets Mandy just past that foreboding buccaneer to a small area meant for hanging coats. There, he backs her against a wall.

"What can you do for *me*?" he quietly asks her. As he does, he steps really close and touches the loose blonde braid hanging over her shoulder. Toys with that braid, too, letting his fingers slip into the woven hairs.

"*Yeah*," she whispers, watching him with her heavily lined eyes. She manages to also drop her order pad in her half-apron pocket, then reach for one of his tattooed arms. Draws a finger from his wrist up to his shoulder. "You alone?" she asks with a quick glance past him into the tavern.

"I am."

A quick nod from Mandy, then. "Haven't seen you around. Stop by later. We'll catch up," she says with an easy wink.

"Catch up …" Shane repeats, his voice really low. He pauses when several people come into the bar. But as soon as they pass through the alcove, Shane steps even closer to Mandy. His fingers still gently weave into that thick braid. "You mean, have a good time at your place?"

"Something like that. I can wrap a few slices of pie. Have them by my firepit. *End the day on a sweet note*," she murmurs, eyeing his shoulders in that ripped-off tee he's got on. Looks at his eyes next, before letting her gaze drop to his mouth, his neck. Presses closer to him, too.

He smiles as she does. Tips his head. Drops one hand to her waist while the other plays with that soft hair of hers. "Well, now. That's a *very* tempting offer for one tired lobsterman."

Behind them, someone's laughing at the bar. A yell

comes from a rowdy pool game in the back room. And a couple leaves, passing beside them with a sidelong glance as they head out.

"My door's always open for you, Shane," Mandy softly says once that couple's gone. She raises a hand and strokes his face, too.

Shane feels her touch there on his whiskered skin. She strokes his jaw, then slips her fingers to his neck.

Which is when Shane takes that hand—abruptly. Takes it and, still holding it, roughly presses it to the wall she's leaning on. Actually, he's got her firmly locked in place as he drops his voice. "There's a reason I've *never* went through that door of yours, Mandy." He leans closer still, so that his mouth is against her ear. "And you can damn well be sure I *never* will. After that stunt you pulled on Celia?"

Mandy tries to squirm out of his locked hold, but he doesn't let her. Instead, he *tightens* the grip on her hand raised up and pressed to the wall. When some fisherman comes in through the entrance there, Shane slightly pulls back and strokes Mandy's braid again.

"*Shane*," she whispers. "*Come on.* I'm sure Celia was just jealous and twisted up my words. You know, to turn you against me."

Shane barely shakes his head as he looks at her. And his hand toying with her braid? That hand yanks the braid tight, quickly, so that Mandy's head is actually pressed against the wall behind her. He pulls harder, tipping her head up. "Who do you think you are, interfering in *my* life? Trying to sway the course of it."

"*Shane*," she whispers again. "*I just thought maybe—*"

"Thought—what? That I'd wise up and come around to *you?*"

"*Would you just listen to me?*" Mandy quietly pleads.

"Oh, I already did. Listened to every filthy lie you told the love of my life."

"Please, Shane. I—"

"*Do you know what happens to people like you?*" he whispers back, cutting her off. "*Nothing. Because no one gives a damn about your kind.*"

Mandy's eyes drop closed for several seconds before she opens them. But she looks past him, first, before meeting his gaze again.

"Did you think that *bullshit* you fed Celia would *really* clear the slate for you? Scare off my girl?" Shane asks. He leans close again. Releases Mandy's hand and slides his fingers down her face, then drags them along the neckline of her tank top. At the same time, he's tugging that braid again, holding her head back firmly against the wall. "*Didn't work, darling,*" he whispers.

Now? Mandy says nothing. Nothing at all. She just presses her hands hard against his chest and tries pushing him away.

Tries, but he won't have it. He takes one of those hands and locks it between them. He lets go of her braid, too, and gently—so gently—brushes a tear from her face. "You're just crying because you got caught," he says, then subtly— so no one might notice—but *forcefully* punches that wall beside her.

And he knows. The bar goes a little quiet, so he's sure some heads have turned. But it doesn't stop him.

"You should be ashamed of yourself," Shane says, his

voice restrained before he releases the barmaid from her locked-in corner and turns to get his take-out order. "Oh, and one more thing." He turns back just as Mandy's trying to straighten her braid, her tank top. Shane steps real close and tips up her chin. "When I walk in here again with Celia on my arm? You better serve us with a God damn smile."

twenty-five

JASON COULD EASILY GET USED to this sick day thing.

After working in his barn studio most of Monday afternoon, he and Maris get ready for dinner. They'd waited for the construction crew to take off so the house would be quiet. In the kitchen now, they check their menu options. There are plenty—between the meals Elsa, Eva and Kyle had delivered to him during the past weeks. Heck, standing at the overloaded freezer is like standing in an all-you-can-eat buffet line.

"How about this?" Jason asks, pulling out a foil-wrapped container. "It's from Eva."

"What is it?" Maris presses close behind him.

"Platter of her amazing chicken cutlets. She put a few tins of them in my freezer, back at Ted's." Jason walks over to their new stove and sets the oven temp. "Thirty minutes should do it. Want them plain, or in sandwiches?"

"Oh, sandwiches! Slathered with mayo and some of

Elsa's tomatoes." Maris is still at their shiny, new stainless-steel refrigerator. "I'll slice a cucumber, too. Grab a bag of chips?"

Easy. Calm. Quiet.

It's how their dinner goes. The patio table outside is set. Tiki torches there, lit. Maris carries out a platter of savory sandwiches on warmed soft rolls. Thick cheese is melted over the breaded cutlets. Mayo-covered tomato slabs and shredded lettuce top the chicken. All of it—the tender chicken, the fresh veggies—is drizzled with honey mustard and some olive oil, too.

He and Maris drag cuke slices through ranch dressing and drippings on the plates.

They dig into the chip bag.

They eat, and talk, and murmur their pleasure. *Mmm-mm.* And, *God bless Eva Gallagher.*

By the time they've cleaned up and Jason's loading the dishwasher, it's late evening. In the kitchen, the windows are open. Warm salt air drifts in off the bluff. A three-quarter moon hangs high in the eastern sky.

Alone there, Jason walks to the stove. A half-wall of gray-and-brown granite stones forms an alcove arch around the appliance. He runs his hands over the stone, yes, thinking of his father. Behind him, the slider screen scrapes open as Maris comes in from wiping down the patio table.

"All done," she says.

Jason turns to her. She's still in her white sleeveless top over a faded denim skirt. "Want to walk on the beach?" he asks. "It's a nice night. Maybe just need a sweater."

Maris shakes her head.

"No?" he asks.

"No. Everyone will know you're here if they see us. They'll know we're back together."

"Yeah. Guess so."

Maris walks to the sink and rinses off the cloth she holds. "And I'm kind of liking our little secret. It's nice having you all to myself these few days."

"So ... no walk."

She turns to him, tossing up her hands.

"Come on, then," he says, taking one of those hands. "Walk this way."

~

Jason leads her to the jukebox alcove. The house is shadowy now, in the evening. There's only one table lamp on in the living room beyond. So the glass and silver trim of the jukebox glimmers in the low light. Maris looks at the song selection in the old Foley's jukebox. A thousand memories swirl. She can close her eyes and go back a decade or two to Foley's back room. Picture slow dances there—dust floating like stardust as some sultry tune got everyone in each other's arms on hot summer nights.

That's all she wants now—to be in Jason's arms. She could dance like that all night. When he picks a slow song, and as guitar strumming lightly plays, he turns up the volume.

Does something else, too.

He leads her outside to the deck. The only light there comes from the few tiki torches still burning. Their flames flicker in the dark as Jason takes her in his arms. And the night is magical as they sway beneath the night sky. Who knows how many more summer dances they'll have before autumn rolls in? Oh, she'll take as many as she can get.

The singer's voice comes to them now. He sings of being close, and dreaming the night away. And as Jason does hold *her* close, that's what it feels like on this hazy summer night. The salt air is thick. The sea breeze, light. Yes, Maris could be in such a misty dream.

And as the singer mentions a full moon, and of dancing in its light, don't they do just that.

And only that.

They don't talk beneath the starlit sky. Don't whisper.

Jason only holds her in his arms. Maris rests her head on his shoulder. She feels his fingers touch her hair. Tiki-torch flames waver in the night. And beneath the light of the rising moon, they dance on the deck. Pressed close, they sidestep, and sway.

The guitar lightly strums as the song carries to them.

Her dream beneath the moon goes on.

***

Some things, Jason never sees coming.

Things like this.

Like being in the dimly lit living room with Maris later that night. Several candles—tapers and pillars—flicker on the mantel. More candles are clustered within the stone fireplace. That fireplace arrangement is all pillar candles—some tall, some squat. Some on candle holders; some right on the grate. The candle flames cast a soft glow.

And here they are—opening the bottle of wild blueberry

wine Shane gave them last Thursday. *That* night? The idea of sitting alone with Maris and killing this bottle of wine was as far removed from Jason's life as a ship on the horizon.

But didn't life go and surprise him?

Or Maris did, showing up at Ted's like she did Saturday night. And now? This.

Jason pours the dark blueberry wine into goblets and sits with Maris on the couch. She leans into him, lifts her feet to the coffee table and sips the tart, sparkling wine. In the candlelit room, they talk some. And just sit together, quiet some, too.

"Been meaning to show you something," Jason eventually tells her, his voice low.

"What is it?"

He reaches to the coffee table for his cell phone. Flips to a grainy photo on it. "Know who this is?" he asks.

"Wait. Isn't this photograph in one of Neil's scrapbooks?"

"That's right. I snapped a picture of it to see it up close. One of the last photos Neil ever took."

Maris considers the image. "Is that you?"

"No. It's Shane at some coin-operated viewer. In Maine."

"No way." She squints at the image before handing the phone back to him. "So ... Neil went north to see him?"

"More than once. Apparently he stayed in touch with Shane, here and there. Right till the end."

"That's *incredible*," Maris says. "Neil had such connections with people. A true friend."

"Yeah. So Shane called me last Friday." Jason surprises her with that, too, as he sets the phone aside. "He wanted to see where Neil died."

"Oh my God, Jason." Maris, leaning against his chest, slightly turns to his face. "Really?"

Jason nods. He tells her how Shane was pretty broken up at the scene after learning how it all went down. After taking it all in. After hearing how Jason and Neil had gotten a part for the bike and were on their way to lunch, but never made it.

"And you know something?" Jason asks, then sips his wine. And watches all the flickering candles in the room. "Shane wanted to *have* that lunch. That day. Almost like it was some kind of unfinished business in my life."

Maris sits up then, curls her feet beneath her, and says nothing. She just reaches a hand to Jason's neck as he talks. Runs her fingers through his thick hair. In the candlelight. Sips her wine. And listens.

"The thing is?" Jason goes on, swirling the wine in his glass. "Shane really opened up at the crash site. It was fresh for him. He didn't have the past ten years to process it all— Neil dying, my leg gone. Shane's had only days. And he told me he wanted to *go* to that café Neil and I were headed to." Jason sips his wine. Feels Maris' light touch on his hair. "Said he wanted to break bread together."

Jason pauses. The candles flicker around them in the living room of his gabled cottage. Salt air drifts in the windows. He leans forward, too, and lifts the wine bottle off the coffee table. Adds a splash more to his and Maris' glasses. Sets the bottle down and leans back on the couch.

"I asked him, right there on the turnpike. Said this isn't just about having a meal, is it? You know what he said?"

Maris shakes her head, no.

"He said it's about forgiveness."

"Forgiveness? For what?"

"Everything, I guess. Holding the wrong grudges. Situations. We didn't get into it too much. Just some." Jason raises his wineglass—but stops. "Jesus, if you'd told me earlier this summer that me and Shane would ever even sit at the same table? I'd have said ... *That'll be the day*. But hell, it felt *right*, Maris." Jason takes that swallow of wine then, thinking of the lunch he and Shane had. Of sitting across from him at that table and yes, breaking bread. "You know, I can't get my brother back, but I got a beach brother back." He looks at Maris. "That's something I didn't expect."

"*Oh, Jason*," Maris whispers. She reaches over and strokes his jaw. "I'm happy for you. You really are a fortunate man."

Jason sits back on the couch and crooks an arm for Maris to settle against him. She does, and holds his hand looped around her shoulder. It takes a minute or so, long seconds of Jason looking into the candle flames, seconds when he waits until it feels okay to answer her words. "*Sometimes*," he practically whispers then, his voice husky. "Sometimes lately, I *do* feel fortunate."

Still leaning in his shoulder, Maris laces her fingers through his. "I can't tell you how much I missed you," she softly says, looking only at the burning candles as she lies against him.

To that, he closes his eyes and kisses the top of her head.

And they sip their wine until the bottle is killed—just like Shane ordered.

Oh, he knew, Jason is fully aware. Shane knew what

killing that blueberry wine would mean.
      It would mean this. Right now.
      Son of a bitch, he knew.

twenty-six

THIS IS THE BEST PART of the day.

Oh, Elsa knows it after arranging her tomato cart early Tuesday morning. The cart's wire shelves hold shallow crates of ripe tomatoes. A few paper sacks and pretty baskets are filled with them, too. There's also a wooden bin lined with random veggies: cucumbers, late zucchini, a few bell peppers. After opening the cart's sun-umbrella, Elsa adjusts her painted *Tomatoes for Sale* sign. It's tacked onto a garden stake pressed into the inn's green lawn. That done, she also opens a webbed folding chair.

The September sunshine is warm today. It has Elsa sigh as she adjusts her long V-neck tee over black capri leggings and white canvas sneakers before sitting. When she tips her face to the sky then, yes, she believes early morning is truly the best part of the day. Nothing's happened to put a damper on it. The hours are filled with possibility. With her eyes closed behind her sunglasses, there's only sweet birdsong and a warm sea breeze lifting off the Sound. In minutes, though, she hears something. It's a golf cart zipping down the street—but slowing at her inn.

"Hey, Elsa," Kyle calls out from the driver's seat as he parks roadside.

Elsa lifts her big sunglasses to the top of her head. "My first customer of the day!"

Kyle gets out of the golf cart. He wears wet swim trunks, and his hair is slicked back. There's a towel draped around his neck, too.

"Did you have your regular morning swim I've heard about?" Elsa asks, standing now.

"Sure did," he says, pressing that towel to his damp face. "And look at you, branching out into a new business!" He approaches the cart and lifts a ripe tomato near a pile of paper bags. "I can sure use a bunch of these. I'll make fresh BLTs at the diner."

"What about the bag I dropped off with Lauren the other day?"

"That batch is long gone, Elsa. Devoured by the fam." As he says it, Kyle lifts an empty bag before turning to the crate selections.

"Those are Jet Stars," Elsa says, pointing to one crate. "And Big Boys, over there."

"I'll go with those. Good sandwich slicers," Kyle decides, pulling a few bills from his wallet. "It's too bad the inn opening hit a snag," he says as Elsa puts the money in her cashbox. "But if things don't work out … DeLuca's Farm Stand?"

"Ha!" Elsa turns back to him. "I like that. But for now, it's just a little something keeping me busy. And my garden harvest won't go to waste."

Kyle nods. "Even better? Research shows that when you have a *variety* of daily activities—like this here—you're more likely to have balanced emotions. *Emodiversity*, I think it's called. Which is really beneficial."

"How so?" Elsa asks, sitting again in her webbed chair.

Kyle drops several Big Boys into his empty bag. "Well, the same way someone might be a well-rounded individual? By having a variety of activities, you're also experiencing different *emotions*—making you well-rounded in *that* department. Balanced." He adds one last plump tomato to his bag, then folds the top of it. "Emodiversity actually makes you better able to handle different life situations." As he says it, Kyle climbs into his golf cart. "So keep it up, Elsa!" he calls out, then pulls into the street. In a second, he beeps his golf cart horn and slows, yelling back to her, "Hey, here comes the commish!"

Elsa looks past him and sees Cliff in the security cruiser. As Kyle waves to Cliff and takes off, Cliff is pulling up curbside—right in front of the inn.

"Mrs. DeLuca," Cliff says after parking and getting out of the car. He's in full commissioner uniform—from black cap to black polo shirt. Both are inscribed with gold stitching spelling out the word: *Commissioner.* But ... wait. Is he pulling a ticket pad out of his khaki pants pocket?

"Cliff!" Elsa puts on her sunglasses again and watches him with trepidation. "What are you doing out so early?"

"On my way to pick up Nick," he says, now taking a ballpoint pen from his shirt pocket. "We're continuing with the hurricane safety package distribution. But that's neither here nor there," he says, squinting at her tomato cart as he approaches. "*This* is what concerns me."

Elsa stands now. "My tomato cart?"

"Well, yes. I'm afraid I might have to shut down this unauthorized business."

"*Unauthorized?*" Elsa sputters, looking from her charming cart to Cliff. "*Business?*" She picks up a tomato and shakes it at him. "Are you telling me that this violates some ordinance? Number ... T—for tomato—dot 32067 or some such thing?"

"The question is: Are you turning a *profit* on those tomatoes?"

"How should I know? I charge a few dollars on my garden harvest, and my customers get a sack of fresh vegetables. And ... and the money goes to décor—like those doilies. And supplies, like little baskets. And paper bags. So you see? *Everyone* benefits! My food doesn't go to waste, and my neighbors eat healthy."

Cliff plucks a tomato from one of the open baskets and inspects it. "But Elsa," he says, "this was most certainly *not* approved by the Board of Governors."

Elsa tips her head and watches Cliff. There was no hello from him. No inquiry as to how she's been, or how her day's going. No kiss. No chatting. So he's actually being persnickety today. She briefly lowers her sunglasses and peers at him over the top of the frame as he sniffs—*sniffs!*—a Jet Star.

"What are you, the local food inspector?" she asks, hands on hips now.

"You know how things operate here," Cliff answers, returning the tomato to the basket. He backs up then and eyes her garden-staked *Tomatoes for Sale* sign. "The rules ...

are the rules. It's only fair to everyone that way."

"Fair?" Elsa steps closer. "Did you jog this morning, Cliff?"

"I did." He glances at her, then walks around her cart as he jots a note on his ticket pad.

"Well, I don't think the endorphins kicked in," Elsa tells him while following behind him.

"Endorphins?" he asks over his shoulder.

"Yes! Aren't they supposed to make you *happy*?"

Cliff keeps walking. Now he stops at her cashbox and taps it with that pen, then writes more on his pad.

"Did you have your fresh-squeezed orange juice?" Elsa asks when she comes up behind him.

"Is there a reason you're so concerned about my morning routine?"

"Well, it seems you got up on the wrong side of the futon today," she shoots back.

"I can assure you I didn't. And now I'm off to pick up Nick. He'll drive while I announce which residents are to visit the pavilion for their hurricane safety kit." Cliff turns, shields his eyes and looks to the street. "Sea View Road families today. *Might first have to replace the batteries in my megaphone*," he says to himself. "But *this*," he goes on, motioning his ticket pad to her utterly charming tomato cart, "is unacceptable. I'm sure some neighbor *will* file a grievance with the BOG."

"I can't believe you!" Elsa stands beside Cliff and eyes the cart while he writes out a ticket. "This isn't a *commercial* business. It's just a ... a *community* thing. Do you really want my tomatoes to go to waste?"

"Listen. If money exchanges hands," he says, scratching

his chin, "that likely classifies the business as a commercial endeavor." Cliff rips the ticket from his pad and gives it to her. "I'm feeling lenient, so that's just a warning—until I do some research," he adds, heading back to his car. Once in the driver's seat, he opens the window. "I'll have to review the Stony Point handbook and get back to you," he calls out. "Good day, Mrs. DeLuca."

Elsa, clutching that ticket with her hands still on her hips, stamps her sneakered foot. "*Oooh*," she mutters as he peals out toward the distant guard shack. "*Oh, you … you …*" she whispers, shaking a fisted hand in his direction before turning away. "*Oh!*"

~

Tuesday morning, Jason still can't believe he's actually home—just like that.

But he is. And before work—filming at the Fenwicks', then back to the Beach Box gut—he stops in his barn studio.

And literally stops in place.

He drops his work duffel and lunch bag at the door and inhales that faint scent of barnwood and old tools. Maddy's with him and lies in the patch of sunlight coming in through the skylights. So Jason heads to his big office desk and thumbs through a pile of bills and envelopes that came in the mail. The double sliders are open behind him, and he hears waves breaking out on the bluff. Seagulls, too, crying as they swoop low. Then there's the sound of truck doors slamming outside, and men's voices. The construction crew is showing up on this last day of the kitchen reno.

And now? Quiet. Just the muffled sounds of a late-summer day.

Wait. There's a distant voice. A familiar one, at that. One that has Jason rush to the step outside and take notice. He gives a whistle to Maddy—and away they go. That familiar voice grows louder as they cross the lawn around the side of the house. From behind some overgrown hedges, Jason gets a passing glimpse of the Stony Point security cruiser slowly rolling by the house. Nick must be driving, because Cliff is speaking through a megaphone planted at the open passenger window.

"*Attention Sea View Road residents,*" Cliff's amplified voice rings out. "*Please report to the pavilion this morning. It's your pick-up day for the Hurricane Emergency Kit, and this will be your only notice. Detailed safety brochures will be distributed. Free wind-up radio with built-in flashlight and phone charger included. Proof of residency required in form of parking sticker or piece of mail. Remember. Safety preparedness starts with awareness.*"

A moment's pause, then it begins again as the car inches further down the street.

"*Attention Sea View Road residents. Please report to the pavilion this morning …*"

~

Normally, Jason would've swung by the pavilion and picked up their kit himself. But he can't risk being discovered back at home. So he leaves Maddy in the barn—away from the kitchen construction zone—and heads to Maris' writing shack. Maybe she has a few minutes and can pick up their hurricane kit. On his way there, though, he thinks the shack must be on fire—what with the smell of smoke he's getting. So he hurries closer, right away.

"*Maris?*" he calls out, heading to the partially open door.

When he stops in the shack's doorway, Maris leaps up and spins around. She's wearing a loose gray tank top with ripped-denim Bermuda shorts. As she turns to him—he can't miss it—she's also hiding a lit cigarette behind her back. Her *other* hand, the one clutching a half-eaten powdered doughnut, is *frantically* waving the air in some lame attempt to clear the smoky space. Oh, and she also turns her head way to the side as she exhales a cloud of smoke.

Jason just stands there—stock-still. "So that's where everything went," he says.

"*What?*"

"My doughnuts. The ones you said are no good for me. And my cigarette stash."

"Damn it, Jason." Maris' hair is in a low ponytail, and she tucks several fallen wisps behind an ear. Takes a few puffs of that cigarette, too. "My nerves are … *shot!* So I needed something to take the edge off. Because I can't *deal* with this anymore!"

"With writing?"

"No! Well, yes." She takes another hasty cigarette puff as she glances at her laptop, too. "Writing *and* the kitchen reno." One more quick drag of that cigarette. "I mean, the *noise*. The intrusion!" she says while exhaling that smoke, then waving it away with that doughnut-laden hand. "*And* Mitch is waiting for a consult with me. So I have to polish the first three chapters that he'll review. And I can barely focus with all the commotion here!"

Jason takes a cautious step closer to his frazzled wife.

"The reno's almost done, sweetheart," he says. Then takes another step. "It'll be over later today and the crew gone for good." He steps closer. "*So just breathe,*" he practically whispers.

"Yeah," she tells him, looking over her shoulder at the flipped hourglass and scattered papers. "*I'm breathing all right,*" she manages to gripe with another cigarette puff.

Jason reaches forward and takes the lit cigarette from her fingers. He takes a drag, too, before tamping it out in a cigarette-butt-overflowing seashell she's using for an ashtray. "And one more thing," he says then. "You can take a writing break. I think you need one."

"What?" Maris asks, glancing at that tamped-out cigarette.

"Cliff drove by with his megaphone-announcement. Today's our street."

"Our street for what?"

"It's Sea View Road's turn. We got our time slot to get to the pavilion in the parking lot. Today *only.* We have to pick up our hand-crank radio and hurricane safety kit. Cliff's been up and down the road two times on his megaphone."

"Is *that* what I heard?" Maris asks while going in for another powdered-sugar doughnut bite.

Jason looks at her, then reaches his hand to her face. "Hold on. You've got a little something there," he says, brushing powdered sugar from her cheek. And stepping closer. And lightly tugging her half-fallen ponytail.

Maris touches his whiskered jaw, leans in and manages to kiss him while still holding her doughnut piece. "Wait, Jason," she interrupts, pulling back. "I'm a mess. I'm smoky. I'm powdery."

"And beautiful as ever," he says, cradling her face and deepening that sugary kiss.

Maris presses closer—stopping only to drop her doughnut on the desk before getting back to some necking. And whispering his name.

He feels it, too, the way she smiles into their kiss right as he feels her up—sliding his hands up her hips, along her sides and over the swell of her breasts. One hand keeps going, wrapping around her shoulders, her neck, and embracing her. While they toy with that kiss, as she opens her mouth to his and they get into it—right there in the shack—his other hand discreetly drops to her desk and lifts the cigarette pack there. Silently, their kisses now flirting with *serious* fooling around, Jason drops that pack of cigarettes into his cargo shorts pocket—far away from his anguished novelist-wife.

twenty-seven

OKAY, SO THE STONE TRESTLE is becoming a really familiar sight. Not that Shane minds. And midday Tuesday—the five-hour drive from Maine behind him— he's there again. He's veering off Shore Road and driving beneath the tunnel of brown stones. Has a certain thought, too, as he does.

"*The trestle giveth?*" he asks himself. "*Damn straight.*" Because hell, he got his brother back here. Got his old friends back, too. *And* got a fighting chance to love someone. Celia. "*Just hope to God that trestle never taketh away,*" he whispers, emerging from the tunnel and stopping at the guard shack there. He rolls down his window and tips up his newsboy cap. "Where's Nick?" he asks a uniformed guard new to him.

"Distributing hurricane gear at the pavilion." The guard, clipboard in hand, approaches Shane's truck. "Where you staying?"

Shane hitches his head, left. "Over on Sea View."

"Let me get this for the log. Name?"

"Bradford."

"Street address?"

"Don't know the number. Renting a place called *This Will Do*."

When the guard jots it down and backs away with a nod, Shane adjusts his cap and drives on.

But he doesn't drive to his little bungalow. There's a different cottage needing a drive-by. Celia's guest cottage. As he approaches the three-story, shingled Ocean Star Inn, he notices a wire tomato cart on the front lawn—which is as good a cover as any. Parking there, he gets out, picks a sack of tomatoes and leaves a few dollars in the tin cashbox.

He's doing something else, too. He's looking around for Elsa's car—which isn't here.

So he takes a chance.

First up? Drop the tomato sack in his truck. Second? Reach past an old Frisbee on the passenger seat for a bag there. That done, he heads around the inn and swings behind the guest cottage to Celia's back porch. When she doesn't answer his knock, Shane tries the screen door— and it opens. So quickly, he takes Aria's seashell wind chime out of its bag and hangs it in one of the screened windows.

Still no sight of Celia or the baby, though.

So he takes the roundabout way back toward his parked truck. Strolling the grounds beside the inn, he comes upon the *inn*-spiration walkway. Ornamental dune grasses border it, and white conch shells dot the surrounding dark mulch. Shane pauses and reads Elsa's latest chalked message there. The words are a little faded, but he can make them out: *Sea, speak to me.*

"*Hmm,*" Shane quietly says. Almost seems like a little plea for guidance. He glances over at Elsa's inn, then heads across the lawn toward her Sea Garden.

Which is when he spots Celia.

She's wearing a chambray button-down and frayed black shorts. Her straw fedora is on her head as she waters the hydrangeas behind the inn's wide veranda. A light spray of water spews from the hose she holds; Aria's in her playpen nearby.

Shane comes up behind Celia. Still, he takes a cautious look both ways before talking.

"There she is," he says then.

Celia quickly looks over her shoulder. "Shane! You're back!"

"That I am."

"But what are you doing *here*?"

"Bought some tomatoes." He motions to the front of the inn where the cart is, then bends over the playpen and shakes Aria's little hand. "Saw that the coast was clear," he adds, walking to Celia then. "Elsa's car is gone."

"Really?" Celia turns and looks toward the driveway while still spraying the hydrangeas. "I didn't realize she'd gone out."

"*And* I left something for you on your back porch." As he says it, Shane stops behind her. He gently wraps his arms around her waist and kisses her cheek.

"You left something for *me*?" Celia leans back into his embrace. "What is it?"

"You'll see." He taps her fedora. "So goodbye for now," he says, backing away.

"That's *it*? You're leaving?" she asks, spraying a shrub

heavy with pale blue hydrangea blossoms.

"Ah. *Just* pulled in under the trestle. Really have to unpack and unkink. And it's risky hanging around here. You tempt me too much." He keeps backing away as Celia waters the bushes—and watches him from beneath that straw fedora. "So ..." Shane goes on, still backing up. "So long to the woman who loves me but can't say it." He tips his newsboy cap at her.

Celia says nothing. But she also doesn't let him get away with his shenanigans. She gives him a quick dousing of hose spray—getting him to sidestep on the lawn.

Shane pulls out his wallet once he's out of water-reach. Holds the wallet up, too. "That's okay," he calls, tugging out her note. "Got it in writing now."

~~

As Jason wraps up work at the little Beach Box job site, his cell phone dings with a text. He can't get to it, though. Not while inspecting the rough framing for the old cottage's brand-new vaulted kitchen ceiling. The homeowners wanted to give an illusion of space in the tiny room.

"That'll do the trick," Jason tells the contractor on this job. As they walk out the demo'd cottage's front door, Jason takes off his hardhat. "Remember. The finish work on that ceiling is all beadboard, guy."

"Got it," his contractor assures him as Jason hands him his hardhat.

They keep talking shop right there on the scrubby front yard—until a familiar pickup slowly drives by.

"Yo, Barlow!" Shane calls out from the driver's seat.

"Heads up, loser," he yells, flinging a red Frisbee out the window.

Jason lunges for it and makes the catch. "Rematch on the sand, one of these days!" he calls back as Shane takes off. Turning back to his contractor, Jason spins the Frisbee his way. "Tanner, catch."

"You son of a gun." Tanner makes the catch and reads the imprinted Frisbee. "Rockport, Maine, huh?"

"Yeah. Guy's a lobsterman. Thinks he's the shit." Jason takes the Frisbee back. "And he probably is. Now we all set here, Tanner?"

"Yeah, we're good. Later, man."

When Jason's cell phone dings again, he heads to his SUV parked on the road. Tosses the Frisbee in, leans on the vehicle and checks his phone. The text is from Kyle.

Bro. Need me to drop off dinners at Sea Spray tonight? You must be running low on healthy meals.

Jason answers Kyle's text—without letting on that he's back home with Maris. *Nah. I'll pick up*, his thumbs type. *Make me a couple. I'll freeze one.*

Okay, so the last part's a lie. Because like hell Kyle's dinners will end up in the freezer. As he gets into his SUV, Jason knows exactly what'll happen. Those dinners will end up on his and Maris' plates tonight, in their renovated—and finally completed—kitchen.

Yep, and so he texts Maris the good news.

Thirty minutes later, Jason's walking into the Dockside Diner. The place is hopping; booths are full; weathered buoys hang from the ceiling like pendant lights; fishing net on the wall is laced with starfish and seashells. Jason grabs a stool at the busy counter right as Kyle saunters out from the kitchen. He's wearing his full chef apron and carrying two insulated take-out bags.

"Here you go, guy," Kyle says as he walks over.

"Thanks, man. What's on the menu?"

"Homemade meatloaf here," Kyle tells him, raising one bag. "Honey-dipped fried chicken in the other. Have that one tonight. The meatloaf will freeze better."

"Got it."

"There's a big spinach salad in there, too. With mushrooms, bacon, egg. The works. Gotta eat your greens."

"Keeping me healthy?" Jason asks.

"Someone has to. And hey, still on that shaving strike, huh?" Kyle asks, setting the bags on the counter and giving Jason's jaw a slap. "Guess I'll know you're back home when your face is smooth again."

"Yeah. It is what it is, Bradford," Jason tells him, keeping his reunion with Maris under wraps. "My hands are tied."

Kyle crosses his arms and squints at Jason. "What'd I tell you already? About this being *divorce* season." When Jason waves him off, Kyle persists. "Couples try to rekindle their relationships during the warm summer months—like you and Maris, right? And by the *end* of summer? They realize they can't stand being together and head to divorce." He points at Jason on the stool. "And you're *still* apart, at summer's end, my friend."

"We'll get there." Jason stands and pulls out his wallet. "Don't worry, Kyle."

"Maybe you have to work on your compromising."

"Compromising?" Jason slaps a twenty and a ten on the counter.

Kyle looks past him and gives a wave to a customer at a stool further down. "Take care, Smithy."

"You too, Kyle. Good grub, as always," this Smithy says as he heads out.

"Now, Barlow," Kyle goes on to Jason. "Are you giving at *all*, in your marriage? Or just being your obstinate self. Because listen, dude," Kyle says as Jason puts away his wallet and reaches for the bags. "Sit yourself down a sec and really *listen*," Kyle insists, moving the bags out of reach.

"Fine." Jason sits again and eyes the countertop dessert case. "But throw some of those frosted brownies in my bags *while* I'm listening, would you?"

As Kyle does, he explains that studies show happy couples practice the art of compromising. That when they feel like their opinions matter, they're truly happy. "So, you know. Try some *meeting halfway*. Take turns deciding on things, like which movie to go see. Or what to cook. Or what color to paint a room. Shit like that. It *works*, man," Kyle maintains as he sets two wrapped brownies in a bag.

"Really?" Jason stands to leave now. "And what do *you* do to compromise in your marriage?"

"Me?" Kyle pushes Jason's take-out bags across the counter. "Okay, nothing. All right? Because I *know* better," he says. "Hell, I let Lauren do *whatever* she wants."

⌒

Funny thing is, Jason thinks about that the whole way home. Compromise. Maybe Kyle's onto something. Or else he's onto something even more significant—letting his wife have *all* the say.

When Jason walks into his gabled cottage on the bluff later, he steps over the dog chewing a knotted-rope bone at the slider. "*Hi there, girl,*" he quietly says, then notices the kitchen. The room is striking—and done. It's obvious Maris worked to clean it up and get it shining once the construction crew left.

"My God, Maris," Jason calls out. "Kitchen looks incredible."

"Hey, babe. Isn't it something?" Maris asks, turning into the room.

"I'm in awe." Jason, still holding the diner food, looks around the sleek and glimmering space. "Want to come work for me? Husband-and-wife design team?"

Maris just laughs him off before reaching for dishes in the cabinet. "Kyle still think you're at Sea Spray?" she asks.

"Yep. And that I'm freezing some of this," Jason says as he drops the take-out bags on the counter. "Not that I'm devouring it all with you tonight."

As Maris sets placemats and dishes and silverware on their new kitchen table, Jason takes in the final design details installed today. Especially that denim-blue island anchoring the space. The island's new quartz top is marbled white with veins of silvery-gray and blue. You can't help but feel the sea in all the colors. He looks from that stunning island—to the two small crystal chandeliers above it.

"Um, sweetheart?" Jason asks, turning to Maris as she lifts the meatloaf container out of a bag. "These pendant chandeliers? I thought we were going with something more ... *coastal.*"

"We did," Maris says. "That's coastal *bling*," she explains while lifting a slab of brown-gravy-drizzled meatloaf onto Jason's plate. "You got barnwood floors, and rustic ceiling beams. And the stonework around the stove in honor of your dad." She looks at Jason, smiles and shrugs. "And I got the glam."

Jason looks at the two cone-shaped chandeliers. Their glass drops are suspended from a silver filigreed crown. The glittering reflections of those glass drops cast a low light on the room. He gives one last look at them, and thinks about Kyle's compromise talk.

"Okay," Jason says, turning to Maris sitting at the table now. She's spearing a forkful of spinach salad.

"So you like them?" she asks.

"I do," he tells her, sitting and squeezing her hand. "I really do."

twenty-eight

JASON GOT HIS LIFE BACK, all right.

That night, after The Dockside's take-out dinner, he's back at it—in his barn studio. Maris took the kitchen cleanup so he could get some prints done. He sits at his drafting table now. Blueprints are spread out around him. Markers, too, as well his architectural scale. The double slider is open to the late-summer night. Crickets slowly chirp. The distant sound of breaking waves drifts into the barn. It's in this kind of quiet that Jason's lulled into the thick of work. His mind swims with numbers and calculations and dimensions. Time passes unnoticed.

Until a sharp one-two knock on the slider gets him looking over—right as Shane opens the slider screen and walks in. Wearing a plaid button-down loose over a tee and jeans, he stops just inside the door.

"Shane, hey," Jason says.

"Maris keeping you out of the house still?" As he asks,

Shane tips up that newsboy cap of his.

"Yeah, something like that," Jason bluffs, rolling his stool back from the drafting table. "How about you? Boat still busted?"

"That it is. When I drove by you earlier with the Frisbee toss? I'd just got back from a trip home. Had some stuff to take care of in Maine. Truck registration. Paid some bills," Shane tells him. As he steps into the studio, he's also taking in its visual details. "Figured a night walk was in order now. Stretch my legs after one long-ass drive."

"I'll bet."

"Yeah. So I saw your barn all lit up from the street and hooked a left here." Shane walks further in, veering over to the massive framed photographs hanging on the wall. Brass picture lights illuminate the photos from above. There are grand shingle-style New England cottages and pristine painted bungalows and gabled summer homes. "You do these?" Shane asks, motioning to them all.

"I did."

Shane gives a low whistle as he slowly walks past them.

"So what are you up to? Heading to Celia's?" Jason asks. He spins his stool around and leans an elbow on the drafting table.

"No." Shane talks while scrutinizing the framed pictures. "We really can't press our luck here. I saw her earlier, when I first got back."

"So you *are* pretty serious about her. But a hell of a situation you're in."

That gets Shane's attention. He looks over at Jason. "Hey, I can say the same about you, my friend. You're working in your barn, yet *banished* from your house? *Also* a hell of a situation."

"And *you're* changing the subject," Jason reminds him. "Which I'm going to hold you to. What are your intentions with Celia, anyway?"

Shane laughs. Rubs the back of his neck, too, but gets serious when he turns to Jason. "Intentions," he repeats. "In a perfect world?"

"Yeah."

Shane walks to the stairs to the loft. He glances up them, but sits himself on a lower step. Puts his elbows on his knees and talks. "My intentions in a perfect world." He takes a long breath of the damp sea air. "Be married by December. Spend Christmas with my new wife and daughter. Yep, that's right. Get the paperwork started to adopt Aria, too."

"Jesus Christ, Shane." Jason pulls back and squints at him. "*Seriously?*"

"Dead serious." He turns up those hands hanging over his knees. "Problem is, Celia doesn't know *any* of this. *And* it would send her running for the hills—in two seconds flat."

"Damn straight it would." Jason glances out the double slider to his house. "We sure don't live in that perfect world, do we?"

"Afraid not." Shane stands then and heads over to the wall shelves lined with Neil's journals—some leather and canvas, some ragged, some twine-wrapped. "So, instead of all that?" Shane says over his shoulder as he pulls out a journal. "I'll be a hundred miles out to sea come December. Lobstering federal waters and hoping to survive another winter on the Atlantic."

"That's tough, man."

"Yeah." Shane's flipping through a journal. "These Neil's?" he asks, not looking up.

"Pretty much. His observations, notes. Photos, sketches. They're an archive for just about everything I need for Barlow Architecture. It's how I keep my brother around."

"I can get that." Shane returns the journal to its shelf, then wanders closer to the enormous stuffed moose head mounted at the top of the stairs. "Now *that* looks familiar. From Foley's?"

Jason stands. "The bona fide original," he says. "From the good old days." Rolling up a blueprint, he drops it in the tube rack beside his table.

"How the hell'd that old moose end up here?" Shane asks, resettling his cap.

"Swiped it from Foley's after it closed down. Long story, you had to be there."

Shane nods and keeps wandering around the barn studio. He ends up at Jason's drafting table and turns another blueprint there. "So what're *you* doing? Working?"

"You bet."

"At this hour?" Shane asks. Now he moseys over to Jason's big L-shaped desk and lifts a handful of unopened mail. "Too busy to even take a break?"

Jason sits again at his drafting table and picks up a marker. "Hell, no rest for the weary, I guess."

"Or the wicked."

Jason looks up from lining a T-square over a print and drawing a measured line. "Come again?"

"But the wicked are like the troubled sea, when it cannot rest, whose waters cast up mire and dirt."

Jason gives a short laugh. "Quoting the Bible, are you?"

"That I am. Book of Isaiah. *There is no peace, saith my God, to the wicked,*" Shane recites, sitting on the edge of Jason's massive desk. "So … no rest for the wicked," Shane adds. "It's a proverb, meaning evildoers will face *eternal* punishment. But," he continues, tapping one of those envelopes on his hand, then standing and straightening the desk chair before heading to the double slider. "In modern day? It's loosely come to mean one's *work* never ceases."

"Ain't that the truth," Jason says, plugging numbers into his calculator now.

"Yeah." Shane opens the slider, then turns back. "So, Barlow. *You* are either busy—*or* you're an evildoer." With that, Shane tips his newsboy cap and walks out into the night.

～

Evildoer or not, busy or not, Jason works another hour before turning off his swing-arm lamp and locking up the studio. Crossing the dewy night lawn, he looks down toward the street to where Shane took off. Then he looks toward his house across the yard. Lamplight shines in the windows. He walks closer, spotting a large seascape painting on a wall. The dog is inside. Maris is there, too.

Evildoer or not, busy or not, one thing Jason knows for sure right now. He has plans for the evening. He's going in the house, crashing with Maris on the couch in front of the TV—and relishing those fudge brownies from the diner, too.

twenty-nine

THE NOISE GETS JASON TO jolt awake.

Lying in bed Wednesday morning, he opens his eyes. It's still dark out. So he props himself up on his elbows, shakes off some grogginess and glances at the bedside table.

"*Shit,*" he whispers, reaching to his alarm clock. With the clock in his hand, he drops back down on his pillow and shuts off the *beep-beep-beeping* alarm. The room is quiet now. A slight breeze drifts in the open windows. But there's no sound of the gulls feeding on the bluff. No morning birdsong. It's too early, thus the darkness outside.

"Wait a minute." Jason brings the alarm clock close to his face. He squints through the darkness at the time. "What the hell?" he asks himself. Twisting around, he sets the clock back on the bedside table. There's a brass ship-wheel paperweight there, too, anchoring some of Maris' manuscript pages. He'd read a page or two aloud to her last night, in bed.

But his clock is all messed up.

He gently nudges Maris beside him beneath the sheet. "Why is my clock going off twenty minutes early?"

"Oh," she says, her voice heavy with sleep. "I reset it."

"Reset it? *Why?*"

She turns on her side and touches a lock of his hair. "Because in case you might've forgotten, I love you."

Lying on his back, Jason looks at her next to him. "That's why you ... set my alarm early?"

"Well," she says, touching his hair again. His neck, too. Traces her fingers there. "*And* so we can do this." She moves closer and kisses his shoulder. Leaves more sleepy kisses on his arm. Lifts his hand and kisses his palm, his fingers. "*You said how we lost time*," her drowsy voice whispers.

"We did," he answers, watching her.

"So I'm slowly getting those minutes back, Jason Barlow."

"And I'm right there with you."

Wearing her silky nightshirt, Maris moves a leg over him and straddles him then. Her sleep-mussed hair hangs forward. Her fingers lift the bottom of his T-shirt and pull it over his head. "Getting twenty minutes back—starting right now," she says, bending low and kissing him, her kisses soft as the sea air drifting in the windows and grazing his skin.

～

This is the only time Cliff has—*after* distributing hurricane safety kits all morning and *before* the BOG meeting later this afternoon. He has thirty minutes, tops. Enough time to stop at Elsa's. He carries a small box up her walkway and thinks she must've been cutting flowers this morning. Looks like she left some on her front stoop.

"Or not," he says under his breath after climbing the stoop stairs. The flowers at her inn's door are an obvious arrangement *delivered* there. Setting his box on a porch table, he pulls a folded note from the bouquet and gives a quick skim.

Just a midweek bouquet today, Elsa. Snagged one of Carol's latest creations. The beach grass reminded me of that enchanted path of yours. —Mitch

"*Enchanted* path?" Cliff says, then looks over the porch railing to the secret path at the far end of the backyard. It's obviously not a secret anymore. After returning the note to the bouquet, Cliff gives a quick knock at the door, grabs up the box he brought—along with the flowers—and goes inside. Passing beneath the Mason-jar chandelier, he heads down the main hallway. Passes Jason's mighty fine grandfather clock near the inn's reception desk, too.

And smells the sweetest aroma—simmering tomato sauce.

Juggling the flowers and his box, Cliff walks to the kitchen. "Elsa?" he calls out on his way there.

~

"Cliff?" Elsa calls back from the stove. "I'm in the kitchen." Two pots of tomato sauce bubble on the burners. While stirring the sauce with a wooden spoon, she hears him approach.

"Called your street earlier for the hurricane safety kit. Didn't you hear the megaphone?" Cliff asks, turning into the kitchen. "Nick and I were up and down this road in the security cruiser. You were supposed to pick this up at the pavilion."

While he's talking, Elsa hears him dropping things on her marble kitchen island. "Well, I meant to," she says, still stirring without looking back. "But I got tied up on the phone, still wrangling legalities from Sal's estate."

"Figured something was up. And that's a darn legitimate excuse. Is it going okay?"

"Slowly, but surely," Elsa answers, still stirring.

Cliff comes up behind her. He plucks a spoon from her silverware drawer, lifts the second pot's lid and dips the spoon for a sauce sample. "You've been cooking batches?"

"Some for Maris, for dinner in her new kitchen. Some for Eva. And especially some for Celia." Elsa taps her wooden spoon on the edge of the copper pot. Cliff's beside her in his full commissioner uniform—black inscribed cap, and black inscribed polo shirt over khaki pants. He's cupping a sauce-dripping spoon, too. "The sauce for Celia is a peace offering," she admits.

"Peace offering?" Cliff asks, then slurps that spoonful of tomato sauce.

"She's upset at the way I've handled things here with the inn." Elsa sets her spoon on the counter and turns away from the stove. "*Oh!* Those are *beautiful*," she says, hurrying to a flower arrangement on her island. There are white beach roses, and mini sunflowers, and stems of blue larkspur—all mixed in with sweeping blades of beach grasses. They're arranged in a glass vase wrapped in thin rope at the vase neck. Touching the flowers, she turns to Cliff. "Are these for me?"

"I'm *assuming*," he says, still going at the sauce. "Since I found them on your stoop."

"You mean, they're not from you?"

"No."

As he explains how he just brought them in, a text message dings on Elsa's cell phone. It's charging on her island-top, so she picks it up to read the message.

The message from Mitch!

On my way to a faculty meeting. Dropped something on your front porch.

Oh, something's *dropped*, all right, Elsa thinks while clearing the text. Dropped all over her—a cold sweat! Her eyes drop closed, too, right as she hears Cliff's question from the stove.

"Who's texting you?" he asks.

"What?" Elsa looks from Cliff to her phone. "Oh, that. It's nothing. Just Maris with a kitchen question." Elsa plugs her phone back in, then discreetly plucks the note from the flowers. Opens it a smidge, too—just enough to read it.

Cliff walks closer, still holding his sauce spoon. "So … who are the flowers from? That's quite an arrangement."

"The flowers?" Elsa folds their accompanying note. "Carol, actually!" And it's not a lie, she tells herself. The note said this was *Carol's* latest creation.

"Carol?"

"Yes, Carol Fenwick. For … for my cart! That's it. My tomato cart. Which is actually hers, and she's letting me borrow it." Elsa slips that note into a pocket on her sand-colored lounge jumpsuit. "Carol thought the flowers could

218

… *zhuzh* up my tomato display."

Cliff sits on a stool at the island now. He takes off his gold-stitched *Commissioner* cap and sets it aside. "That cart is *still* illegal, you know. Flowers or not. Just because Carol has BOG approval for *her* flower business does *not* mean her cart is legal on *your* property."

"Yes, well." Elsa sits at the island, too. She reaches to that flower arrangement and traces a finger over a white beach rose. "It's *temporary*, that cart."

"And that there tomato cart of yours is an addendum to the BOG agenda. Got a meeting today, and majority rules on the cart's fate."

"*Basta!* You're relentless! My tomato side hustle will be done soon enough, Cliff. So can't you turn a blind eye?" When there's nothing from Cliff—no answer, no words—Elsa just meets his steady gaze and waits.

"Turn a blind eye on *what* exactly, Elsa?" he quietly asks.

Elsa goes silent now. A moment passes between them. "*What do you mean?*" she finally whispers to Cliff.

"Listen, Elsa …" Cliff picks up his cap and fidgets with it. They're sitting side by side—their arms practically touching—as the kitchen goes *really* quiet. He sets down his cap and adjusts a wayward sunflower in the bouquet. "Is there something you maybe want to tell me?" he asks then.

A beat of silence falls between them. But only a beat—because it's interrupted by two sharp raps at Elsa's side kitchen door. "Aunt Elsa!" Maris calls out as she opens that door and rushes into the kitchen. "Tomato sauce time!" she says.

Yes, saved by her niece. When Elsa hurries across the room, Maris gives her a big hug.

"Oh, Cliff!" Maris says, backing out of that embrace. "You're here, too."

"On my way out, actually." Cliff stands now. "And running late."

"Wait." Elsa takes a step in his direction. And stops. Lightly tosses up her hands with a small smile. "Cliff."

Cliff looks long at her. "Got to go," he says. "That BOG meeting's a few hours off. Have to get things in order." Putting on his cap, he looks over at Elsa again.

Elsa takes a quick breath. Steps closer to him, too. "Okay," she quietly says, stopping when Cliff gives a wave and turns to leave. "And, well. Thanks for the hurricane safety kit!" she calls after him.

"Oh! I picked up ours yesterday! It's really great," Maris says. She rummages through Elsa's box and lifts the crank radio. "This is *so* practical, Aunt Elsa. It charges your *phone*, too."

"Yes." Elsa watches Cliff hurry down the hallway to the front door. "Cliff thinks of everything."

"You do, too. And I can't thank you enough for making some extra sauce for me."

Elsa turns to Maris now. Wearing a Stony Point Beach tee with denim cutoffs, she's plucking a spoon from the drawer and headed to the sauce pots. "Why don't you come back later, Maris? You can have dinner *here*."

"No, no," Maris says after swallowing a spoonful of sauce. "I'm writing. And under deadlines. *Ooh*, did I tell you?"

"Tell me what?" Elsa asks, joining Maris at the stove.

"*Mitch* offered to be my editor. You know, for *Driftline*?"

"He *did*?"

"Yes, it's the best news. But things have also been *crazy*

busy with my kitchen reno. So I could use a good pasta dinner—at home. I'll squeeze in some writing and it'll be a … a *working* dinner."

As Elsa spoons sauce into a container for her, she glances at Maris waiting there. Something about her gets Elsa's attention. Maris' eyes, they're just sparkling. And her smile comes so easy.

"Oh, is that for my sister?" Maris asks, spotting an empty container labeled with Eva's name. "I'm headed over there for an afternoon coffee break. She wants to catch up after being away at her conference. So I'll bring her sauce too, okay?"

"All right. Let me get that one ready. There's an insulated tote there, on the island," Elsa says, hitching her head in that direction. "But are you *sure* it's no trouble carrying all this?" she asks, dipping a ladle into the sauce-filled pots on the stove.

"None at all. I have my golf cart outside," Maris tells her while dropping *her* secured sauce container into that tote. And as soon as she's got Eva's sauce tucked in too, she whisks herself out the side door again.

Elsa follows after her, stopping in the doorway and watching. Maris carefully sets the insulated tote in her golf cart, then climbs in herself. As she does, Elsa looks past her for any sign of Cliff.

But there's none. He's gone.

When Maris toots her golf cart horn and zips off, Elsa waves. Still standing in the doorway, she also pulls Mitch's folded note from her pocket and gives it another read.

And assumes—looking out toward the street—that yes, Cliff read the note, too.

thirty

THE BEACH IS QUIET MIDDAY.

Shane sits beneath the shade pavilion on the boardwalk. His hands joggle two good skipping stones he picked up on the sand. On the beach in front of him, the noon sun shines bright. A few late-season sunbathers have their umbrellas and chairs set near the water. Some walkers stroll by, too. Tide's coming in, so the waves are a little choppy.

But in his pocket of shade? Summertime quiet. The only sound is the creaking noise coming from the boat basin behind him. The pull of the current brings the small motorboats and rowboats docked there to life. The vessels creak and sigh against the pilings and posts.

Until another sound gets his attention.

It's Celia wheeling Aria's stroller over the boardwalk planks. The stroller's tires *thumpity-thump* as they approach. Shane waits there on the bench. The long blue sundress Celia's got on flutters in a light sea breeze; her straw fedora keeps the sun off her face.

"I got your text about crossing paths here," Celia says as she wheels the baby into the shade. "Boy, life's a lot more complicated here than it was in Maine."

"Want to move up there? Join me?"

"Shane!" She lightly swats his arm.

"Can't fault a guy for trying." Shane drops his skipping stones in his cargo shorts pocket, then pats the bench seat beside him. "Was worth a shot, anyway."

Celia sits with him then. Squeezes his hand, too. "What've you been up to this beautiful Wednesday? Besides skipping stones."

Shane leans forward and pats Aria's arm. "Hey there, little one. Enjoying a walk with your mama?" he asks, then sits back and turns to Celia. Moves a wisp of hair from her cheek. "Had breakfast at the diner. Go there as much as I can now, actually. To see Kyle," he says.

"Becoming a regular, are you?"

Shane nods. "Feels good, too. My brother's so busy, it's the only place I can connect with him. So I ate there, then stopped at the hardware store."

"Hardware store? Did something break?"

"No. But that guard shack at the trestle is looking pretty sorry. Kind of neglected, actually, with lots of peeling paint. So I grabbed some paint chips. Going to sway the commish to gussy it up." As he says it, Shane leans forward, picks up the plush lion rattle in Aria's stroller and gives the lion a gentle shake for her. "Listen," he says, looking back at Celia. "I really wanted to ask you something."

"What is it?"

"You having dinner with Elsa today?"

"No." Celia stands and lifts Aria from her stroller. She settles the baby on her lap when she sits again. "We actually had an argument this week."

"Oh, no."

Celia nods with a sad smile. "It wasn't good."

"Well, we can talk about it tonight."

"Tonight?"

"Yeah. Have dinner with me?"

Celia tips up her fedora. "I don't know, Shane. It's risky. Cliff's driving up and down all the streets still, blasting his hurricane safety reminders." She shakes her head. "He might spot you around. Or see my car at your place."

"No, no." Shane bends to Aria and points to a low-flying, squawking seagull. "*Look!*" he whispers as Celia shifts the baby in the bird's direction. "We'll go out," he says then to Celia. "You, me and the baby. Take separate cars and meet up."

"Where?"

Shane looks out at the September-blue sky. The salt air is warm today. He looks at Celia beside him, then. "Lobsterland. Aria will love it there, on the water. And Noah will fix us up some good eats."

⁓

If ever there was a moment when the saying *Home Sweet Home* meant something, this is it. Right now. Right as Jason walks inside his own house at day's end. He's carrying his work duffel and car keys—and is beat.

And smells some *comforting* aroma that he tries to place. Wait. Yes, it's tomato sauce simmering on the new stainless-steel stove. In the rest of the kitchen, recessed lights cast a glow on the gray-painted cabinets. On the gray stonework around the stove, too. And Maris' crystal pendant lights glimmer over the white-swirled island top. Hell, if a new kitchen will get Maris cooking like this, he's all for it. By the time he closes the slider behind him, Maddy's at his feet. Maris is standing in the dining room doorway, too.

"Good evening, Jason," she says, then crosses the kitchen and kisses him.

"Maris." He takes in the sight of her. She's wearing an elegant black satin shell loose over really faded skinny jeans. Her star pendant hangs from a gold chain around her neck. Her hair is down, with thick gold hoop earrings shining beneath it.

"Here," she says, helping him off with his blazer. She drapes it over her arm and takes his duffel from him, too. "Your table's waiting for you," she tells him then, beckoning him to follow her to the dining room.

Well. He might as well be in heaven. Their painted farm table is set for two. Beneath the low light of the black lantern-chandelier, vintage blue-and-white china plates are set on fringed gray placemats. Slightly tarnished silverware is set on cloth napkins. Crystal goblets sparkle. Pillar candles flicker atop two silver-metallic pedestals. Those sit beside a centerpiece—a tree-bark box filled with lavender spikes covered in purple blossoms. The paned windows are open to the warm evening.

Maris pulls out his chair. "The flowers are from Carol, when she was here to dinner when you guys were camping."

Jason nods, and slowly sits when Maris heads back to the kitchen. He hears her filling Maddy's bowl with kibble.

And he knows—now's the time. Quickly, he pulls out his cell phone and rapidly thumbs the keys. *Fast, fast.* Into his contacts, adding names, typing his message. That done, he sets the phone aside and fully takes in the beautiful room Maris arranged. A plate of sliced, crusty bread is on the table. Beside it? A dish of dipping olive oil with herbs. There's a bottle of Lambrusco. A ready-made salad filled with greens and fresh tomato wedges and sprinkled with cheese. Some sinful, frosted dessert is on the sideboard.

All the while, Maris is rattling dishes in the kitchen, and stirring things in pots on the stove.

"You made all this?" Jason calls over his shoulder.

"Yes, I did. I toiled in our new kitchen *all* afternoon," Maris calls back as she brushes through some utensils. "Your wife has many tricks up her sleeve …"

"Uh-huh." Jason rubs his jaw while sitting back at the elaborately set table. "Any of those tricks called Elsa?" He eyes the loaf of bread. "And maybe Maritime Market's dinner-to-go aisle?"

"Jason Barlow!" Maris' voice carries from the kitchen. "You're doubting me? I made this pasta myself, yes I did. I opened the spaghetti box and put the pasta in boiling water." As she says it, she walks into the dining room. Her both hands hold a large platter of spaghetti and meatballs. "Dinner is served," she quietly says, setting the platter on the table.

Jason reaches for the Lambrusco and fills their goblets. "A toast to the chef, then."

Maris sits across from Jason. She lifts her wineglass, too, and clinks his glass. "Yes. A toast to me," she says with a nod before sipping her wine.

They settle in. Over salad, they talk about their day. About the segment taped for *Castaway Cottage*.

"Filmed in Addison, actually," Jason lets on.

"Addison? Why?"

"There's a lighting repair shop there. What a place. It's called Lighting Lodge and is in an old carriage house. Run by a guy named Winter. Dean Winter. He's refurbishing the huge brass-and-copper masthead light that will hang in the Fenwicks' belvedere."

"Oh, sounds beautiful. A masthead light from an actual *ship*?"

"It is. Dates to the early 1900s and was originally an oil lamp. Dean's converting it to electric." Jason sips from his wine goblet. "Trent filmed the segment when Mitch picked out the light at the salvage yard, so we want to follow that light's journey to the cottage. Got some good footage of the refurbishing."

Maris nods and stabs a forkful of salad. She tells Jason that she's coming down the homestretch with Neil's book. But before she can say more, they're interrupted by Jason's phone. Text-message dings rapidly start up, one after the other after the other.

"*What* is going on?" Maris asks, twirling a forkful of spaghetti. "Is that Trent?"

Ding. Ding.

Jason's glancing at his phone. "No," he says, scrolling the phone screen.

Maris eats that spaghetti, then sets down her fork.

"Gimme," she says around the food—all while reaching for the phone in Jason's hand.

Ding.

Jason leans way back, out of her reach.

Ding.

"Jason!"

"Okay. They're all replies to a group text."

"Wait. A text from you?"

He nods, then lifts half a saucy meatball to his mouth. "Let me read it," he says, scrolling to the original message with his other hand. *"Boardwalk meeting tomorrow. Sunrise. Please be there."*

"Oh my God, Jason." Now Maris sits back in her chair. "Is that what I think it is?"

"What do you think it is?"

"Our secret?" Maris picks up her fork and twirls more spaghetti. "That we're telling everyone we're back together?"

"I think it's time." Jason sets down his phone and finishes that half-eaten meatball. "On the beach tomorrow," he says while chewing. "We can tell them there, all at once. One shot, done."

"Let me see what they're saying." When Jason slides his phone to her, Maris reads the messages. "Eva's bringing muffins," she begins, tucking her hair behind an ear. "Elsa dibs a coffee carafe. And Shane says he's never been to a boardwalk meeting. And—huh."

"What?"

"Kyle says this better be good news."

"Kyle, man—he'll be happier than we are. Lord, has he been after me to fix things."

Maris reaches over and squeezes Jason's hand, then reads more. "Ha! Celia says she'll bring Aria." Maris scrolls a little more. "And knowing how the meetings go, she's bringing the swear jar, too."

"Good one, Celia," Jason says, digging into his spaghetti.

"And your sister?" Maris waits until Jason looks across the table at her. Candles flicker between them. The lantern-chandelier drops golden light on their antique china. "Paige?" Maris continues.

Jason watches her with his dark eyes. His whiskered face is a little tired when he nods for her to go on.

"Paige says it's so good to hear from you." Before she reads more, Maris feels her eyes tear up. She glances from the text message to Jason—then whispers the rest as her voice catches. *"And that she's really pulling for us."*

~

Yep, it was an hour of heaven, that dinner. There's no mistaking it. Sitting there at the table, eating good food, talking. When Maris is turning on their dishwasher later, Jason puts away a clean pot. With the kitchen in order, the day ended just the way he likes. He comes up behind Maris at the counter and wraps his arms around her. The silk of her black tank top is cool to the touch.

"I'm going to unwind," he says, pressing his mouth close to her ear. "In the living room, okay? Take my leg off. Maybe have an extra glass of that Lambrusco."

"You should. Downtime's so important, Jason." Maris leans back into him. "But would you help me with something first?"

229

"Anything, sweetheart."

Maris turns and dries her hands with a dishtowel. "I have some framed artwork I'd like to hang in the kitchen." She nods in the direction of their new pedestal kitchen table. There's a blanket draped over something there. "Help me get those on the wall?"

He looks from her to the blanket, then walks in that direction. "What is it?"

"Lift it and see."

Jason looks back at her, then reaches for the blanket. Behind it, he sees two large, distressed-white picture frames. Some of the wood grain shows beneath the paint on the frames. But it's what's *in* the shabby frames that gets to him. Faded blue bandanas—*Neil's* bandanas—are mounted behind the glass of each frame. The bandanas are pressed and taut, showcasing the swirls of blue and white his brother favored. The blues and whites of the sea. Knowing now that this is what Maris was working on in her loft, Jason turns to her behind him.

"I really wanted to do this for you," she tells him.

"Maris," he begins. "This is *unbelievably* thoughtful."

"I'd like them hung right here," she quietly says while pointing to a freshly painted empty wall beside the kitchen table. A salty breeze drifts in the open windows. Her voice is just as soft. "So Neil's always a part of our home," she says, taking one of the frames. "Our *meals*," she goes on, holding the framed blue bandana to the wall. "Our *lives*."

thirty-one

IT TAKES A LOT TO surprise Shane.

A whale surfacing in the Atlantic can do it. Especially when the whale twists and falls back into the sea—and the spray of its splash reaches Shane's face on deck. A rogue wave can surprise him, too, washing over the boat as it tries to take him back into the ocean. And those storms that seem to spin up unannounced, right out of the water? There's a certain surprising glory to their writhing winds and driving rain.

Now he can add boardwalk meetings to his list of surprises.

That's right. Stony Point boardwalk meetings.

Because early Thursday morning? He thought that he'd be the first one there. He got up before dawn, showered and had a quick coffee. After throwing on his jeans, a tee and his old leather boat shoes, he grabbed his navy zip sweatshirt and left the cottage right at sunrise. And as he passed the coastal cottages on Sea View Road, his view was of that sun seemingly climbing out of Long Island Sound. A majestic sight, indeed.

But surprising? No.

The surprise comes when he heads down the footpath and turns onto the boardwalk. Walks the planks and sees people setting up under the pavilion. Heck, Elsa and Paige are unfolding the legs of a portable table and centering the table on the boardwalk.

"Paige," he hears Elsa saying as she hands over a bag. "Put out these cups. I've got the coffee, here." Elsa turns to the boardwalk bench and lifts a fancy carafe.

Seriously? Shane thinks. *For a boardwalk meeting—all this?*

He walks closer and notices Eva there, too. She's fussing with a *smorgasbord* of food.

"I was too nervous to make something myself," she's telling the others. "So I practically bought out Scoop Shop's bakery case." She turns to see Shane then. "Shane! Help yourself," she says, motioning to the spread on Elsa's table.

"Don't mind if I do," he replies, taking in the ... the *event* being orchestrated here. Elsa and Paige call out their hellos as he surveys the paper-wrapped egg sandwiches, and plastic-wrapped blueberry muffins, and little bags of tater tots, and sugar doughnuts. "Heard a lot about *these*," he says, taking an egg sandwich and ketchup packet.

"Oh, those are *divine*," Elsa calls over from her coffee-carafe fussing.

Shane nods. "Let me try one for myself." He grabs a paper plate from the table and settles a ways down on the boardwalk bench—right as Lauren and Kyle approach from the far end. So as Shane lifts the top of his croissant and ketchups his melted-cheese-covered egg sandwich, he listens to the gossip.

From Lauren: *Hey, guys. What do you think's going on?*
And Eva: *I tried to get it out of Maris last night, but she wouldn't return my voicemail. Gave me nothing.*
Paige adds: *Which makes me worried.*
Lauren pipes in: *Well, was Maris even invited? She wasn't on the group text.*
And Kyle: *Please don't let it be a divorce—which is why she wouldn't be here.*

As Kyle says it, he's grabbing a muffin off the table and heading Shane's way.

"Yo, Kyle," Shane says around a mouthful of ketchuped egg sandwich.

"What's happening, bro?" Kyle sits beside Shane and rips off a hunk of muffin.

"Not much. Just taking in the hoopla here," Shane tells him. "Seriously, all this ... for an *announcement?*"

"You have no idea," Kyle tells him while chewing his muffin piece.

Just then, Shane looks to the right when he hears a *thumpity-thump* sound. It's Celia wheeling Aria's stroller down the boardwalk. Over a striped tee and white skinny jeans, Celia's got on that black denim jacket Shane bought for their Maine trip. The jacket hangs open and is cuffed at the sleeves.

"Hey, guys," Celia says, approaching them now.
Shane hitches his head to her. "Good morning, Celia."

"And look at that *baby*." Kyle leans forward and tickles a finger beneath Aria's chin. "She's getting so big."

"She is, by leaps and bounds," Celia says, wheeling past them to the women now.

The boardwalk quiets then, when Shane notices only the lapping waves on the beach. A few seagulls soar low. The rising sun glints on the rippling Sound. But that quiet is broken by the thud of jogging footsteps now.

"Okay, Judge," Matt's telling Cliff beside him. Matt's got on nylon jogging pants and a loose muscle tee; Cliff's wearing a color-block tracksuit of matching tee and shorts. "Let's cool off," Matt instructs. He grabs hold of the top of the boardwalk seatback and starts some lunges. "Stretch it out."

Shane watches, still chowing down on that sinful egg sandwich that everybody's right about. Pops a few tater tots in his mouth, too, right as Nick approaches. He's in full security uniform—khaki button-down shirt with black epaulets, black shorts and black sneakers.

"Nice threads, dude," Shane tells him.

"Yeah, and I've got some nice premade tickets for you." Nick pulls a handful of paper notices from his shirt pocket. "I just *knew* this crew would be breaking *every* rule in the book. Food on boardwalk. Running on boardwalk. Unruly behavior."

"What the *hell*?" Kyle asks. "Who's being unruly?"

"Oh, *someone* will. In due time," Nick assures him.

As Nick's talking, Celia approaches again. Except now, she's holding a jar of money.

Nick, meanwhile, is handing Kyle and Shane prewritten food-violation tickets, then distributing tickets to the

234

others. "Here you go," Nick says with each handout. "Here you go. Here you go," right down the line.

But Celia? She stops in front of Kyle and gives that money jar a shake.

"Oh, no," Kyle groans, sitting back and stuffing the last of his muffin into his mouth.

"Oh, yes. Pay up, buster," Celia orders him. "I heard, as did Aria, the swear word you just said—sullying my baby's ears."

"You kidding?" Shane asks, as if he doesn't already know the swear jar story. "You're fined for saying—" He abruptly stops with a glance at Celia before *safely* finishing. "H-E-double-hockey-sticks?" he asks Kyle.

"Apparently." Kyle pulls a five-dollar bill from his wallet and drops it in the jar. "Celia's keeping us on the straight and narrow with her swear jar."

Just then, an argument starts up. Shane walks with Celia to the table for a cup of coffee as the debate begins: cinnamon versus chocolate-frosted doughnuts.

Oh, chocolate-frosted. The more chocolate, the better.
But cinnamon's lighter, no?
Heck, my vote's for chocolate. With cinnamon, all those sugar grains fall off—right onto your desk, or clothes.

Shane, watching this all go down from the sidelines, notices something, though. Worry creeps into the debate. These guys just can't help it—they're *really* distracted by the intent of Jason's invite here. And they voice that concern, too.

Too bad Vinny couldn't make it. Moral support for Jason.
Vinny's getting the kids to school, then going to work himself.
Chocolate's high calorie.
And sugar grains aren't?
But has anyone talked to Jason?
His message was really cryptic! And it was only from him, too.
Not Maris.
Listen. Back to the doughnuts. Studies prove that chocolate helps
reduce memory decline.
Well, cinnamon gives an energy boost!

Then? Nothing.

Nothing but silence—except for the gentle waves lapping onto the sand. And the whistle of a light sea breeze. And the clanking of the halyard cable on the tall flagpole in front of the boardwalk.

Silence until a *new* sound begins.

Footsteps get them all to slowly sit on the boardwalk bench, nudge each other, whisper.

Shane sees it, too—the way *everyone* here is glued to this nail-biter initiated by Jason's text yesterday. As those footsteps near, some of the friends lean forward for a better look. For a hint of the announcement to come. Others sit back, tip their faces to the warm sun and just wait.

So Shane sits, too—coffee in hand. He's beside Celia now, and they both silently turn to watch Jason and Maris approach together beneath the morning sunshine.

But he can't read them. They're moving slowly. Jason's in an open denim jacket over a loose tee and black cargo shorts. Maris, beside him, wears a cropped white blazer over a V-neck top, utterly shredded jeans and white leather mules.

And they're *both* as poker-faced as can be.

～

The first thing Jason notices is this: All eyes are on them.

Which he'd expected.

What he *didn't* expect is how serious the moment would actually be. That seriousness is visible on *everyone's* face. Elsa, Eva and Matt. Cliff. Celia. Nick, even. *All* of them. Three weeks of worry shows itself in everyone's eyes, in their solemn expressions. Three weeks of concern is there. Three weeks of scrapped-together hope.

Maris leans into him, whispering, *"I'm here for you, Jason. Always."*

And he knows. She's repeating her wedding vow promising to be by his side. Always.

So Jason takes a deep breath of the morning's salt air, first. Then—right there on the boardwalk as they stroll the sandy planks—he links hands with Maris, bends and kisses her head.

And that's all it takes.

That hand-holding. That kiss.

The gang just *erupts*. Okay, with some trepidation, but they do. There are some *Whoops!* A few people start clapping. There's a sharp whistle. And Jason shakes his head when he notices that Kyle's eyes are actually moist.

Kyle's also the first to stand—in his black tee over black chef pants. It's obvious he'll be on his way to the diner after this meeting. "Don't break our hearts," he warns Jason.

"*Don't* let this be goodbye."

"It's not," Jason says when he and Maris stop in front of everyone. "I'm *never* saying goodbye to this beautiful lady." He turns then, cradles Maris' face and kisses her again. "We found our way back," he says, brushing a wisp of hair from her face.

"And wanted to announce it to you all together." Maris wraps an arm around Jason and leans into him as she says it.

"Wait." Nick raises his hand from where he sits. "Found your way back. Does that mean you're *living* here again? *Deets*, Barlow!"

Jason laughs. "I've been living here since Saturday night."

Okay, now they *all* erupt—for real. *No* one can be contained.

Elsa, pressing her hands together: *Oh! Finalmente! I was so worried.*

Paige: *Thank heavens! You both made it. And you behave now, Jason.*

Eva, stamping her foot: *Oh my God, Maris. You didn't even tell me!*

Shane, counting on his fingers: *So … Sunday. Monday. Tuesday. Wednesday. That's four full days you've been back?*

Maris: *We really needed that alone time. Just for us.*

Nick: *Sexy time, huh, Jason? Finally got some action?*

Kyle: *Watch it there, Nick.*

Matt: *Whatever. The Barlows are back.*

But it's Celia who's first to hug them both. "I'm so happy for you two," she tells Maris. And to Jason, in the hug, she whispers, "*Shane and I really hoped for this. Especially*

THE GOODBYE

since we all had dinner together."

Jason backs up a step and nods. And thanks her.

Suddenly then, it's like he and Maris are in the receiving line at a wedding. There are backslaps from the guys. People shake their hands. Give quick kisses and exclamations. Elsa dabs at tear-filled eyes. Lauren sighs with relief. Cliff gets everyone lined up and grabs a picture for the Stony Point newsletter.

"Okay," Eva says. "I was *hoping* this would be the news. *So* ..." She picks up a bag from the bench where she'd been sitting. "So I saw these at Scoop Shop and, all right, I bought them." She digs into the bag and gives out party noisemakers with glitter-fringed blowouts. There are spinners, too, and all kinds of noisy gizmos.

Jason believes the racket now is unlike any the beach has *ever* heard.

Hoots and rattles and unrolling paper-tube horns and squawker whistles.

Nick tells Jason, "She took you back, you lucky dog," then gives his metal party spinner a whirl.

And when Jason's not shaking hands with one, or talking to another, Shane approaches.

"So here's *my* announcement," he says, quieting the group before shoving up his sweatshirt sleeves. "I'd like to buy you and Maris a drink tonight. At The Sand Bar. Hope everyone can make it, first round's on me."

"I'm actually playing there tonight!" Celia calls out.

"Seriously?" Maris asks.

Celia nods. "I got a gig there."

"Oh, I can't wait. Will you be playing your own songs?" Maris asks.

"*Maybe* one or two, with some old favorites. It's just a short set. Patrick hired me to get the open-mic crowd loosened up." Celia turns to Eva, then. "I was hoping Taylor might babysit?"

"Aw, Cee." Eva drops onto the bench seat. "She *would've*. But it's college fair night at the high school, and Tay's so excited about it. Matt and I are going with her to browse her college options."

"It's okay. Totally get that," Celia says with a nod.

"Celia!" Elsa calls out from further down the bench. She gets up and quickly rushes over. "*I'll* babysit Aria."

Celia turns, and is quiet. "Well, I'm not sure—"

Shane, Jason notices, gives Celia a discreet nudge right then.

At the same time, Elsa clasps Celia's hand. "*Please.*" Her face is serious. Her voice drops low as she stands there in her sleeveless chambray tunic and black lace-trimmed leggings. "Just let me."

Celia looks long at her, but agrees with a small nod.

And all of a sudden, tonight's a party—with much of the gang going out together. Though Lauren and Paige have to bow out, too, the rest will kick back to Celia's singing. They'll toast Jason and Maris. They'll linger together on a late-summer night. Doesn't matter the reason. Just that some part of their world's been righted this morning.

Jason takes Maris' hand now and walks her over to the food-and-coffee table. "You bums save anything for us?" he asks, examining what's left of the offerings there.

And as the friends laugh and eat and drink coffee on the boardwalk beneath the morning sun, Jason gives Maris a cinnamon doughnut and takes an egg sandwich for himself. Maris pours their coffees and they sit with everyone—like they've done so many times before.

Before Jason digs in, though, he just sits there.

And listens.

And watches.

The talk is nonstop now—much of it around full mouths as doughnuts are split, and hunks of muffins ripped off and eaten, and ketchuped tater tots devoured.

All the while the sun is warm; the sand, golden; the ocean stars, sparkling on the calm, blue water.

And Jason knows.

All of it—every single bit—would mean *nothing* to him without Maris at his side.

"Come on," she says, breaking off a hunk of doughnut and holding it out. "Let's trade."

"All right." Jason gives over half his egg sandwich.

"Good?" she asks as he bites into what looks like a cinnamon cloud.

Oh, if she only knew *how* good it all is—the morning, his life now, and yes, the doughnut. Instead he only nods, and goes in for another bite.

thirty-two

IT LOOKS LIKE A CRIME scene.

That's what Elsa thinks Thursday afternoon. In her sleeveless chambray tunic and black leggings, she's sitting on the inn's front porch swing. The sun shines warm; the late-summer air is humid. But the porch overhang keeps her cool in its shade.

Problem is, Elsa's laptop is idle beside her. *Idle*, because she doesn't have the heart to write to Concetta.

Not yet.

Not with that crime scene in her front yard.

Yes, that's what it looks like, that yellow-and-black hazard tape crisscrossed there.

A crime scene.

The tape's familiar to her. Cliff uses it sometimes when CT-TV's filming for *Castaway Cottage*. He'll stick that tape across sawhorses—to keep onlookers back from the camera crew. Or when a boat washed up on the rocks earlier this summer, he used that hazard tape to keep neighbors from pushing too close to the marooned vessel.

Now? Now the bright yellow-and-black tape is stuck— top to bottom in a big X—directly across Elsa's charming tomato cart. Her tomato cart! As if some devious crime went down right here on her beautiful inn grounds. *This* must be why Cliff left the boardwalk meeting early. And he said *nothing* of the matter. Just when Elsa was feeling *so* glad for Maris and Jason, her emotional pendulum swings again.

"*Oh!*" she says, waving off the taped sight and lifting her computer to her lap.

Concetta, Concetta, her fingers begin typing. *You won't believe this one. The waters have gotten so choppy in the sea of my life. As I sit here, my illegal tomato cart is all taped up—and it breaks my heart. I'm not sure if it's because I so loved having it, or because of Cliff. It feels like he's giving me a personal notice by taping off my little side hustle business.*

Elsa looks across the lawn and shakes her head, then continues typing her email.

The Board of Governors did not approve the sale of my tomatoes and shut down my cart. But when Cliff taped up the cart, was he doing more? Is he aware of what's going on with Mitch and shutting ME down? Because Cliff also knows I received a gorgeous flower arrangement—from Mitch. Oh, the white beach roses, and mini sunflowers, and stems of blue larkspur so lifted my spirits, too.

"Did they ever," Elsa says, pausing her typing. The week has not been good.

You see, I was feeling sad after a terrible argument with Celia on Monday. So Mitch's flowers brought a much-needed smile. And then ... Again Elsa looks out at the scene of the crime before finishing her sentence. *This!* she types, attaching a photograph she took earlier of her crime-scene tomato stand. *Concetta, you are a wise woman. Being on the outside and looking in, you have clarity. So can you offer me any advice? Because lately? It seems every move I make—whether with Cliff, or Mitch, or even Celia—is the wrong one.*

Grazie, amica.

~

For the first time in weeks, Jason does it. He walks the beach at Stony Point. Maddy's with him; the late-afternoon sun shines low; a salty breeze lifts his hair. He just got back from a new-client consultation and his workday is a wrap.

And he's happy.

Even Maddy is calm and quietly sloshes in the shallows.

This easy walk reminds Jason, too. No place on earth feels as good beneath his gait as this firmly packed sand at the high tide line. Right here. No place else.

You're back, he hears whispered then as a wave sloshes up onto the beach.

Jason closes his eyes for a moment and lets the sun, the salt air, hit his face. "Sure am," he finally answers while walking the beach. The fishing rocks are up ahead, beyond the Fenwick cottage. "Hey, Mitch's place is really taking shape," he quietly adds, nodding to the cottage on the beach. Some scaffolding has gone up on one side of that lone cottage. New windows will soon be installed in the belvedere. "And my marriage is better now, too. Solid," Jason says in almost a whisper. "Maris is really coming along with your book." There's a moment's pause before he continues. "*And* I fixed things with Shane."

Right move, he barely hears, or the light sea breeze whispers.

Jason stops then, when he also *feels* something brush against his shoulder—a clasp, maybe. He glances back, but nothing's there. Hell. Maybe it was just the wind.

So he keeps walking the tideline. "Celebrating tonight at The Sand Bar," he eventually says, dragging a hand back through his hair. "Life feels good, Neil," he goes on, still walking the beach. But he cuts across it now, toward the dune grasses on the berm. Maddy lopes past, her collar tags jangling. "You witnessing this?" Jason asks. "Things are as good as they've been—"

In a long, long time, a low voice finishes, or the swaying grasses sigh in the salty breeze. Either way, how Jason senses his brother here. He turns and vaguely salutes the sea now, before leashing Maddy and heading home.

~

At his gabled house on the bluff, Jason's sidelined at the front stoop. A package leans on the top step, so he picks up the box, then swings around the side of the house to the back deck.

"*Yes*, perfect timing," Maris says, meeting him at the slider and handing him a bowl heaped with kibble. "I'll take the package, you take Maddy's food?"

He does. While unleashing the dog and setting the dog bowl near the patio table, Maris' voice comes to him again from the kitchen.

"Don't forget to close the deck gate!" she calls out.

So Jason does that, too, keeping the dog stationed on

the deck before he goes inside to the kitchen.

"Oh, *good!*" Maris is saying. She's lifting something from the box she just opened. "This one's for you."

Jason heads to the refrigerator now. "For *me?*" he asks over his shoulder.

"Yes! I got you something."

"Seriously?" Jason sits on a stool at their new island and throws back a swallow of bottled water.

"Here. Try it on." She brings it to him at the island. "It's a new sherpa-lined sweatshirt for nighttime beach walks," she says, holding up the sweatshirt as he slips it on. "I thought you'd like it." She brushes her fingers through his salty, windblown hair, then across his whiskered jaw once the sweatshirt's on.

Jason watches her standing close. She's wearing the same V-neck top and shredded skinny jeans that she wore at the boardwalk meeting this morning. Her hair is down; her gold star pendant glimmers on its braided chain. Her fingers touch his jaw, the sweatshirt collar.

"You think of everything," he tells her.

"Everything?" she asks, turning away then.

"Everything. This amazing kitchen. Keeping me warm."

"Just be sure to save me a walk on the beach, will you?" she asks while throwing out the wrappings from the sweatshirt.

"Deal. But right now? I could go for a snack. I'm *famished,*" Jason says. He takes off the sweatshirt and hangs it on the back of a barstool. "Dinner at The Sand Bar's a long ways off."

"Should you get changed for tonight first?"

"I will, later. Before we go."

"Okay." Maris opens their new stainless-steel fridge then. "So … How about if I cut you an apple to munch on?"

"Yeah, okay. Kyle says they're good for my voice, now that I'm a public speaker, I guess." While Maris stands at the island and slices the cold apple into wedges, Jason grabs the granola container from the pantry. "He told me apples will keep me from clearing my throat," Jason explains, sitting again and pouring a healthy helping of granola onto a small plate.

"Well, eat up." Maris slides over the apple plate before slicing her own apple. "That'll tide you over till supper."

Jason stands then—granola plate in one hand, apple plate in the other. "Think I'll have this in the living room," he says, heading that way. "You coming?"

"In a minute."

And by the time Maris joins him in the living room, Jason's sitting on the couch. His granola dish is on the end table, and he holds the apple dish in his lap. Maris sits on the couch, too, and curls her legs beneath her as she crunches on her own fruit. Meanwhile, Jason's dragging apple wedges through the granola.

"Turn the TV on?" Maris eventually asks. "I want to see the weather for tonight, when we go to the bar."

Jason nods. He reaches for the remote, too, on the end table. But his hand catches on the edge of his dish there, tipping it and sending grains of granola *flying*—on the table, the sofa, his lap, the floor.

"Damn it," he gripes, setting aside his apple plate and plucking up random granola pieces. "It just went *everywhere!*" He leans forward; looks at the pieces on the floor; sits back on the couch; brushes pieces off his black cargo shorts. It seems the more he picks and brushes, the worse the mess.

"No, no," Maris finally says. She sets her apple plate on the coffee table and slides across the couch. "I've got it," she tells him, lifting flecks of granola off the cushion. "I've got it," she repeats, her voice dropping as she picks more granola off Jason's lap. She stops then, looks him in the eye and whispers, *"Don't lift a hand."*

Oh, and he *knows* that tone—so there'll be no argument from him. Instead, he leans back as Maris' fingers search for granola pieces, first. Softly, softly her fingers find little pieces in the seams of his cargo shorts, then brush clean the fabric. She moves to his tee next, gently untucking it, too.

"Just checking," she whispers, brushing the shirt fabric now. "That granola is *so* problematic, the way it goes everywhere. And we have to get it all," she adds, lifting that tee off over his head. "Wouldn't want it, well, falling behind the couch cushions now, would we?"

"Can't have that," Jason says.

Says it right as Maris straddles him on the couch. She sits there murmuring little granola worries as she bends low, lifting her fingers through his hair. She leans closer. *"Looks good,"* she whispers, then kisses his head, his ear. *"Good here, too,"* she murmurs, her kisses covering his neck, his jaw. *"And here,"* she says, her mouth moving to his— right as *his* hands slip beneath that V-neck tee that's not on *her* much longer, either.

And sometimes you know. You just know. Like he does now as Maris shifts and gets him to lie on the couch. She squeezes in beside him, too—wearing nothing but her black lace bra and shredded skinny jeans.

Jeans his hands are reaching down to unzip and slip off.

Yep, he knows. The best part of his day this Thursday? Spilling that granola dish, after all.

thirty-three

A COUPLE OF HOURS LATER, Maris watches the roadside scenery as Jason drives to The Sand Bar. The maple trees are heavy with green leaves. The sun has almost set; the horizon is violet-red. A pale mist rises above passing marshes where wild, golden grasses cascade. All of the evening colors are rich, and blurred at the edges somehow, like an old photograph in a scrapbook. A picture you brush a finger across, remembering when.

After pulling into the bar, she and Jason cross the parking lot. The salt air hangs heavy. It's quiet, this late-summer lull.

Suddenly, though, the lull is broken.

There are footsteps—rushing footsteps. And someone's arms reach around Maris from behind. She quickly looks over her shoulder and can't help the instant tears in her eyes. Still, those strong arms wrap around her sides and clasp in front of her. Those arms covered in denim shirtsleeves shoved up to the elbow. It's Kyle—yes, all six-feet-two of him in that denim shirt and dark tan jeans—standing behind her, resting his scruffy chin on her shoulder and hugging her close.

All while laughing. And smiling. And lifting her off her feet! And saying how *good* it is to see her and Jason here—*together.* That they made it through. Kyle's happiness cannot be contained. And with good reason, too, Maris knows. Heck, she *cried* in his diner when Jason left. And she later worked *with* Kyle plotting the camping weekend intended to remind Jason of all he has. Then there were the diner meals Kyle whipped up for the both of them. Many delivered personally right to Sullivan's cottage.

Yes, Kyle's been there for Jason—*and* her—through all of this. Completely.

So when Kyle hugs her from behind, Maris squeezes his hands in front of her and leans back into him—smiling, too. "*I know, Kyle. I know,*" is all she says before the three of them climb the few stairs to the propped-open bar door.

～～

Inside, it's more of the same. Decorative wood pilings wrapped with nautical rope stand at either end of the bar. Patrick, reaching overhead for a wineglass *behind* the bar, calls out, "Hey, *hey.* It's the Barlows!" As he does, a sharp whistle also comes from a booth in the shadows. Shane sits there and motions them his way. So Maris veers in that direction while Jason and Kyle hang out with Patrick for a few minutes.

"Not sure I've ever seen my brother more illuminated,"

Shane says to Maris when she sits across from him. "Kyle's over the moon that Jason's got his bride back."

"Yeah," Maris agrees. She glances over to Kyle at the bar. Standing there, he's lifting a pitcher of beer and turning to the booth. Jason high-fives Patrick and turns, too. Maris watches as Jason crosses the shadowy room. He'd changed into a light brown tee partially tucked into ripped denim shorts rolled at the cuff. A brown beaded bracelet and big leather watchband are on his wrist; low-top sneakers on his feet. His dog-tag chain shows at his neck. His overgrown dark hair is wavy in the humidity; his whiskered jaw is scruffy. When Maris turns back to Shane across the table, he's sitting there and watching *her*. "*Okay*," she admits with a wink. "So maybe I'm a little over the moon about Jason, too."

"And *that*, Mrs. Barlow, is a good thing," Shane says with a nod, right as Kyle and Jason squeeze into the booth.

"Hey, Shane," Kyle says, setting the pitcher down. "Patrick says you got this one."

"That's right. Least I can do for our old friends," Shane answers, then lifts the pitcher and fills four glasses. "Here's to you, Jason and Maris. Together. Stay that way now, you hear?" With that, he raises a glass.

They all do, drinking and laughing to a round of *Cheers!* and *Salute!*

Maris leans into Jason beside her then, and brushes her fingers across his jaw.

A waitress walks by carrying a tray of draft beer to another booth.

And several mounted big-screen TVs are filled with the jewel-green outfields of a late-season ballgame. Pin-striped players hit line drives and slide into bases in a cloud of dust.

And casual laughs and conversations come from surrounding tables.

Then there's the briny salt air drifting in through the bar's open door and windows.

"It's really a great day," Kyle says, lifting his glass for another swallow. "Second best of the summer, since my vow renewal."

It truly *is* a great day. Maris knows it as they settle in with their menus, and as they get distracted with talking and catching up, then deliberate meals before finally placing their dinner orders.

Which is when Patrick introduces the first of the night's entertainment.

"Singer-songwriter Celia Gray is here to get us started—on open-mic night," he announces from the stage area. An amp and microphone stand are set up there near a tall stool. "Let's give Celia a round of applause, folks."

Celia walks out from the shadows. She's wearing a loose gray V-neck tee over silver metallic skinny jeans and open-toe black leather booties. A turquoise pendant hangs from a silver chain around her neck.

"Good evening," she says, settling on that stool with her acoustic guitar. Her fingers pluck the strings and play a few gentle arpeggios. Her silver thumb ring glimmers as she does. "I'm really happy to be here with you tonight," she goes on, sitting beneath a ceiling spotlight. "And want to begin with an old, familiar tune. One that asks a question we can all relate to every now and then."

Several claps ring out in the dark bar. When they do, Celia's fingers softly play the same arpeggio before strumming chords on the guitar. "*Are you lonesome ... tonight?*" her voice sings then. "*Do you miss me ... tonight?*"

Maris turns to Jason when he stands and extends a hand. "Dance with me?" he asks.

Wordlessly, she nods—her eyes suddenly moist while she leaves the booth.

Jason takes her hand and looks at her for a second, then silently leads her to the small dance floor.

⌒

Shane watches only Celia. Beneath that one spotlight, all her silver glimmers. Her auburn hair is down and tucked behind an ear.

"*Does your memory stray ... to a bright summer day?*" Celia's breathy voice sings. She leans to the side and turns her face to the mic. Her eyes briefly close as she goes on. "*When I kissed you ... and called you sweetheart?*"

"Man, too bad Lauren's missing this tonight," Kyle says.

Shane glances at him. "She at home with the kids?"

"Sure is. School night. But she'd have *loved* this." Kyle nods to Celia beneath the spotlight. "She's good, isn't she?"

"Yeah." Shane grabs his harmonica from his shirt pocket. "So shove over. I'm going to jam with her for Jason and Maris."

On his way to the small stage area, though, Shane's intercepted by Cliff and Nick coming in through the propped-open bar door. He quickly points them to Kyle's booth, then joins Celia onstage. Standing a little behind her, he waits while she strums an interlude between verses. She pauses then, and glances over at him with a slight nod.

Shane takes the sign to bring in more melody—with his harmonica. His riff builds as he manipulates the instrument, as his hands wrap around it and he gives a vibrato to certain musical phrases. All the while, Celia's strumming is so soft, just a whisper of an accompaniment to him. So his harmonica plays the song's next verse. He slows the melody and keeps it bluesy as the words run through his mind: *Do the chairs in your parlor seem empty and bare? Do you gaze at your doorstep ... and picture me there?* That faint vibrato lingers before he gives the song back to Celia to close the verse.

Funny, though. It's Jason and Maris who steal the show. The crowd's gone full-on silent while watching them move together. They are the only couple dancing in the shadows. Jason's casual in his tee, big watch and rolled-cuff shorts; Maris, ever stunning in a black lace moto jacket over a camisole and her shredded jeans. And from the way they hold each other, and press close, Shane can see—anyone can. There ain't no way in hell those two are lonesome. Not tonight. Not anymore.

"Is your heart filled with pain?" Celia sings then, her voice tremulous. She slows the song even more now. *"Shall I come back again?"* her words ask, rising in a singing whisper before pausing. *"Tell me, dear,"* she finally sings, turning to watch Jason and Maris barely sway together. *"Are you lonesome ... tonight?"* Her fingers, they linger with the song, fading it out in another arpeggio before raucous applause rises from the shadows.

As it does, Shane walks over to Celia. With a hand on her shoulder, he bends low and talks in her ear. *"You still coming over later?"* he quietly asks.

Celia clasps his hand on her shoulder and only nods—
before Shane turns away and gets himself offstage and back
to the others in the booth.

~

Eventually, their meals are delivered.

Deluxe burgers and fries and onion rings are set on the
tables. There are pickles. Ketchup and mustard, too. All of
it gets shifted here, passed there, drizzled with this, dunked
in that. While they eat, and kill that pitcher of beer, Celia
plays on. They pause to listen to her sing, then get
sidetracked with talk. At one point, Shane manages to pull
several paint chips from his pocket.

"What're those for?" Jason asks.

"The guard shack," Shane says with a nod to Cliff in the
next booth. "That shack's looking shabby these days,
Commish."

And so a new deliberation begins. Green? Or brown?
What about gray? Paint chips go around one table, then get
passed to the other. Back and forth. Here and there. The
words here and there, too.

Green, maybe?
That's what's there now. What about gray? It's more modern.
Not sure. How about brown?
Brown's neutral, at least.
*C'mon. Anything's better than what's peeling off that shack
now.*
Did you know there's a psychology to paint colors?
You fall for that shit, Kyle?

No, listen. Greens are soothing ... natural.
What's gray's meaning?
Stable and secure. But also gloomy!

"All I know is anything pale shows the dirt," Nick says around a mouthful of cheeseburger.

Shane sees Celia coming before anyone else does. Her set is done and someone else took the open mic now. Gorgeous in her silver get-up, Celia's crossing the shadowy bar to his booth. She catches Shane's eye, too—managing a slight wink unnoticed by the others. When she sets down her guitar case and slides a chair to the end of the booth, the paint talk gets briefly interrupted.

"You rocked it," Kyle says, high-fiving Celia.

Others jump in with more enthusiasm. With, *Great show!* And, *Brought down the house.* And, *So good!*

"Thanks, guys." Celia pulls her chair close and eyes the table of food and drinks. "Is there a dinner here for *me?*" she tentatively asks. "I'm starved now."

"Oh, sure," Shane says. He slides over a covered plate from the center of the table. "Grilled cheese and tomato. French fries on the side."

"We kept it warm for you," Maris adds, lifting the top plate off the meal.

"Excellent." Celia pulls the plate closer. And after ordering a soda from the waitress and pouring ketchup on her fries, she asks about the paint chips spread across the tables.

"Those are for the guard shack," Shane feigns an explanation. He'd already told Celia about his stop at the hardware store for the paint chips earlier. "Needs a facelift," he says.

"But before we pick a color," Cliff interrupts from the neighboring booth, "there's something *more* important to consider," he says while lifting his half-eaten burger. "The real question is, *who's* going to paint that shack?"

And—that's all it takes. Deliberations begin anew with everyone comparing work schedules, and why they can or cannot swing a paintbrush to help out.

"Speaking of work," Shane says. "I had dinner with Noah last night. He's got a new gig starting this fall."

"Seriously?" Kyle asks. "Your old captain on the lobster boat? Back in your juvie days?"

"That's right. Guess the state of Connecticut plans to retrieve lobster traps abandoned in Long Island Sound—most of the traps from when the industry went belly-up here," Shane explains. "All the shoreline will be scoured and cleaned up. And Noah's one of the old-timers they've contracted to assist."

"I read something about that in *The Day*," Jason says, sipping his beer. "Shit, to put together an entire coalition, there must be a ton of traps out there, no?" Jason asks.

"Could be as many as a *million* ghost traps in all of Long Island Sound. They're polluting our waters, and killing marine life," Shane tells them. "And it's an *immense* undertaking, tracking down those abandoned traps and hauling them out. So someone experienced, like Noah, is like a living radar—and a real asset. He'll know right where to look."

"But doesn't Noah run a seafood restaurant now?" Celia asks, then sips from her glass of soda.

Shane turns to her. And knows. Knows that *she* already knows all of this—Celia and Aria were *with* him at that restaurant last night. Shane nods and goes along with her cover. "Place called Lobsterland," he says. "Guess he's hiring a temporary manager to run the place while he's out on the Sound again."

And as they talk about Noah returning to lobstering in this new capacity, Celia says she really has to get going.

"Elsa's babysitting," she mentions, pressing a napkin to her mouth before standing. "Don't want to keep her waiting."

"Celia." Maris grabs her purse, too. "Can you give me a lift home?"

"Of course!" Celia says, bending for her guitar case.

"You're leaving?" Jason asks Maris.

Maris nods. "I want to get an early start writing tomorrow." She squeezes out of the booth and joins Celia. "Because I'll have to wrap early, remember?" she reminds Jason. "We have to drop my car at the dealer, after dinner."

"Car trouble, Maris?" Cliff asks from their other booth.

"No. I need new tires before winter. Grabbing an oil change, too," she says, hooking her chain purse strap on her shoulder. "The service department's open half day Saturdays, and I've got a slot."

"What about Friday night fishing, dude?" Nick asks Jason.

"I'll meet up with you guys later," Jason says. "After the car's dropped off."

As Maris kisses Jason goodbye, and as Celia waves to the tables, Cliff stands, too. "I'll walk you ladies out and head back myself," he says, scooping up all those paint chips. "Got some early morning hurricane safety distribution to tend to. Last day of it." He motions to Nick. "Come on. It's getting late."

Nick stands, too. "Yeah. Fine, boss."

"Might be past your bedtime anyway," Kyle tells him.

Which Nick can't ignore. He gives Kyle's shoulder a good shove on the way out.

"Later, Cliff," Jason says to the departing crew. "Catch you at home, Maris."

"Drive safe," Kyle adds, grabbing a few onion rings at the same time.

"Take care, Maris. Celia," Shane calls out. When they turn and wave, he tells them, "See you around sometime."

~

The three of them—Jason, Kyle and Shane—linger in the booth. The talk comes easy. Burgers are finished. The last of fries, downed. Finally, the three of them walk to the bar where Kyle orders a side of nachos and cheese.

"This round's on me," Jason tells Patrick as he sits at the bar.

"Okay," Shane adds, sitting on the stool beside Jason. "Then give us a pitcher, too, bartender."

"Will do. And hey, Barlow. Nice dance earlier, with your wife," Patrick says while mixing a drink. "You guys looked good."

"We *are* good." Jason props his elbows on the bar. "Doing great."

"That's what I like to hear." Patrick sets that mixed drink down for a waiting customer. At the same time, Kyle's nacho platter is ready. "Grab that, would you?" Patrick tells Kyle. "Got another customer in line, then I'll bring your pitcher over."

"No prob," Kyle tells him, lifting the nacho tray.

As they get off their stools and turn toward the booth, Jason's lagging behind to pay the tab. "Yo, Patrick," he calls, taking a step backward. "We're all squared away," he says, tapping the cash.

"Thanks, Barlow," Patrick answers from the other end of the noisy bar. "I'll bring your brew in a minute."

"No rush," Jason calls again while taking another step backward—and nearly tripping on a customer sitting with a small group at a nearby table.

"Watch it, peg leg," the guy tells him.

"*What?*" Jason quickly looks down at his prosthetic leg as though maybe something's wrong with it, then looks to the guy and turns up his hands.

"I *said*, watch where you're going, peg leg," the guy repeats as his friends at that table snicker.

Shane and Kyle turn back. And Jason sees it all. He sees *them* look at his prosthesis, too, extending beneath his cuffed denim shorts. Then they look at the asshole sitting at a small round table.

"Did you just say what I *think* you said?" Kyle asks, still holding the nachos while stepping closer.

"What are you, deaf?" the guy throws back.

A few customers at another nearby table go quiet. But some open-mic duet is singing onstage. And a rowdy pool game is going down in the back room. So things are a little chaotic.

"Come on." Standing in the shadows, Shane cuffs the offending guy's shoulder. "Stand up on those *two* legs of yours, loser, and let's hear that again."

"Hey, man," Jason says, pulling Shane back. "Leave him alone. Just let it be."

"You kidding me?" Shane shoves up the shirtsleeves of his loose button-down. "This guy needs to learn some fucking manners."

"Ease up," Jason persists, giving Shane a push toward their own booth. "Believe me," Jason tells him and Kyle. "I've heard it all. Doesn't matter."

"Damn straight it does." Kyle throws a look over his shoulder as he sets the nachos at their booth.

"Eh, maybe another time it would. But it's been a long, hot day," Jason says. He sits in the booth and is actually glad to see Patrick approaching with their pitcher. "Just what we need," he tells the bartender.

"Listen, my friend." Patrick glances over his shoulder, then at the three of them. "Everything okay? Things looked a little stirred up back there."

"Yeah," Shane assures Patrick. "It's nothing," he says, waving off that jerk. "We're good."

After clapping Jason's shoulder, Patrick heads back to the bar.

And it's true. They're good.

Jason's just glad to pour one last cold one and bullshit with the Bradford brothers. And chill. They have some laughs. Shane tells a seafaring tale. Kyle mentions he's planning a speed-dating night at the diner soon—anything to help the perennial sinking September numbers.

Yep, Jason's relieved. They dodged a grenade tonight.

Dodged a stinkin' bar fight.

All's good.

～

Yeah, right.

Jason should've known.

He *should've* known when Shane said he was off to the men's room. At the same time, Kyle said he wanted a nacho refill and headed to the bar.

Problem is, Jason doesn't catch on until he notices that both brothers—taking roundabout ways to get there—are actually slipping out the bar's side door.

Which gets Jason quickly looking to the table where that slur went down. Of course, the offending dude is no longer there.

"*All's good, like shit,*" Jason whispers, sitting back in the booth. He checks his watch to see just how long it'll take Shane and Kyle to give that guy a piece of their mind. Piece of their fists, too—knowing the Bradford boys.

So Jason just sits alone there. Sips that beer. Half-watches the ballgame going into late innings on a big-screen TV. Checks his watch again and hopes he doesn't hear sirens approaching to break up some parking lot brawl.

It doesn't take long for the outdoor event to come to an end.

Ten minutes later, two hulking shadows make their way through the bar. There's some stealth to their steps. Not much is said between them, either.

But the telltale signs are there. Kyle's dragging a hand through his messed hair. And his T-shirt is torn ragged beneath his denim shirt. Behind him, Shane's clenching and unclenching a hand, then shaking it out. They're both winded, too.

"Oh no, man," Jason says when they sit in the booth seat across from him. "You didn't."

Shane lifts the pitcher and pours the last of the beer into his and Kyle's glasses. "Didn't what?" he asks.

"Come on, you went after that guy?" Jason motions to the empty seat at the small table near the bar. Then he looks at Shane. His face is damp. He wipes a bead of perspiration from his brow. "You're going to get yourselves arrested, for Christ's sake," Jason tells them.

"Nah." Kyle fans his now-sweaty tee fabric. "Didn't do enough to get arrested." He swigs from his beer glass, then leans over the table. "Just enough to shake that asshole up—calling you peg leg."

Shane looks at Jason, then toward the propped-open bar door. He leans back and also swallows a mouthful of beer. Catches his breath some. "Left the motherfucker with a little limp, that's all," he finally lets on. "It'll fade in a few days." He leans forward and reaches an arm across the table. Slaps Jason's shoulder, too. "Got your back, man. Always got your back."

thirty-four

SHANE PULLS UP TO HIS rented cottage an hour later. When he does, his pickup's headlights catch Celia's car parked there. No doubt she's waiting on his back porch. So he kills the truck engine, drags a hand through his hair, blows out a long breath and gets out. Heading down the wood-planked walkway, he passes some scrubby beach grasses before climbing the seven olive-painted porch steps. A few lanterns are lit—some on the half-wall, some on the old table. The lantern flames flicker in the night. Out beyond, the moon's rising over Long Island Sound.

Celia's sitting on that half-wall and leaning against a porch post.

"Sorry I'm late," Shane says, walking to her and lightly kissing the side of her face. "Me and my brother had to beat the shit outta someone."

"*What?*"

"Yeah. Some prick bothering Barlow at the bar, calling

him a peg leg." Shane hoists himself up on the wall, too. "We'll see whose gait's a little off now."

"Oh my God. Shane! Are you all right?" Celia asks, leaning forward in the shadows.

Shane nods and tells her the story—from Jason backing into the guy, to the dirtbag letting loose with his mouth. Sitting on the porch wall, Shane tells more. Tells how Kyle nudged him to get things going when they saw the guy leaving. How they slipped out the side door and tracked the loser down in the parking lot.

"Jason didn't even know what we were up to," he explains to Celia, his voice low. "Not at first, anyway." He pauses then, before describing how he and his brother put the guy in his place. Landed a few blows. Did just enough damage so he'll think twice before opening his contemptible mouth like that again. "But we're okay. Me and Kyle," Shane says. "Hell, thought my brawl days were behind me. But it was pretty offensive, hearing this guy rip into Jason. And it made me so mad."

"Oh, Shane." Celia gets off the wall and walks to him. She touches his face, runs her fingers through his hair. "It must've been awful. You *sure* you're okay?"

"I am. Been through a helluva lot worse out on the Atlantic. Seriously. The guy didn't even know how to fight."

"Can I get you anything? Something to drink inside?"

"Nah. It's nice just sitting out here in the quiet." Shane looks over toward the Sound. Silver moonlight falls on the dark water there. "How about you?" he eventually asks.

"What about me?"

"You get Maris home okay?"

"I did. We talked a little on the ride."

"About what?"

"Well? About us. She was really supportive."

"That right?"

"Yeah. And ... I *liked* talking to her about us. Like that there *is* an us."

"There definitely is. Now, come here," he says to Celia then, pulling her close to where he's sitting on that wall. Kisses her, too. "You sang beautifully tonight, you know."

She nods, stroking his jaw. "It felt right being there. *Especially* for Jason and Maris." Celia hoists herself back on the half-wall and leans against her post again.

Shane shifts over and leans against the post facing her. They talk, then, about nothing—and everything. She mentions she can't stay too late, with Elsa babysitting at the guest cottage. Shane talks about his brother, and regardless of the scuffle, it was good having a beer with him. He also encourages Celia to try to work things out with Elsa. Celia nods, and mentions her adult-ed staging class starting up in the fall.

Time passes. The salty air is damp. Small waves lap at the tiny beach beyond his backyard.

"Oh, I meant to tell you ..." Celia hops off the wall and gets her purse from the porch table. "I received something today," she says, brushing through her bag. "In the mail."

Shane laughs when he sees his envelope in her hand. "My letter. Did you read it?"

"Not yet." She tears open the envelope and pulls out the note, then sits on an old whitewashed bench. A tarnished lantern flickers atop a rusted milk can there. So Celia leans into that illumination and reads Shane's brief note aloud.

"What's it going to take for my ears to hear those three words?" She looks over at him. "That's it?"

From where he sits on the wall, Shane turns up his hands. "I told *you* those three words. *I love you.* And I do. And I also know you wrote those words in the note you left me. But I was just wondering what it would take for you to *voice* those words," he says.

Celia silently reads the note again, then looks across the porch to him. "For me not to be *afraid* to say them."

He nods—feeling a little sad for her then. In a beat of silence, they just look at each other—Shane still on the wall, Celia sitting on the bench.

"Come on," she says a moment later. Standing, she opens the screen door to the kitchen. "Let's go inside. I'll show you another way."

~

And show him, she does. With her every touch, every kiss, every murmur in the darkness of his cottage bedroom, Shane feels her love.

And it's enough for him. Whether Celia's too afraid to *say* she loves him, or thinks it's too soon, he won't push her further. She's been through the unimaginable this past year, and sometimes he can't believe she ever even let him into her life.

Now he's got an arm crooked beneath his head as he lies in bed. He's watching her, too, while she puts on her silver-metallic jeans, first. Sitting on the edge of the mattress, she then hooks on her bra and pulls over her loose gray tee. She has to get home now, he knows that. So they don't say much. But Shane *also* knows he's about to change that quiet.

"Got something to tell you," he admits, still watching her from beneath the sheet.

Celia's standing now, and straightening her top over those silver pants. She just glances back at him.

"Heard from the captain this morning," he goes on. "Boat's headed out Monday."

"*It is?*" she whispers, half-tucking her shirt.

Shane nods. "I have to hit the road tomorrow."

"Friday? So soon?"

"You know how it is. Got to stock up on some food. Pack a duffel for my time on the water. Captain's got a lot of catching up to do to get out of the red. Don't know how long he'll have us out there this trip."

Celia looks at him, then scoops his tee off the end of the bed. She holds it for a long second, then walks closer and swats him good with it.

"Hey, *hey!*" he calls, ducking aside.

"You *knew* you were leaving all this time?" she says. "Why didn't you *tell* me?" she asks with another tee-swat.

"Just did." Shane takes the T-shirt from her and pulls it over his head. "Come on, Cee. I didn't want the whole night to be about goodbyes."

"*Yeah*," she sighs. "I get it." She sits on the edge of the mattress beside him now. Grabs his jeans, too, from a nearby chair and gives them to him. "It's just something we have to get used to, I guess. Your leaving."

As he puts on his jeans, she walks to his dresser and brushes her hair, then bends to the mirror and dabs on some lip gloss.

"Listen, I'll let you know as soon as I get more details from the captain," Shane says, standing and pulling up his pants. "But I'm sure I won't be around much now. Got to get working again."

"I know, Shane. God, I'll miss you, though."

"Me, too," he tells her, adjusting his tee over his jeans.

Celia nods, looking from him to her watch. "How long a drive is it, do you think, from The Sand Bar back to my cottage?"

"Twenty, twenty-five minutes. Give or take," Shane says, buckling his belt. "Why?"

"Elsa wanted me to text her when I leave the bar. You know, I'd be driving alone and she wants to be sure I make it safely." As she says it, Celia pulls her cell phone from her purse and texts Elsa. "Okay, done. She thinks I'm leaving the bar now," Celia says then. "So. We have twenty minutes." She pauses and sets the timer on her phone. "What do you want to do?"

～

Minutes later, they're in the living room. The hour is late. Thin checked curtains hang limp at the open windows. The air is a little dank; the room, shadowy beneath the unpainted, planked-wood ceiling. Celia sits on the gray rattan sofa. She's all dressed again in the silver outfit from her singing gig—right down to her silver thumb ring—and ready to go home. Elsa's expecting her in twenty minutes.

Those twenty minutes they've got to fill.

There's a chair near the blue and green glass fishing floats hanging in the corner. Shane slides that chair over.

He places it on the other side of the distressed painted trunk in front of that sofa. So the trunk is between them now, and an old checkerboard is all set up on top of it.

Shane pulls a dime from his jeans pocket and sits in that chair. Holding that dime, he tells Celia, "Call it. Winner goes first."

"Tails."

Shane flips the dime onto his other hand. "Tails. Your move."

And so it begins.

The twenty-minute countdown.

No one glances at their watch, though. They pretty much don't look up from the checkerboard at all. Instead, each leans forward—elbows on knees—and studies the checker pieces.

But something *is* happening; Shane can tell. At least for him, it is. And from the sad look Celia fights on her own face as she puts up a brave front, he imagines it's happening to her, too.

With each silent nudge of a checker on the checkerboard, there's some question or thought *neither* dares say.

Celia's first move: *When will I see you again?*
Shane's next: *How are we going to do this?*
Another diagonal nudge of a checker: *Are you happy?*
A jumped checker: *I miss you already.*
Another diagonal slide: *Will this work?*
And another: *I wish I could come with you.*
A kinged piece: *Wish I could stay.*

They both jolt a little when Celia's phone timer sounds.

271

She reaches for the phone, stops the alarm and gives Shane a sad smile.

"Well," he says, standing then. "We'll pick up with the game whenever I'm back, okay?"

"I'd like that." Celia lifts her purse from the sofa and stands, too.

"I'll leave the board just the way it is. Won't move a thing." Shane nods to the checkerboard—stopped midgame.

"*Okay*," Celia barely says. She walks around the sofa and passes a silver tin pitcher filled with beach grasses.

"Give Aria a hug for me?" Shane asks.

A nod from Celia. "*I've got to go*," she whispers then, heading to the cottage's front door.

Shane follows behind her. When she turns to him before stepping outside, he cradles her face and kisses her. He's surprised, too, by the intensity of that kiss. By the way neither wants to part.

But they do. They separate reluctantly, their kiss ending in several small kisses trying to hold on.

Finally, Celia's fingers trace his jaw right before she turns and walks outside.

Shane follows again, but only to the front porch this time. Neither one of them says a word. Least of all— goodbye.

Shane just stands there in the night and listens to her footsteps heading to her car.

Hears the thud of her car door.

Watches as she backs out onto the road and drives away.

thirty-five

THIS CERTAINLY ISN'T HOW ELSA planned on spending her Friday morning. Not dressed in her garden clothes—typical long tee over black capri leggings and slip-on sneakers. Not with her hair tied back with a rolled paisley bandana. But it's warm—even for September. And while closing up her tomato cart, she figured dust would rise; her hands would get dirty; her brow, sweaty.

She presses a hand to that brow, but suddenly hears someone approaching.

"Nice thing about being back home?" a voice asks from behind her.

Elsa turns to see Jason there. His dark, wavy hair looks damp from a shower. His unshaven face is scruffy. "And what's that?" she asks back.

"I get to walk to work."

"Well, that's not the *only* nice thing," Elsa answers, opening her arms wide to him. "You also get hugs."

Wearing a gray button-down over brown carpenter shorts and serious work boots, he laughs. Walks closer and takes that hug, too.

"*Oh, I've missed you being around,*" Elsa whispers right into it.

When he backs up, though, Jason's eyeing the mess on her lawn. "What are you up to here?"

Elsa looks at the lawn, too. Shallow wooden crates are askew on it, crates that held her tomatoes. Her *Tomatoes for Sale* sign is flat on the grass, along with some decorations—faded conch shells; a bouquet of wispy beach grasses tied together in a square glass vase. There's a big clump of yellow hazard tape, too.

"Aren't you *selling* your excess tomatoes?" Jason presses, taking a closer look at her random lawn items. "Surely your crop is still going strong."

"It is." Elsa lifts a shallow wood crate of tomatoes off her now-defunct tomato stand. "But I just have no time," she says, setting the old crate on the grass. "I've been too busy being in trouble with several people."

"Several?" Jason asks, removing the cashbox from the cart.

Elsa nods. "Celia."

Silently, Jason only looks at her with a raised eyebrow.

"There've been some mishandlings with the inn," Elsa quietly explains, taking the cashbox from him. "I've overstepped, and now I need to fix things."

"Okay." Jason squints through the bright morning sun at her. "Who else are you in trouble with?"

"Well, there's Mitch."

"Huh. Which leads us to Cliff?"

"Yes. Cliff." Elsa sets the cashbox on the lawn and lifts the spent yellow tape she'd peeled off the cart earlier. "Who actually shut *down* my tomato operation," she says, giving the balled-up tape a shake.

"What?"

"He did. The BOG did *not* approve my tomato cart." She drops the tape then. "And Cliff wouldn't grant an exception."

"Well," Jason says, lifting a little blue jay garden spinner off the cart. "That's the judge's way. You know that," he says, giving her the blue jay. "The rules are the rules."

"So are the rules of the heart," she answers. "And honestly? My heart's a little tangled up right now."

"Careful there, Elsa," Jason says over his shoulder as he closes the cart's umbrella. "And make damn sure you *listen* to that heart of yours."

"Oh, a lot of good *that's* been doing me." She lightly tosses the bird whirligig on the lawn. "Anyway, my tomato biz is over—just like my inn. And now I've got to bring this cart back to Carol."

"I'll do it," Jason tells her as he lifts the closed umbrella from its cart clamp. "I'm going to the Fenwicks' anyway, for work."

"You're filming dressed like that?"

Jason glances down at his outfit, including the heavy boots. "It's a construction site, don't forget. I've got a window guy there today, talking corrosion from the salty elements. And condensation. Glass impact resistance, too, for when those big storms hit. He'll explain which windows are best for a place right on the water, like Mitch's." Jason checks his watch. "I have some time still, so I'll walk your cart over. No problem."

"Oh, fine. *Fine*," Elsa huffs now. She scoops her cashbox and that idled blue jay spinner off the lawn, then heads to her fenced-off garden around back. "I'll start bringing all this to my shed."

～

As Jason's sliding an extra mesh shelf back into place on the cart, a vehicle pulls up to the curb.

"Hey, Barlow," Shane says through the pickup's open window. He tips up his newsboy cap. "What's doing here?"

"Shane." Jason snaps that shelf secure then turns to the truck. He eyes Shane's face beneath that cap. "How you feeling today? No bruises from that brawl last night?"

"Nah. That guy was a wuss. I'm good."

"Well, I appreciate it. But you *could've* let it go."

"For you, I couldn't. And sometimes ... you know. Someone's just *cruisin'* for a bruisin'. So my brother and I were glad to oblige you." Shane motions to the mess on the lawn now. "What's going on here? Thought Elsa was selling her tomatoes."

"She was. Until the Board of Governors shut her down."

"No shit. They closed that little stand?"

"Yeah." Jason rolls up his shirt cuffs and glances to the cart. "She's not too happy about it. I'm giving her a hand dismantling it all."

"Well, I'm glad I caught you," Shane says as he gets out of his parked truck. Leaning against the closed door, he crosses his arms. "I'm headed back to Maine."

"Really. Back to the boat?"

"Be out to sea Monday. So I'm on my way home, saying my goodbyes to folks."

"Celia know?"

"She does. Told her last night. And I'm swinging by the diner next. Want to grab a coffee with Kyle before I leave."

"That's good. Be a long haul out on the water this time?"

"Seems it. Captain's got a helluva catch-up to play." Shane adjusts his cap. "Listen, Elsa around?"

"She's in the garden shed. Putting away her things there." As he says it, Jason sets the folded umbrella on top of the cart.

"And here she is now," Shane says, tipping that cap of his at Elsa.

"Shane!" Elsa calls as she approaches. She's pulling off her garden gloves, too. "I *thought* that was you. Are you leaving us already?"

"That I am. Hitting the road and the high seas."

"You come back soon, you hear? I always have a pasta dish with your name on it," Elsa reminds him.

"And you remember *my* offer," Shane tosses back at her. "If you ever feel like a trip north, be *sure* to get in touch. I'd be plenty offended if you didn't."

"Oh, Shane." Elsa hurries to him and gives him a hug. "*Dio ti benedica*," she whispers, then backs away, squeezing his hand. "God bless you on the ocean."

"Thanks, Elsa. Do appreciate that," Shane tells her.

"Oh! And *please*," she insists, scooping the last two bags of tomatoes from her now stripped-and-empty tomato stand. "Take these. Bring some to the boys on the boat."

"I surely will," Shane says, taking the bags from her.

Bending then, Elsa picks up the remaining empty crates

on her lawn. "Until next time," she calls to Shane as she heads to her shed again.

Shane gives a wave, before turning to Jason. "And here *I* go," he tells him, clapping Jason's shoulder before backing away. "Take care, my friend," Shane says.

"You, too, guy. Calm seas."

Shane nods, then gets into his truck. "Hey, there's one more thing I wanted to tell you," he says through the open window.

"And what's that?"

"Want you to know how happy I am for you and Maris. Truly," he says, patting a hand to his heart.

"Me, too." Jason releases the brakes on the tomato cart's wheels. "My life just doesn't work without her," he admits while maneuvering the cart toward the street. "You know what I'm saying?"

"I'm starting to." Shane's leaning over the steering wheel and turning the truck's ignition. "Starting to," he repeats with a wave before slowly driving off then.

Jason just nods. Watches Shane go, too.

thirty-six

WHAT A DIFFERENCE A WEEK makes.

Working in her writing shack after lunch Friday, Maris is nothing but glad for that difference.

Last week, before Jason was back home, her words swam out of focus. Her sentences didn't flow together. More than she wrote, she *worried* about everything—Jason, her marriage, her ongoing kitchen reno. At the keyboard then? Her fingers hit the *Delete* key more than any other.

This week? Jason's home and the kitchen's done. Life's good. And Maris can barely keep up with her typing hands. With the shack door propped open to the sunny September day outside, and with the salt air drifting in with the sound of waves on the bluff, she does it. She flips her pewter hourglass again and keeps going in this latest *Driftline* passage ...

She lifts the bottle of red wine off the counter and gives it a swirl. "Enough for me," she whispers, emptying the last few drops into her glass. Turning then, she walks through the candlelit kitchen into the living room. She's barefoot, and the frayed hem of her black bell-bottoms drags on the floor.

More candles flicker in that living room. On the mantel. Clusters of them on the console at the bottom of the stairs. On an end table. Melting wax dribbles down what's left of the tapers and pillars. In the wavering light, she makes someone out sitting on the sofa. His stocking feet are raised to the coffee table. A pillow's propped behind his head. He's smoking a joint. The pungent scent fills the room.

"What are you doing?" she asks.

"Watching TV."

She turns to the black TV screen. "You are not. There's no power."

"I'm waiting for my supper, too," he says, hitching his head to the fireplace.

She looks there, where someone else is sitting in a folding chair and leaning toward the burning logs. He's holding two roaster forks over the open flame. Several hot dogs are stuck on the fork's prongs. Another friend turns into the living room just then.

"Ooh, make mine burnt," she says. "I'll go get the buns." When she returns with a bag of them, she sits cross-legged near the hearth.

It's quiet as they wait for dinner now. Quiet except for the wind howling outside the plywood-covered windows. There's the sound of splashing waves, too, rolling in beneath the elevated cottage on the beach. That's a sound she still hasn't gotten used to. It unnerves her with the thought that the whole cottage could get washed out to sea. Another one of the guys saunters in and lands on the couch, too. He takes a hit of that joint going around the room. Right about then, the fireplace chef puts a few of the roasted hot dogs on a plate.

THE GOODBYE

"That burned enough for you?" he asks, holding the plate out toward the woman still sitting by the hearth.

⌒

Maris just can't stop. The words in her mind are reeling past, faster than her fingers can type. Burnt hot dog talk. And a flirting scene with the wine drinker. And the liquor getting restocked with bottles stolen from a neighboring cottage. And the hurricane party that ensues, well into the night. The music on the battery-operated radio. The heavy scent of cut flowers.

Only one thing stops her fingers from typing—her phone dinging with a text message. It's Jason. He must be on some break at a job site. So Maris turns her phone and reads the message.

> *Early pizza at Ronni's tonight?*
> Maris thumb-types back: *Meet me there.*
> From Jason: *About 4?*
> Maris: *It's a date, babe.*
> And Jason: *We'll drop your car off at dealer's after.*
> Maris again, with a fish emoji: *Then good luck fishing with the guys!*

Sliding her phone aside, Maris notices the top bulb of her pewter hourglass is empty again. Empty! Another hour's gone by—*already*. So with the afternoon sun shining through the shack's open door, and a random robin singing in the maple tree outside, and Maddy dozing by her feet, she flips the hourglass once more.

Lifts her fingers to the keyboard and types away.

$\sim$

"Fried zucchini does *not* count as a vegetable, Jason Barlow," Maris says later that afternoon.

Jason sits across from her at the window table in Ronni's Pizza. "Why not?"

"Because it's fried in all that oil, which counters the health benefits of the vegetable."

Jason dips a toasted bread-crumb-coated zucchini stick into ranch dressing. "But the zucchini is still in there. And it *is* a vegetable, regardless."

Maris reaches for a zucchini stick from his plate and dips it into the dressing. Her eyes flutter closed with the flavor.

"*Aha!*" he says, pointing another zucchini at her over the table.

"*Okay, fine,*" she whispers around another mouthful. "My God, are these good."

They talk then, about their day. About Maddy, and how she's more herself now that Jason's back. About the latest window segment filmed for *Castaway Cottage* that morning. About Maris' intense writing session that afternoon. She sits there wearing a distressed denim vest over a long, black tank-top dress. Her hair is pulled back in a low twist, so Jason notices the blue topaz earrings he'd given her.

And he also thinks he can just look at her talking there— for hours.

A large window is beside them. Across the street, behind patches of scrubby grass, the railroad tracks run by. Beyond those are East Bay, then Long Island Sound further out.

282

Above it all, the vast sky is as blue as the sea. The late-afternoon sun shines brilliant on the rippling water.

Jason waits until they're digging into their hot chicken-and-eggplant pizza to tell Maris about the bar fight last night. But first, he has to clarify something with her. He lifts a slice of pizza off its silver pedestal and sets it on a plate for her. "Note the eggplant," he says with a nod. "More fresh vegetables."

"That's right, Jason. You have to be careful with what you eat," Maris says, lifting the cheesy pizza piece and biting in. "I want you healthy and around for a long time."

"Okay, okay." Jason takes a slice for himself. "Now listen. You missed some epic stuff at the bar last night, after you and Celia left."

"I did? Like what?" Maris asks while chewing.

Jason folds the thin slice of pizza in his hand and takes a double bite. "Shane and Kyle?" he begins, wiping pizza sauce from his lip. "They laid into some guy outside, in the parking lot."

"What do you mean—laid into him?"

"Roughed him up some, I guess."

"Like ... got in a fight? A fistfight?"

Jason only nods.

"Oh my God! What happened?" Maris asks.

"The dude gave me a hard time when I backed into him in the bar. Called me some names."

"Names?"

Jason turns up a hand. "Peg leg, pretty much."

"Oh, Jason." Maris reaches across the table and squeezes his hand. "*I'm sorry*," she whispers.

"Eh. I've heard it all in the past decade. Some people

just don't hold back. Don't think. Whatever. They're not even worth a response."

"But it's still so hurtful," Maris says, sipping from her iced water. "Why didn't you tell me last night?"

"You were sleeping when I came up," Jason explains while biting into his pizza. "I didn't want you to get rattled at bedtime."

Maris gives him a small smile. "Oh, *wait*," she says, grabbing his hand again. "Train!"

That train is so far off that Jason knows. She's been waiting for one ever since they sat down. No way would she let him win their ongoing competition of who notices an approaching train first. He feels it, then. The slight rumble in the air before that Amtrak blows past outside their window—the train's whistle carrying back long after it's gone by.

"Anyway," Maris continues, as if nothing happened. Well, there might be *some* smugness in her tone now—for the train win. "I'm not surprised Kyle and Shane came to your defense."

"Did they ever. Said they left the guy with a little limp."

"*Aargh*," Maris says, shaking her head.

"I know. They had it in for him." Jason pushes his plate away and sits back. The pizza joint is crowded. Wooden chairs scrape on the floor. Pizza trays are slid in and out of the ovens. The phone rings with take-out orders. "Shane actually left for Maine this morning," Jason tells her.

"He did?"

"Yep. Back on the boat Monday—none the worse for wear," Jason admits, just as their waiter approaches for their dessert order.

284

Oh, how Maris has missed this.

Easy pizza dinners with her husband. Easy talk. Easy looks. It's everything.

They split a piece of chocolate lava cake topped with vanilla ice cream—and devour it now in heaping spoonfuls.

"Hang on," Jason says when the cake is almost gone. He leans across the table and lightly touches her jaw. "You have a little chocolate on your face. Right there."

Maris pulls back. "Jason Barlow. Nice try ..."

"*What?*"

She quickly slides the cake dish out of his reach. "Sure. While I'm busy getting my mirror out of my purse and checking my face, *you're* busy finishing the last hunk of chocolate cake!"

"No, you *really* have some chocolate there." He reaches across the table again and dabs a napkin on her chin. As he does, Maris sees that he still hasn't shaved since being home, so whiskers cover his jaw. And at the end of a warm, muggy September day, his dark hair is wavy in the humidity. After he sets aside the napkin, he leans back and cuffs the sleeves of his gray button-down.

"Okay, *thanks*," Maris relents. "But there's still the issue of the cake. *What* are we going to do about the last piece with its oozing fudge lava and melting ice cream?"

Jason only shrugs.

"Thumb war?" she asks. "Coin toss? Or, I know. Rock-paper-scissors."

Jason just shakes his head. "You can finish it, sweetheart."

"Me? Why?"

He lifts her spoon and scoops up a glorious cake-and-fudge-and-ice-cream dollop. "Because I love you," he says, leaning forward and feeding her the sweet mess. "That's why."

⁓

Out in the parking lot, Jason opens the back of his SUV. Maris stands beside him holding the pizza box while he shoves aside his fishing pole and tackle box. "I'm going to grab a couple hours of fishing when we get home," he says, taking the leftover pizza from her.

"You should, babe. And look at that moon," she tells him when he closes the SUV liftgate. "It'll be really nice out on the rocks, the way it's shining."

Jason takes in the sight of that moon hanging low and heavy in the sky. "Looks full."

"It does. And you just relax fishing with the guys, okay?" Maris is saying as they walk to her car beside his SUV. "Take it easy."

"I will. It'll give me a chance to pin down Cliff, too. He hasn't been talking much since his proposal never happened."

"So you'll see how he's doing?"

"Yeah."

"Okay, and while you're fishing, I'll review the chapters I'm getting ready for Mitch."

"Sounds good. Is that your spare key?" he asks as she unlocks her car door. "For the dealer's drop-off box?"

She tosses her purse on the passenger seat. "It is. I'll fill out the envelope there and we'll be good to go." She turns to Jason. "You'll follow me?"

"I will. Be right behind you."

"*Okay*," she whispers, then gives him a quick kiss. "Bye, babe."

Jason gets in his SUV and follows her out of the parking lot. Traffic is sparse when they turn onto the main drag and drive a few miles toward Stony Point. It's early evening, when closed storefronts glimmer beneath low lighting. A few miles later, the setting sun casts a red hue over salt marshes they pass. Rowboats are anchored in a calm inlet. The horizon is smudged with violet.

Jason follows as Maris takes a right and heads in the direction of the car dealer. This winding street is more residential and wooded as they veer away from the coastline. Shanties and cabins are set back off the road. They pass a farm stand shuttered for the day. Shadows grow long. That pastel sky shimmers behind tall oak and pine trees. And that rising moon—it hangs heavy behind the outstretched tree branches. As Jason follows behind Maris' car, it's quiet, too, in the SUV. He leaves the radio off and opens his window halfway. The misty evening air breezes in. It's warm still, a last breath of summer.

Far ahead, a motion catches his eye. It's a deer in a grassy area off to the right. The animal isn't grazing, but is a flash of tawny movement as it bounds from the grass right into the street. Thankfully, Maris sees the deer, too. Her brake lights briefly flicker. So Jason knows she's watching that deer leap past while she's driving.

But Maris must be watching that *fleeing* deer still—off to her left.

Because she's *not* braking for the next deer on her right. No red taillights come on as *that* deer bounds out of a stand of trees.

"Shit, *shit!*" Jason says aloud in his vehicle. "To your *right*, Maris! Look! There's another one!"

Everything's a flash, then. A blur that happens in only seconds.

And in those seconds, he knows. Maris' attention is on the first deer. *Not* the second one coming up behind it.

Not until it's too late.

Jason can't miss that it's too late—and there's *nothing* he can do.

Maris doesn't see that second deer leaping into the street until the animal's right in front of her moving car. She slams on the brakes.

Hard.

Hard enough for those damn brake lights to come on—steady now. Steady and veering from side to side as her car fishtails across the road. A sound comes, too. It's her locked tires squealing over the pavement.

"*No, no, no, no,*" Jason whispers, watching it all go down. "*Maris.*"

He grips his steering wheel and slows up. And leans forward to watch closely through his windshield—as if he can steer Maris out of this. Can somehow help her.

Instead, helpless, Jason only sees it all.

Sees the very last rays of sunlight glimmer on the metal of Maris' skidding car.

Sees her car spinning sideways now.

The tires screeching.

The deer mid-leap—its white tail flashing.

A blur of red brake lights and out-of-control car weaving on the twilight's gray pavement.

The beach friends' journey continues in

THE
BARLOWS

The next novel in The Seaside Saga from

New York Times Bestselling Author

JOANNE DEMAIO

Also by Joanne DeMaio

Also by Joanne DeMaio

Beach Cottage Series
(In order)
1) The Beach Cottage
2) Back to the Beach Cottage

Standalone Novels
True Blend
Whole Latte Life

The Winter Series
(In order)
1) Snowflakes and Coffee Cakes
2) Snow Deer and Cocoa Cheer
3) Cardinal Cabin
4) First Flurries
5) Eighteen Winters
6) Winter House
—And More Winter Books—

For a complete list of books by *New York Times*
bestselling author Joanne DeMaio, visit:

Joannedemaio.com

About the Author

JOANNE DEMAIO is a *New York Times* and *USA Today* bestselling author of contemporary fiction. The novels of her ongoing and groundbreaking Seaside Saga journey with a group of beach friends, much the way a TV series does, continuing with the same cast of characters from book-to-book. In addition, she writes winter novels set in a quaint New England town. Joanne lives with her family in Connecticut.

For a complete list of books and for news on upcoming releases, visit Joanne's website. She also enjoys hearing from readers on Facebook.

Author Website:
Joannedemaio.com

Facebook:
Facebook.com/JoanneDeMaioAuthor

Made in the USA
Middletown, DE
02 August 2022

70466432R00179